THE BILLIONAIRE AND BABIES COLLECTION

The men in this special 2-in-1 collection rule their worlds with authority and determination. They're comfortable commanding those around them and aren't afraid to be ruthless if necessary. Independent and self-reliant, they are content with their money and lack of commitment.

Then the babies enter their lives and, before they know it, these powerful men are wrapped around their babies' little fingers!

With the babies comes the awareness of what else might be missing. Seems the perfect time for these billionaires to find the women who will love them forever.

Join us for two passionate, provocative stories where billionaires encounter the women—and babies—who will make them complete!

If you love these two classic stories, be sure to look for more Billionaires and Babies books from Harlequin Desire.

JANICE MAYNARD

In 2002 Janice Maynard left a career as an elementary teacher to pursue writing full-time. Her first love is creating sexy, character-driven, contemporary romance. She has written for Kensington and NAL, and is very happy to be part of the Harlequin family—a lifelong dream by the way! Janice and her husband live in the shadow of the Great Smoky Mountains. They love to hike and travel. Visit her at www.janicemaynard.com.

Look for more books from Janice Maynard in Harlequin Desire—the ultimate destination for powerful, passionate romance! There are six new Harlequin Desire titles available every month. Check one out today!

USA TODAY Bestselling Author

Janice Maynard

and

USA TODAY Bestselling Author

Katherine Garbera

THE BILLIONAIRE'S BORROWED BABY

AND

BABY BUSINESS

 HARLEQUIN® BILLIONAIRES AND BABIES

Recycling programs
for this product may
not exist in your area.

ISBN-13: 978-0-373-60981-9

The Billionaire's Borrowed Baby And Baby Business
Copyright © 2014 by Harlequin Books S.A.

The publisher acknowledges the copyright holders
of the individual works as follows:

The Billionaire's Borrowed Baby
Copyright © 2011 by Janice Maynard

Baby Business
Copyright © 2008 by Katherine Garbera

Printed in U.S.A.

CONTENTS

THE BILLIONAIRE'S
BORROWED BABY

Janice Maynard

For the next generation: Anastasia, Ainsley, Allie, Sydney, Olivia, Dakota and Samuel Ellis.

Chapter 1

It was a hot, beautiful Georgia morning, but all Hattie Parker noticed was the taste of desperation and panic.

"I need to speak to Mr. Cavallo, please. Mr. *Luc* Cavallo," she clarified quickly. "It's urgent."

The thirtysomething administrative assistant with the ice-blue suit and matching pale, chilly eyes looked down her perfect nose. "Do you have an appointment?"

Hattie clenched her teeth. The woman had an expensive leather date book open in front of her. Clearly, she knew Hattie was an interloper and clearly she was doing her best to be intimidating.

Hattie juggled the baby on her hip and managed a smile. "Tell him it's Hattie Parker. I don't have an appointment, but I'm sure Luc will see me if you let him know I'm here."

Actually, that was a bald-faced lie. She had no clue if Luc would see her or not. At one time in her life he had been Prince Charming, willing and eager to do anything she wanted, to give her everything she desired.

Today, he might very well show her the door, but she was hoping he would remember some of the good times and at least hear her out. They hadn't parted on the best of terms. But since every other option she had considered, legal or not, had gone bust, it was Luc or no one. And she wasn't leaving without a fight.

The woman's expression didn't change. She was sheer perfection from her ash-blond chignon to her exquisitely made-up face to her expensive French manicure. With disdain, she examined Hattie's disheveled blond hair, discount store khaki skirt and pink cotton blouse. Even without the drool marks at the shoulder, the outfit wasn't going to win any fashion awards. It was hard to maintain a neat appearance when the little one grabbed handfuls of hair at regular intervals.

Hattie's legs felt like spaghetti. The stoic security guard in the lobby had insisted that she park her stroller before entering the elevator. Seven-month-old Deedee weighed a ton, and Hattie was scared and exhausted, at the end of her rope. The last six weeks had been hell.

She took a deep breath. "Either you let me see Mr. Cavallo, or I'm going to pitch the biggest hissy fit Atlanta has seen since Scarlett O'Hara swished her skirts through the red Georgia dust." Hattie's chin trembled right at the end, but she refused to let this supercilious woman defeat her.

Scary lady blinked. Just once, but it was enough to let Hattie know that the balance of power had shifted. The other woman stood up with a pained sigh. "Wait here." She disappeared down a hallway.

Hattie nuzzled the baby's sweet-smelling head with its little tufts of golden hair. "Don't worry, my love. I won't let anyone take you, I swear." Deedee smiled, revealing her two new bottom teeth, her only teeth. She was starting to babble nonsense syllables, and Hattie fell more in love with her every day.

The wait seemed like an eternity, but when Luc's assistant finally returned, the clock on the wall showed that less than five minutes had elapsed. The woman was definitely disgruntled. "Mr. Cavallo will see you now. But he's a very busy man, and he has many other important commitments this morning."

Hattie resisted the childish urge to stick out her tongue at the woman's back as they traversed the hallway carpeted in thick, crimson plush. At the second doorway, the woman paused. "You may go in." The words nearly stuck in ice woman's throat, you could tell.

Hattie took a deep breath, no longer concentrating on her would-be nemesis. She kissed the baby's cheek for luck. "Showtime, kiddo." With far more confidence than she felt, she knocked briefly, opened the door and stepped into the room.

Luc ran a multimillion-dollar business. He was accustomed to dealing with crises on a daily basis. The ability to think on his feet was a gift he'd honed in the fires of corporate America.

So he wasn't easily thrown off balance. But when Hattie Parker appeared in his office, the first time he'd seen her in over a decade, his heart lodged in his throat, his muscles tensed and he momentarily forgot how to breathe.

She was as beautiful now as she had been at twenty. Sun-kissed porcelain skin, dark brown eyes that held hints of amber. And legs that went on forever. Her silky blond hair barely brushed her shoulders, much shorter than he remembered. He kept the width of his broad mahogany desk between them. It seemed safer that way.

As he struggled with shock, he was stunned to realize the woman he had once loved was holding an infant. Jealousy stabbed sharp and deep. Damn. Hattie was a mother. Which meant there was a man somewhere in the picture.

The sick feeling in his gut stunned him. He'd moved on a long, long time ago. So why was his chest tight and his pulse jumping like a jackrabbit?

He remained standing, his hands shoved in his pockets. "Hello, Hattie." He was proud of the even timbre of his voice.

"Hello, Luc."

She was visibly nervous. He indicated the chair closest to him and motioned for her to sit. For a brief moment, Luc caught a glimpse of sexy legs as Hattie's skirt rode up her thighs. The baby clung to her neck, and Hattie wriggled in the chair until she was modestly covered.

He examined her face, deliberately letting the silence accumulate in tense layers. Hattie Parker was the girl next door, a natural, appealing beauty who didn't need enhancement. Even dressed as she was in fairly unflattering garments, she would stand out in a room full of lovely women.

At one time, she had been his whole world.

And it irked him that the memories still stung. "Why are you here, Hattie? The last time we had sex was a lifetime ago. Surely you're not going to try and convince me that baby is mine."

The mockery and sarcasm made her pale. He felt the pinch of remorse, but a guy needed to wield what weapons he could. The man he was today would not be vulnerable. Not ever again.

She cleared her throat. "I need your help."

He lifted a brow. "I'd have thought I would be the last person on your go-to list."

"To be honest, you were. But it's serious, Luc. I'm in big trouble."

He rocked on his heels. "What's her name?"

The non sequitur made Hattie frown. "This is Deedee."

Luc studied the baby. He didn't see much of Hattie in the child. Maybe the kid took after her dad.

Luc leaned over and punched the intercom. "Marilyn...can you come in here, please?"

It was a toss-up as to which of the two women was more horrified when Luc phrased his next request. When Marilyn appeared, he motioned to the baby. "Will you please take the little one for a few minutes? Her name is Deedee. Ms. Parker and I need to have a serious conversation, and I don't have much time."

Hattie wanted to protest, he could tell. But she reluctantly handed the baby over to Luc's assistant. "Here's a bottle. She's getting hungry. And you'll need this bib and burp cloth. You don't want to let her ruin your nice suit."

Luc knew his assistant would be fine. She might be a cold fish, but she was relentlessly efficient.

When the door closed, Luc sat down in his leather office chair. It had been specially ordered to fit his long, lanky frame. He steepled his hands under his chin and leaned back. "So spill it, Hattie. What's going on in your life to make you seek me out? As I recall, it was *you* who dumped *me* and not the other way around."

She flushed and twisted her hands in her lap. "I don't think we need to go there. That was a long time ago."

He shrugged. "All right then. We'll concentrate on the present. Why are you here?"

When she bit her lip, he shifted in his chair uneasily. Why in God's name did he still have such vivid memories of kissing that bow-shaped mouth? Running his hands through that silky, wavy hair. Touching every inch of her soft, warm skin. He swallowed hard.

Hattie met his gaze hesitantly. "Do you remember my older sister, Angela?"

He frowned. "Barely. As I recall, the two of you didn't get along."

"We grew closer after our parents died."

"I didn't know, Hattie. I'm sorry."

For a moment, tears made her eyes shiny, but she blinked them back. "Thank you. My father died a few years after I graduated. Lung cancer. He was a two-pack-a-day man and it caught up with him."

"And your mother?"

"She didn't do well without Daddy. He did everything for her, and without him, the world was overwhelming to her. She finally had a nervous breakdown and had to be admitted to a facility. Unfortunately, she was never able to go back to her home. Angela and I sold the house we grew up in...everything Mom and Dad had, but it wasn't enough. I practically bankrupted myself paying for her care."

"Angela didn't help?"

"She told me I should back off and let the state look after Mother...especially when Mom retreated totally into an alternate reality where she didn't even recognize us."

"Some people would think your sister made sense."

"Not me. I couldn't abandon my mother."

"When did you lose her?"

"Last winter."

He looked at her left hand, but it was bare. Where was her husband in all this? Was the guy a jerk who bailed on Hattie rather than help with the mom? And what about the baby?

Suddenly, it became clear. Hattie needed to borrow money. She was proud and independent, and things must be really bad if she had humbled her pride enough to come to him.

He leaned forward, his elbows on the desk. No one who knew their history would blame him if he kicked her out. But though his memories of her were bitter, he didn't have it in him to be deliberately cruel, especially if a child was involved. And though it might be petty, he rather liked the idea of having Hattie in his debt…a kind of poetic justice. "You've had a rough time," he said quietly. "I'll be happy to loan you however much money you need, interest free, no questions asked. For old times' sake."

Hattie's face went blank and she cocked her head. "Excuse me?"

"That's why you're here, isn't it? To ask if you can borrow some money? I'm fine with that. It's no big deal. What good is all that cash in the bank if I can't use it to help an old friend?"

Her jaw dropped and her cheeks went red with mortification. "No, no, no," she said, leaping to her feet and pacing. "I don't need your money, Luc. That's not it at all."

It was his turn to rise. He rounded the desk and faced her, close enough now to inhale her scent and realize with pained remembrance that she still wore the same perfume. He put his hands gently on her shoulders, feeling the tremors she couldn't disguise.

They were practically nose to nose. "Then tell me, Hattie. What do you need from me? What do you want?"

She lifted her chin. She was tall for a woman, and he could see the shades of chocolate and cognac in her irises. Her breathing was ragged, a pulse beating at the base of her throat.

He shook her gently. "Spit it out. Tell me."

She licked her lips. He could see the tracery of blue veins at her temples. Their long separation vanished like mist, and suddenly he was assaulted with a barrage of memories, both good and bad.

The soft, quick kiss he brushed across her cheek surprised them both. He was so close, he could smell cherry lip gloss. Some things never changed. "Hattie?"

She had closed her eyes when he kissed her, but her lashes lifted and her cloudy gaze cleared. Astonishment flashed across her expressive features, followed by chagrin and what appeared to be resignation.

After a long, silent pause, she wrinkled her nose and sighed. "I need you to marry me."

Luc dropped his hands from her shoulders with unflattering haste. Though his expression remained guarded, for a split second some strong emotion flashed in his eyes and then disappeared as quickly as it had come. Most men would be shocked by Hattie's proposal.

Most men weren't Luc Cavallo.

He lifted a shoulder clad in an expensive suit. The Cavallo textile empire, started by their grandfather in Italy and now headquartered in Atlanta, had made Luc and his brother wealthy men. She had no doubt that the soft, finely woven wool fabric was the product of a family mill. His mouth twisted, faint disdain in his expression. "Is this a joke? Should I look for hidden cameras?"

She felt her face go even hotter. Confronting her past was more difficult than she had expected, and without the baby to run interference, Hattie felt uncomfortably vulnerable. "It's not a joke. I'm dead serious. I need you to marry me to keep Deedee safe."

He scowled. "Good Lord, Hattie. Is the father threatening you? Has he hurt you? Tell me."

His intensity made her shiver. If she really had an abusive husband, there was no doubt in her mind that Luc Cavallo would hunt him down and destroy him. She was making a hash of this explanation. "It's complicated," she said helplessly. "But no, nothing like that."

He ran two hands through his hair, mussing the

dark, glossy strands. The reminder function on his BlackBerry beeped just then, and Luc glanced down at it with a harried expression. "I have an appointment," he said, his voice betraying frustration. "Obviously we're not going to resolve this in fifteen minutes. Can you get a sitter for tonight?"

"I'd rather not. Deedee has been through a lot of trauma recently. She clings to me. I don't want to change her routine any more than necessary." And the thought of being alone with Luc Cavallo scared Hattie. This brief meeting had revealed an unpalatable truth. The Hattie who had been madly in love with Luc was still lurking somewhere inside a heart that clung to silly dreams from the past.

He straightened his tie and strode to the other side of his desk. "Then I'll send a car for you." As she opened her mouth to protest, he added, "With an infant seat. We'll have dinner at my home and my housekeeper can play with the child while we talk."

There was nothing ominous in his words, but Hattie felt her throat constrict. Was she really going to try to convince Luc to marry her? Who was she kidding? He had no reason at all to humor her. Other than perhaps sheer curiosity. Why hadn't he shown her the door immediately? Why was he allowing her to play out this odd reunion?

She should be glad, relieved, down on her knees

thanking the good lord that Luc wasn't already married.

But at the moment, her exact emotions were far more complicated and far less sensible.

She was still fascinated by this man who had once promised her the moon.

Chapter 2

What did one wear to a marriage proposal? While the baby was napping, Hattie rummaged through the tiny closet in her matching tiny apartment, knowing that she was not going to find a dress to wow Luc Cavallo. The only garment remotely suitable was a black, polished cotton sheath that she had worn to each of her parent's funerals. Perhaps with some accessories it would do the trick.

In a jewelry box she'd had since she was a girl, her hand hovered over the one piece inside that wasn't an inexpensive bauble. The delicate platinum chain was still as bright as the day Luc had given it to her. She picked it up and fastened it around her neck, adjusting the single pearl flanked by small diamonds.

Though there had been many days when the wolf was at the door, she had not been able to bring herself to sell this one lovely reminder of what might have been. She stroked the pearl, imagining that it was warm beneath her fingers....

They had skipped their afternoon classes at Emory and escaped to Piedmont Park with a blanket and a picnic basket. She was a scholarship student...his family had endowed the Fine Arts Center.

As they sprawled in the hot spring sunshine, feeling alive and free and deliciously truant, Luc leaned over her on one elbow, kissing her with teasing brushes of his lips that made her restless for more. He grinned down at her, his eyes alight with happiness. "I have an anniversary present for you."

"Anniversary?" They'd been dating for a while, but she hadn't kept track.

He caressed her cheek. "I met you six months ago today. You were buying a miniature pumpkin at Stanger's Market. I offered to carve it for you. You laughed. And that's when I knew."

"Knew what?"

"That you were the one."

Her smile faded. "College guys are supposed to be counting notches on their bedposts, not spouting romantic nonsense."

A shadow dimmed the good humor in his gaze. "I come from a long line of Italians. Romance is in our blood." His whimsical shrug made her regret tarnishing the moment. Lord knew she wanted it to be true, but her mother had drummed into her head that men only wanted one thing. And Hattie had given that up without a qualm.

Being Luc Cavallo's lover was the best thing that had ever happened to her. He was her first, and she loved him so much it hurt. But she was careful to protect herself. She had a degree to finish, grades to keep up. A woman had to stand on her own two feet. Depending on a man led to heartbreak.

Luc reached into the pocket of his jeans and withdrew a small turquoise box. He handed it to her without speaking.

If she had been able to think of a polite refusal, she would have handed it back unopened. But he looked at her with such naked anticipation that she swallowed her misgivings and removed the lid. Nestled inside the leather box was a necklace, an exquisite, expensive necklace.

Hattie knew about Tiffany's, of course. In fact, back in the fall she'd been in the store at Phipps Plaza with one of her girlfriends who was in search of a wedding gift. But even on that day, Hattie had felt the sting of being out of place. She couldn't af-

ford a key chain in those swanky glass cases, much less anything else.

And now this.

Luc ignored her silence. He took the necklace from the box and fastened it around her neck. She was wearing a pink tank top, and the pearl nestled in her modest cleavage. He kissed her forehead. "It suits you."

But it didn't. She was not that woman he wanted her to be. Luc would take his place one day with the glitterati. And Hattie, with or without the necklace, would wish him well. But she wasn't "the one"... and she never would be.

A car backfired out on the street, the loud sound dragging Hattie back to the present. With a mutinous scowl at her own reflection, she closed the jewelry box with a defiant click. Luc probably didn't even remember the silly necklace. He'd no doubt bought pricey bling for a dozen women in the intervening years.

The afternoon dragged by, the baby fussy with teething...Hattie nervous and uncertain. It was almost a relief when a nicely dressed chauffeur knocked at the door promptly at six-thirty.

The pleasant older man took Hattie's purse and the diaper bag while she tucked Deedee into the top-of-the-line car seat. It was brand-new and not smeared with crusty Cheerios and spit-up. The baby was charmed by the novelty of having Hattie sit across from her. A game of peekaboo helped distract them both as the car wound its way from the slightly run-down neighborhood where Hattie lived to an upscale part of town.

Though it had been ten years since Hattie and Luc's college breakup, they had never crossed paths after graduation. It was a big city, and they moved in far different spheres.

West Paces Ferry was one of the premier addresses in Atlanta. Decades-old homes sat side by side with new construction created to resemble historic architecture. Even the governor's mansion called the narrow, winding avenue home. Luc had recently purchased an entire estate complete with acreage. Hattie had seen the renovation written up in a local magazine.

The article, accompanied by photos of Luc, had no doubt been responsible for this crazy decision to throw herself on Luc's mercy. Seeing his smiling face after so many years had resurrected feelings she believed to be long dead.

Perhaps it was a sign....

The old home was amazing. Azaleas and forsythia bloomed in profusion on the grounds. A lengthy driveway culminated in a cobblestone apron leading to the imposing double front doors. Luc stepped out to meet them almost before the engine noise had died. His dark hair and eyes betrayed his Mediterranean heritage.

He held out a hand. "Welcome, Hattie."

She felt him squeeze her fingers, and her skin heated. "Your home is beautiful."

He stepped back as she extracted Deedee. "It's a work in progress. I'll be glad when the last of it is finished."

Despite his disclaimer, and despite the small area of scaffolding at the side of the house where workmen had been repairing stonework, the interior of the house was breathtaking. A sweeping staircase led up and to the right. The foyer floor was Italian marble, and above a walnut chair rail, the walls were papered in what appeared to be the original silk fabric, a muted shade of celadon. A priceless chandelier showered them in shards of warm light, and on a console beneath an antique mirror on the left wall, a massive bouquet of flowers scented the air.

Hattie turned around in a circle, the baby in her arms quiet for once, as if she, too, was awed. "It's stunning, Luc."

His smile reflected quiet satisfaction. "It's starting to feel like home. The couple who lived here bought it in the 1920s. They're both gone now, but I inherited Ana and Sherman. He wears many hats… driver is only one of them."

"He was very sweet. I felt pampered. And Ana?"

"His wife. You'll meet her in a moment. She's the housekeeper, chef, gardener…you name it. I tried to get them both to retire with a pension, but I think they love this house more than I do. I get the distinct feeling that I'm on probation as the new owner."

As promised, Ana entertained Deedee during dinner while Luc and Hattie enjoyed the fruits of the housekeeper's labors—lightly breaded rainbow trout, baby asparagus and fruit salad accompanied by rolls so fluffy they seemed to melt in the mouth.

Luc served Hattie and himself, with nothing to disturb the intimacy of their meal. Surprisingly, Hattie forgot to be self-conscious. Luc was a fascinating man, highly intelligent, well-read, and he possessed of a sneaky sense of humor. As the evening progressed, sharp regret stabbed her heart. She was overwhelmed with a painful recognition of what she had lost because of her own immaturity and cowardice.

He refilled her wineglass one more time. "I suppose you're not nursing the baby."

She choked on a sip of chardonnay. An image of Luc in her bed, watching her feed a baby at her breast, flashed through her brain with the force of a runaway train. Her face was so hot she hoped he would blame it on the wine. She set the glass down gently, her hand trembling. Unwittingly, he had given her the perfect opening.

"The baby's not mine," she said softly. "My sister Angela was her mother."

"Was?"

Hattie swallowed, the grief still fresh and raw. "She was killed in a car crash six weeks ago. My brother-in-law, Eddie, was driving…drunk and drugged out of his mind. He got out and left the scene when he hit a car head-on. Both people in the other vehicle died. Angela lingered for a few hours…long enough to tell me that she wanted me to take Deedee. I was babysitting that night, and I've had the baby ever since."

"What happened to the baby's father?"

"Eddie spent a few days behind bars. He's out on bail awaiting trial. But I guarantee you he won't do any time. His family has connections everywhere. I don't know if we have the Mob in Georgia, but I wouldn't be surprised. Eddie's family is full of cold, mean-spirited people. Frankly, they scare me."

"I can tell."

"At first, none of them showed any sign of acknowledging Deedee's existence. But about two weeks ago, I was summoned to the family compound in Conyers."

"Eddie wanted to see his child?"

She laughed bitterly. "You'd think so, wouldn't

you? But no. He was there when I arrived with her. A lot of them were there. But not one single person in that entire twisted family even looked at her, much less asked to hold her. They kept referring to her as 'the kid' and talked about how she was one of theirs and so should be raised by them."

"That doesn't make any sense given their lack of enthusiasm for the baby."

"It does when you realize that Eddie thinks Deedee will be his ace in the hole with the judge. He wants to portray the grieving husband and penitent dad. Having Deedee in the courtroom will soften him, make him more sympathetic to the jury."

"Ah. I take it you didn't go along with their plan?"

"Of course not. I told them Angela wanted me to raise her daughter and that I would be adopting Deedee."

"How did that go?"

She shivered. "Eddie's father said that no custody court would give a baby to a single woman with few financial means when the father wanted the child and had the resources to provide for her future."

"And you said…?"

She bit her lip. "I told them I was engaged to my college sweetheart and that you had a boatload of money and you loved Deedee like your own. And then I hightailed it out of there."

Luc actually had the gall to laugh.

"It's not funny," she wailed, leaping to her feet. "This is serious."

He topped off her wineglass once again. "Relax, Hattie. I have more lawyers than a dog has fleas. Deedee is safe. I give you my word."

Her legs went weak and she plopped into her chair. "Really? You mean that?" Suspicion reared its ugly head. "Why?"

He leaned back, studying her with a laserlike gaze that made her want to hide. He saw too much. "My motivation shouldn't matter…right, Hattie? If I really am your last resort?" Something in his bland words made her shiver.

She licked her lips, feeling as if she was making a bargain with the devil. "Are you sure you're willing to do this?"

"I never say anything I don't mean. You should know that. We'll make your lie a reality. I have the best legal counsel in Atlanta. Angela's wishes will prevail."

"I'll sign a prenup," she said. "I don't want your money."

His gaze iced over. "You made that clear a decade ago, Hattie. No need to flog a dead horse."

Her stomach clenched. Why was it that he could make her feel so small with one look?

When she remained silent, he stood up with visible impatience. "I know you need to get the little one in bed before it gets any later. I'll have my team draw up some documents, and then in a few days, you and I can go over the details."

"Details?" she asked weakly.

His grin was feral. "Surely you know I'll have a few stipulations of my own."

Her throat tightened and she took one last swallow of wine. It burned going down like it was whiskey. "Of course. You have to protect your interests. That makes sense." For some reason she couldn't quite fathom, the specter of sex had unexpectedly entered the room. Her mouth was so dry she could barely speak.

Surely lawyers didn't use legalese to dictate sex…did they?

Suddenly an unpalatable thought struck her. "Um…Luc…I should have asked. Is there anyone who will… I mean…who is…um…"

He cocked his head, one broad shoulder propped against the door frame. His face was serious, but humor danced in his eyes. "Are you asking if I'm seeing anyone, Hattie? Isn't it a bit late to worry about that…now that you've told everyone I'm your fiancé?"

Mortified didn't begin to describe how she felt. "Not everyone," she muttered.

"Just the Mob?" He chuckled out loud, enjoying her discomfiture a little too much. Finally, he sobered. "You let me worry about my personal life, Hattie. Your job is to take care of yourself and that little girl—" He stopped abruptly. "Speaking of jobs...what happened? Why aren't you teaching?"

She had majored in math at Emory and had gone directly from college to a high school faculty position.

"I had to take a leave of absence for the rest of the year when the accident happened."

He sobered completely now, stepping close enough to run a hand over her hair. She'd worn it loose tonight. "You've been through a hell of a lot," he said softly, their bodies almost touching. "But things will get better."

She smiled wistfully. "Somedays it seems as if nothing will ever be the same."

"I didn't say it would be the same."

For some reason, the words struck her as a threat. She looked up at him, their breath mingling. "What do you get out of this? Why did you agree to back up an impulsive lie by a woman you haven't seen in ten years?"

"Are you trying to talk me out of it?"

"Tell me why you agreed. I was ninety percent sure you'd throw me out of your office on my fanny."

"I can be kind on occasion." The sarcasm was impossible to miss.

She searched his face. It hurt knowing that it was as familiar to her as if they had parted yesterday. "There's something more," she said slowly. "I can see it in your eyes."

His expression shuttered. "Let's just say I have my reasons." His tone was gruff and said more loudly than words that he was done with the conversation.

He was shutting her out. And it stung. But they were little more than strangers now. Strangers who had once made love with passionate abandon, but strangers nevertheless.

"I have to go."

He didn't argue. He ushered her in front of him until they entered a pleasant room outfitted as a den. Ana, despite her years, was down on an Oriental rug playing with a sleepy Deedee.

Hattie rushed forward to scoop up the drowsy baby and nuzzle her sweet-smelling neck. "Did she nap for you at all?"

Ana stood with dignity and straightened the skirt of her floral cotton housedress. "She slept about forty-five minutes…enough to keep her awake until you can get her home and in bed. Your daughter is precious, Ms. Parker, an absolute angel."

"She's not my daughter, she's my niece…but thank you." Did the housekeeper think Luc had brought his love child home for a visit?

Her host grew impatient with the female chit-chat. "I'll walk you out, Hattie."

Sherman waited respectfully by the car door, making any sort of personal conversation awkward. Luc surprised Hattie by taking Deedee without ceremony and tucking her expertly into the small seat.

She lifted an eyebrow. "You did that well."

He touched the baby's cheek and stepped aside so Hattie could enter the limo. "It's not rocket science." He braced an arm on the top of the car and leaned in. "I'll look forward to seeing you both again soon."

"You'll call me?"

"I'll get Marilyn to contact you and set up a meeting. It will probably only take a couple of days. You need to go ahead and start packing."

"Packing?" She was starting to sound like a slightly dense parrot. What had she gotten herself into? Luc was helping her, but with strings attached. She had known his every thought at one time. Now he was an enigma.

His half smile made her think of a predator anticipating his prey. "You and Deedee will be moving in here as soon as the wedding is over."

Chapter 3

Two days later, Luc tapped briefly at his brother's office door and entered. Leo, his senior by little more than a year, was almost hidden behind piles of paperwork and books. A genius by any measure, Leo masterminded the financial empire, while Luc handled R & D. Luc enjoyed the challenge of developing new products, finding the next creative venture.

Leo was the one who made them all rich.

It was a full thirty seconds before his brother looked up from what he was doing. "Luc. Didn't expect to see you today."

The brothers met formally twice a month, and

it wasn't unusual for them to lunch together a few times a week, but Luc rarely dropped by his brother's sanctum unannounced. Their offices were on different floors of the building, and more often than not, their customary mode of communication was texting.

Luc ignored the comfortable, overstuffed easy chair that flanked Leo's desk and instead, chose to cross the room and stand by the window. He never tired of gazing at Atlanta's distinctive skyline.

He rolled his shoulders, unaware until that moment that his neck was tight. He turned and smiled. "What are you doing on May 14?"

Leo tapped a key and glanced at his computer screen. "Looks clear. What's up?"

"I thought you might like to be my best man."

Now Luc had Leo's full attention. His older sibling, though still a couple inches shorter than Luc's six-three, was an imposing man. Built like a mountain, he looked more like a lumberjack than a numbers whiz.

He escaped the confines of his desk and cleared a front corner to lean on his hip and stare at his brother. "You're pulling my chain, right?"

"Why would you say that?"

"Three weeks ago I suggested you bring a date to Carole Ann's party, and you told me you weren't seeing anyone."

Luc shrugged. "Things happen."

Leo scowled, a black expression that had been known to make underlings quake in terror. "I can read you like a book. You're up to something. The last time I saw that exact look on your face, you were trying to convince Dad to let you take the Maserati for a weekend trip to Daytona."

"I have my own sports cars. I'm not trying to pull anything."

"You know what I mean." He changed tack. "Do I know her?"

Luc shrugged. "You've met."

"How long have *you* known her? It's not like you to go all misty-eyed over a one-night stand."

"I can assure you that I've known her for a very long time."

"But you've just now realized you're in love."

"A man doesn't have to be in love to want a woman."

"So it's lust."

"I think we've gotten off track. I asked if you would be my best man. A simple yes or no will do."

"Damn it, Luc. Quit being so mysterious. Who is she? Will I get to see her anytime soon?"

"I haven't decided. We've been concentrating on each other. I don't want to spoil things. Just promise me you'll show up when and where I say on the fourteenth. In a tux."

The silence was deafening. Finally, Leo stood up and stretched. "I don't like the sound of this. When it all goes to hell, don't come crying to me. Your libido is a piss-poor businessman. Be smart, baby brother. Women are generally not worth the bother."

Luc understood his brother's caution. They had both been burned by love at a tender age, but thankfully had wised up pretty fast. What Leo didn't know, though, was that Luc had a plan. *Revenge* was a strong word for what he had in mind. He didn't hate Hattie Parker. Quite the contrary. All he wanted was for her to understand that while he might still find her sexually attractive, he was completely immune to any emotional connection. No hearts and flowers. No protestations of undying devotion.

He was no longer a kid yearning for a pretty girl. This time *he* had the power. *He* would be calling all the shots. Hattie needed him, and her vulnerability meant that Luc would have her in his house... in his bed...under his control. Perhaps *revenge was* too strong a word. But when all was said and done, Hattie Parker would be out of his system...for good.

Hattie was ready to scream. Moving anytime was a huge chore, but add a baby to the mix, and the process was darned near impossible. She'd finally gotten Deedee down for a nap and was wrapping breakables in the kitchen when her cell phone rang. She jerked it up and snarled, "What?"

The long silence at the other end was embarrassing.

"Sorry," she said, her throat tight with tears of frustration.

Luc's distinctive tones were laced with humor. "I don't think I've ever heard you lose your temper. I kind of like it."

"Don't be silly," she said, shoving a lock of damp hair from her forehead. "What do you want?"

"Nothing in particular. I was checking in to see if you needed anything."

"A trio of muscular guys would be nice."

Another silence. "Kinky," he said, his voice amused but perhaps a tad hoarse.

Her face flamed, though he couldn't see her. "To help with moving," she muttered. "I wouldn't know what else to do with them. This mothering thing is hard work."

"Why, Hattie Parker. Are you hinting for help?"

"Maybe." Deedee was a good baby, but being a single parent was difficult. Hattie no longer felt as panicked as she had in the beginning. Much of the daily routine of dealing with an infant seemed easier now. But Deedee had been restless the three nights since Hattie had dined with Luc. Perhaps the baby was picking up on Hattie's unsettled emotions.

And to make matters worse, Eddie had begun sending a harassing string of vague emails and texts. Clearly to keep Hattie on edge. And it was working.

Luc sighed audibly. "I would have hired a moving crew already, but you're always so damned independent, I thought you would pitch a fit and insist on doing it yourself."

"I've grown up, Luc. Some battles simply aren't worth fighting. I know when I'm in over my head."

"I'm sorry. I made a stupid assumption. It won't happen again."

The conversation lagged once more. She looked at the chaos in her kitchen and sighed. "Do you know yet when we're going to sit down and go over the finer points of our marriage agreement?"

"I thought perhaps tomorrow evening. When does Deedee go down for the night?"

"Usually by eight…if I'm lucky."

"What if I come over to your place then, so she won't have to be displaced. I'll bring food."

"That would be great."

"Have you heard any more from your brother-in-law?"

"Nothing specific." No need at the moment to involve Luc in Eddie's bluster. "He likes to throw his weight around. Right now, he's got the perfect setup. I'm babysitting for him, but when he's ready, he'll grab Deedee."

"I hope you don't mean that literally."

"He's not that stupid. At least, I don't think he is."

"Try not to worry, Hattie. Everything is going to fall into place."

For once, it seemed as if Luc was right. Deedee went to sleep the following evening without a whimper. Hattie found an unworn blouse in the back of her closet with the tags still attached. She'd snagged it from a clearance rack at Bloomingdale's last January, and the thin, silky fabric, a pale peach floral, was the perfect weight for a spring evening.

Paired with soft, well-worn jeans, the top made her look nice but casual…not like she was trying too hard to impress. Unfortunately, Luc showed up ten minutes early, and she was forced to open the door in her bare feet.

His eyes flashed with masculine appreciation when he saw her. "You don't look frazzled to me, Hattie."

She stepped back to let him in. "Thanks. Today was much calmer, maybe because the moving company you hired promised to be here first thing in the morning. And I was able to actually take a shower, because the baby took a two-hour morning nap."

As she closed the door, he surveyed her apartment. "No offense, but I don't see any point in storing most of this stuff. Let the movers take the bulk of it to charity, and bring only the things that are personal or sentimental with you."

She bit her lip. It had occurred to her that this subject would have to be broached, but she hadn't anticipated it would come so soon. "The thing is…"

"What are you trying to say?" He tossed the duffel bag he'd been carrying in a chair and deposited two cloth grocery bags in the kitchen. Then he turned to face her. "Is there a problem?"

She shifted from one foot to the other. Luc was wearing a suit and tie, and she felt like Daisy Duke facing off with Daddy Warbucks. "This union won't last forever. After all the money you're spending to help Deedee and me, you shouldn't have to finance the next phase of my life, as well. I thought it might be prudent to have something to fall back on in the future."

He nudged a corner of her navy plaid futon/chair with the toe of his highly polished wing tip, giving the sad, misshapen piece a dismissive glance. "When that happens, I won't cast off you and the child to live with cheap, secondhand furniture. I have a reputation to uphold in this town. Image is everything. You're going to have to face the truth, Hattie. You're marrying a rich man—whether you like it or not."

The mockery in his words and on his face was

not veiled this time. He was lashing out at her for what she'd done in the past. Fair enough. Back then she had made a big deal about their stations in life. Luc's money gave him power, and Hattie had been taught at her mother's knee never to let a man have control.

The man Hattie called "daddy" was really her stepfather. As a nineteen-year-old, her mother had been that most naive of clichés…the secretary who had an affair with her boss. When Hattie's mom told her lover she was pregnant, he tossed her aside and never looked back.

Hattie lifted her chin. "It was never about the money," she insisted. "Or not *only* the money. Look at what your life has become, Luc. You're the CEO of a Fortune 500 company. I'm a public school teacher. I clip coupons and drive a ten-year-old car. Even before I began helping with my mother's finances, I lived a very simple lifestyle."

He curled a lip. "Is this where I cue the violins?"

"Oh, forget it," she huffed. "This is an old argument. What's the point?"

He shrugged. "What's the point indeed?" He picked up the duffel bag. "Dinner will keep a few minutes. Do you mind if I change clothes? I came straight from the office."

"The baby is asleep in my room, but the bathroom's all yours. I'll set out the food."

She had rummaged in the bags only long enough to see that Luc's largesse was nothing as common as pizza, when a loud knock sounded at the door. She glanced through the peephole and drew in a breath. Eddie. Good grief. Reluctantly, she opened the door.

He reeked of alcohol and swayed slightly on his feet. "Where's my baby girl? I want to see her."

She shushed him with a quick glance over her shoulder. "She's in bed. Babies sleep at this hour of night. Why don't you call me in the morning, and we'll agree on a time for you to come by?"

He stuck a foot in the doorway, effectively keeping her from closing him out. "Or why don't I call the police and tell them you've kidnapped my kid?"

It was an idle threat. They both knew it. Hattie had already consulted a lawyer, and a nurse at the hospital had heard Angela's dying request. Nevertheless, Eddie's bluster curled Hattie's stomach. She didn't want to be in the middle of a fight with Deedee as the prize.

"Go away, Eddie," she said forcefully, her voice low. "This isn't a good time. We'll talk tomorrow."

Without warning, he grabbed her shoulders and manhandled her backward into the apartment. "Like hell." He shoved her so hard, she stumbled into the wall. Her head hit with a muffled thud, and she saw little yellow spots.

He lunged for her again, but before his meaty fists could make contact, Luc exploded down the hallway, grabbed the intruder by the neck and put a chokehold on him. Eddie's face turned an alarming shade of purple before Hattie could catch her breath.

Luc was steely-eyed. "Call the cops."

"But I don't want…"

His expression gentled. "It's the right thing to do. Don't worry. I'm not leaving you to deal with this alone."

The response to the 911 call was gratifying. Just before the two uniformed officers arrived, Luc stuck his face nose to nose with Eddie's. "If I ever see you near my fiancée again, I'll tear you apart. Got it?"

Eddie was drunk enough to be reckless. "Fiancée? Yeah, right. If she was telling my daddy the truth about you and her, then where's the fancy diamond ring?"

"I had to order it," Luc responded smoothly. "It happens to be in my pocket even as we speak. But some jackass has ruined our romantic evening."

The conversation ended abruptly as Hattie opened the door to the police. They took Luc's statement, handcuffed Eddie and were gone in under twenty minutes.

In the sudden silence, Hattie dropped into a

chair, her legs boneless and weak in the aftermath of adrenaline. Thank God the baby hadn't been awakened by all the commotion.

Luc crouched beside her, his eyes filled with concern. "Let me see your head." He parted her hair gently, exclaiming when he saw the goose egg that had popped up.

She moved restlessly. "I'm fine. Really. All I need is some Tylenol. And a good night's sleep."

Luc cursed under his breath. "Don't move." After bringing her medicine and water with which to wash down the tablets, he created a makeshift ice bag with a dish towel and pressed it to the side of her head. "Hold this." He lifted her in his arms and laid her gently on the ugly sofa. "Rest. I'll fix us a couple of plates."

He was back in no time. The smells alone made Hattie want to whimper with longing. Her stomach growled loudly.

He put a hand on her shoulder. "No need to get up yet. I'll feed you."

"Don't be ridiculous." But when she tried to sit upright, her skull pounded.

He eased her back down. "You don't have to fight me over every damn thing. Open your mouth." He fed her small manageable bites of chicken piccata and wild rice. While she chewed and swallowed, he dug into his own portion.

Hattie muttered in frustration when one of her mouthfuls landed on the sofa cushion. "See what you made me do…"

"Don't worry," he deadpanned. "A few stains could only help this monstrosity."

She eyed him, openmouthed, and then they both burst into laughter. Hattie felt tears sting the backs of her eyes. She told herself it was nothing more than delayed reaction. But in truth, it was Luc. When he forgot to be on his guard with her, she saw a glimpse of the young man she had loved so desperately.

She wondered with no small measure of guilt if her long-ago defection had transformed the boy she once knew so well into the hard-edged, sardonic Luc. A million times over the years she had second-guessed her decision. It had been gratifying to establish a career and to stand on her own two feet. Her mother had been proud of Hattie's independence and success in her chosen field.

But at what cost?

When the last of the food was consumed, the mood grew awkward. Luc gathered their empty plates. "Stay where you are. You have to deal with Deedee in the morning, so you might as well rest while you can."

She lay there quietly, wondering bleakly how her life had unraveled so quickly. Two months ago she'd been an ordinary single woman with a circle of friends, a good job and a pleasant social life. Now she was a substitute parent facing a custody battle and trying to combat a tsunami of feelings for the man who had once upon a time been her other half, her soul mate. Was it any wonder she felt overwhelmed?

A trickle of water from melting ice slid down her cheek. She sat up and sucked in a breath when a hammer thudded inside her skull. The food she had eaten rolled unpleasantly in her stomach.

Luc frowned as he rejoined her, pausing only to take the wet dish towel and toss it on a kitchen counter. "We probably should make a trip to the E.R. to make sure you don't have a concussion."

"I'll be fine." She knew her voice lacked conviction, but it was hard to be stoic with the mother of all headaches.

Luc put his hands on his hips, his navy polo shirt stretching taut over broad shoulders and a hard chest. "I'll stay the night."

Chapter 4

Hattie gaped. "Oh, no. Not necessary."

"We have the baby to think of, too. You probably won't rest very well tonight, and you'll likely need an extra hand in the morning. I'll sleep on the couch. It may be ugly as sin, but it's long and fairly comfortable. I'll be fine."

Hattie was torn. Having Luc in her small apartment was unsettling, but the encounter with Eddie had shaken her emotionally as well as physically, and she was dead on her feet.

She shrugged, conceding defeat. "I'll get you towels and bedding." She brushed by him, inhaling for a brief instant the tang of citrusy aftershave and the scent of warm male.

When she returned moments later, he was on the phone with Ana, letting her know he wouldn't be home that evening. It touched her that he would be so considerate of people who were in his employ. He was a grown man. He had no obligation to let anyone know his schedule or his whereabouts.

But wasn't that what had drawn her to him in the beginning? His kindness and his humor? Sadly, his personality had an edge now, a remoteness that had not existed before.

She began making up the sofa, but he stopped her as soon as he hung up. "Go to bed, Hattie. I'm not a guest. I don't need you waiting on me. I can fend for myself."

She nodded stiffly. "Good night, then."

He lifted a shoulder, looking diffident for a moment. "May I see her?"

"The baby?" Well, duh. Who else could he mean?

"Yes."

"Of course."

He followed her down the short hallway into the bedroom. A small night-light illuminated the crib. Luc put his hands on the railing and stared down at the infant sleeping so peacefully. Hattie hung back. Her chest was tight with confused emotions.

Had things gone differently in the past, this scene might have played out in reality.

A couple, she and Luc, putting their own daughter to bed before retiring for the night.

Luc reached out a hand, hovered briefly, then lightly stroked Deedee's hair. She never stirred. He spoke softly, his back still toward Hattie. "She doesn't deserve what has happened to her."

Hattie shook her head, eyes stinging. "No. She doesn't. I can't let Eddie take her. She's so innocent, so perfect."

Luc turned, his strong, masculine features shadowed in the half-light. His somber gaze met her wary one, some intangible link between them shrouding the moment in significance. "We'll keep her safe, Hattie. You have my word."

Quietly, he left the room.

Hattie changed into a gown and robe. Ordinarily, she slept in a T-shirt and panties, but with Luc in the house, she needed extra armor.

She folded the comforter and turned back the covers before heading for the bathroom. Well, shoot. She'd forgotten to give Luc even the basics. Taking a new toothbrush from the cabinet, she returned to the living room. "Sorry. I meant to give you this. There's toothpaste on the counter, and if you want to shave in the morning—"

She stopped dead, her pulse jumping. Luc stood

before her wearing nothing but a pair of gray knit boxers, which left little to the imagination. Every inch of his body was fit and tight. His skin was naturally olive-toned, and the dusting of fine black hair on his chest made her want to stroke it to see if it was as soft as she remembered.

Long muscular thighs led upward to… She gulped. As she watched in fascination, his erection grew and flexed. She literally couldn't move. Luc didn't seem at all embarrassed, despite the fact that her face was hot enough to fry an egg.

"Thank you for the toothbrush." A half smile lifted one corner of his mouth.

She extended the cellophane-wrapped package gingerly, making sure her fingers didn't touch his. "You're welcome."

And still she didn't leave. The years rolled away. She remembered with painful clarity what it was like to be held tightly to that magnificent chest, to feel those strong arms pull her close, to experience the hard evidence of his arousal thrusting against her abdomen.

His gaze was hooded, the line of his mouth now almost grim. "Like what you see?"

The mockery was deliberate, she had no doubt… as if to say *you were so foolish back then. Look what you gave up*.

Heat flooded her body. The robe stifled her. She

wanted to tear it off, to fling herself at Luc. But her limbs couldn't move. She was paralyzed, caught between bitter memories of the past and the sure knowledge that Luc Cavallo was still the man who could make her soar with pleasure.

"Answer me, Hattie," he said roughly. "If you're going to look at me like that, I'm damn sure going to take the invitation."

Her lips parted. No sound came out.

The color on his cheekbones darkened and his eyes flared with heat. "Come here."

No soft preliminaries. No tentative approach.

Luc was confident, controlled. He touched only her face, sliding his hands beneath her hair and holding her still so his mouth could ravage hers. His tongue thrust between her lips—invading, dominant, taking and not giving. She was shaking all over, barely able to stand. He kissed her harder still, muttering something to himself she didn't quite catch.

She felt the push of his hips. Suddenly, her body came to life with painful tingles of heat. Her arms went around his waist, and she kissed him back. But when his fingers accidentally brushed the painful knot on her skull, she flinched.

Instantly, he cursed and thrust her away, his gaze a cross between anger and incredulity. "Damn you. Go to bed, Hattie."

If she had been a Victorian heroine, she might have swooned at this very moment. But she was made of sterner stuff. She marshaled her defenses, muttered a strangled good-night and fled.

Aeons later it seemed, she rolled over and flung an arm over her face. Bright sunshine peeked in through a crack between the curtains. She had slept like the dead, deeply, dreamlessly. A glance at the clock stopped her heart. It was nine o'clock. Deedee. Dear heaven. The baby was always up by six-thirty.

She leaped from the bed, almost taking a nose-dive when the covers tangled around her feet. The crib was empty. She sucked in a panicked breath, and then her sleep-fuddled brain began to function.

Luc. Memories of his kiss tightened her nipples and made her thighs clench with longing. She touched her lips as the hot sting of tears made her blink and sniff. Ten years was a lifetime to wait for something that was at once so terrible and so wonderful.

She opened her bedroom door and simultaneously heard the sound of childish gurgles and smelled the heavenly aroma of frying bacon. Luc stood by the stove. Deedee was tucked safely in her high chair nearby.

He glanced up, his features impassive. "Good morning."

The baby squealed in delight and lurched toward Hattie. Luc unfastened the tray and handed her off. "I fed her a bottle and half a jar of peaches. I didn't want to give her anything else until I checked with you." The words were gruff, as if he'd had to force them from his throat.

Hattie cuddled the baby, stunned that Luc had taken over with such relaxed competence. Not that she didn't think he was capable. But she had never witnessed him with children, and she was shocked to see him so calm and in control, especially when Hattie herself had experienced a few rough moments in the last six weeks.

He started cracking eggs into a bowl. "This will be ready in five, and the movers will be showing up shortly. You might want to get dressed. I can handle Deedee."

Hattie held the baby close, realizing with chagrin that she had jumped out of bed and never actually donned her robe. The sheer fabric of her nightie revealed far too much. "She'll be fine with me." Suddenly she noticed the sheaf of legal papers on the nearby coffee table. "Luc...I'm so sorry. With everything that happened, we never did get around to dealing with the marriage stuff."

He popped two slices of bread into her toaster. "No worries. We'll have time later today."

She hesitated, eager to leave the room, but feeling oddly abashed that he had watched her sleeping…without her knowledge. Though they had made love many times when they were together, only once or twice had they enjoyed the luxury of spending the night together.

She cleared her throat. "Thank you for getting up with the baby. I can't believe I didn't hear her."

He shrugged. "I'm an early riser. I enjoyed spending time with her. She's a charming child."

"You haven't seen her throw a temper tantrum yet," she joked. "Batten down the hatches. She has a great set of lungs."

He paused his efficient preparations, the spatula in midair. "You're doing a great job. She's lucky to have you as her mother." His eyes and his voice were serious.

"Thanks." Despite the task he had undertaken, nothing about the setting made Luc look at all domestic: quite the opposite. Luc Cavallo was the kind of man you'd want by your side during a forced jungle march. He possessed a self-confidence that was absolute.

But that resolute belief in his own ability to direct the universe to his liking made Hattie uneasy. In asking for his help, she had unwittingly given him the very power she had refused to allow in their previous relationship. Even if she had second thoughts now, the situation was already beyond her control.

The contents of the small apartment were packed, boxes loaded and rooms emptied by 12:30. Luc had already paid out the remainder of Hattie's lease. All that was left for her to do was turn in her keys to the super and follow Luc out to the car where Sherman was waiting. But there she balked. "I'll follow you in my car."

Luc frowned. "I thought we had this discussion."

"I like my car. I'm sentimentally attached to my car. I'm not giving it away."

The standoff lasted only a few seconds. Luc shrugged, his expression resigned. "I'll see you at the house."

It was a small victory, but it made Hattie feel better. Luc had a habit of taking charge in ways that ostensibly made perfect sense, but left Hattie feeling like a helpless damsel in distress. She had *asked* for his help, but that didn't mean she'd let him walk all over her.

She strapped Deedee into the old, shabby car seat and slid into the front, turning the key in the ignition and praying the car would start. That would be the final indignity.

As their little caravan pulled away from the curb, Hattie glanced in the rearview mirror for one last look at her old life slipping away. Her emotions were not easy to define. Relief. Sadness. Anticipation. Had she sold her soul to the devil? Only time would tell.

Luc experienced a sharp but distinct jolt of satisfaction when Hattie stepped over his threshold. Something primitive in him exulted. She was coming to him of her own free will. She'd be under his roof...wearing his ring. Ten years ago he'd let his pride keep him from trying to get her back. That, and his misguided belief that he had to respect her wishes. But everything was different this time around. *He* was calling the shots.

The attraction was still there. He felt it, and he knew she did, as well. Soon she would turn to him out of sheer gratitude, or unfulfilled desire or loneliness. And then she would be his. He'd waited a long time for this. And no one could fault him. He was giving Hattie and her baby a home and security.

If he extracted his pound of flesh in the process, it was only fair. She owed him that much.

He left them to get settled in, with Sherman and Ana hovering eagerly. After changing clothes, he drove to the office and threw himself into the pile of work that had accumulated during his unaccustomed morning off.

But for once, his concentration was shot. He found himself wishing he was back at the house, watching Hattie…playing with the baby…anticipating the night to come.

He called home on the drive back. It wasn't late, only six-thirty. Hattie answered her cell.

"Hello, Luc."

He returned the greeting and said, "Ana has offered to look after Deedee this evening. I thought we might go out for a quiet dinner and discuss business."

Business? He winced. Did he really mean to sound so cavalier?

Hattie's response was cool. "I don't want to take advantage of Ana's good nature."

"You're not, I swear. It was her idea. Little Deedee has a way of making people fall in love with her. I'll be there to pick you up in twenty minutes."

It was only dinner. With a woman who had already rejected him once. Why was his heart beating faster?

Unfortunately for Hattie, the black dress had to do duty again. This time she had no inclination to wear Luc's necklace. Not for a *business* dinner. She tied a narrow tangerine scarf around her neck and inserted plain gold hoops in her ears.

She was ready and waiting in the foyer when he walked in the front door.

Luc seemed disappointed. "Where's the baby?"

Hattie grimaced, her nerves jumping. "She's taking an early evening nap. I couldn't get her to sleep much at all this afternoon…the uncertainty of a new place, I think. She was cranky and exhausted."

"Too bad. Well, in that case, I guess we can get going."

The restaurant was lovely—very elegant, and yet not so pretentious that Hattie felt uncomfortable. The sommelier chatted briefly with Luc and then produced a zinfandel that met with Luc's approval.

Hattie was persuaded to try a glass. "It's really good," she said. "Fruity but not too sweet."

He leaned back in his chair. "I thought you'd like it."

They enjoyed a quiet dinner, sticking to innocuous topics, and then afterward, Luc reached into a slim leather folder and extracted a sheaf of papers. "My lawyers have drawn up all the necessary documents. If you wish, you're welcome to have a third-party lawyer go over them with you. I know from experience that legalese is hard to wade through at times."

She took the documents and eyed them cautiously. "I have someone who has been helping me with the custody issues," she said, already skimming the lines of print. "I'll get her to take a look." Most of it was self-explanatory. When she reached page three of the prenup, her eyebrows raised. "It says here that if and when the marriage dissolves, I'll be entitled to a lump sum payment of $500,000."

He drummed the fingers of one hand on the table. His skin was dark against the snowy-white cloth. "You don't think that's fair?"

"I think it's outrageous. You don't owe me anything. You're doing me a huge favor. I don't plan to walk away with half a million dollars. Put something aside for Deedee's education if you want to, but we need to strike that line."

His jaw tightened. "The line stays. That's a deal breaker."

She studied his face, puzzled and upset. "I don't understand."

He scowled at her, his posture combative. "You've thrown my wealth in my face the entire time I've known you, Hattie. And now you're using it to protect someone you love. I don't have a problem with that. But I'll be damned when that day comes if I'll let anyone say I threw you out on the street destitute."

Her lip trembled, and she bit down on it...hard. Luc was a proud man. Perhaps until now she had never really understood just how proud he was. She was sure his heart had healed after she broke up with him. But maybe the dent to his pride was not so easily repaired.

She owed him a sign of faith. It was the least she could do after treating him so shabbily in the past. He was an honorable man. That much hadn't changed. She reached into her purse for a pen and turned to the first yellow sticky tab. With a flourish, she signed her name.

He put a hand over hers. "Are you sure you don't want someone to look over this with you?"

She shivered inwardly at his touch. "I'm sure," she said, her words ragged.

He released her and watched intently as she signed one page after another. When it was all done, she handed the documents back to him. "Is that it?"

Luc tucked the paperwork away. "I have a couple of other things I think we need to discuss, but it requires a private setting. We'll be more comfortable at home."

"Oh." Her scintillating response didn't faze him. He seemed perfectly calm. He summoned their waiter, paid the check and stood to pull out her chair. As they exited the restaurant, she was hyperaware of his warm hand resting in the small of her back.

Hattie was silent on the drive back. Her skin

was hot, her stomach pitchy. What on earth could he mean? Sex? It seemed the obvious topic, but she had assumed they might work up to that gradually...after they were married. She hadn't anticipated talking about it so bluntly or openly. They had been as close as two people could be once upon a time. But that was long, long ago.

Was she willing to go to his bed? To be his wife in every sense of the word? He was well within his rights as a husband to insist.

Did she expect him to be faithful in the context of a sham marriage? And if Luc no longer wanted to be intimate with Hattie, was it fair to deny him physical satisfaction?

She wouldn't lie to herself. She wanted Luc.

Dear Lord, what was she going to say?

In a cowardly play for more time, she stalled when they got back to the house. "I'd like to check on the baby and change clothes. Is that okay? It won't take me long."

Luc dropped his keys into the exquisite Baccarat dish on the table in the foyer. "Take your time. I'll meet you in the den when you're ready."

Chapter 5

Wearing ancient jeans and a faded Emory T-shirt, Luc sprawled on the leather sofa and stared moodily at the blank television screen. Was he insane? *Power.* A nice fantasy. Clearly he was fooling himself. What man was ever really in control when his brain ceded authority to a less rational part of his body?

Just being close to Hattie these last few days had caused him to resort to cold showers. He told himself that his physical response to her was nothing more than a knee-jerk reaction to memories… to sensual images of the way he and Hattie had burned up the sheets.

She'd been a virgin when they met, a shy, reserved girl with big eyes and a wary take on the world. As if she was never quite sure someone wasn't going to pull the rug out from under her feet.

He'd been embarrassed to tell her how many girls he'd been with before meeting her. A horny teenager with unlimited money at his disposal was a dangerous combination. In high school, he'd been too concerned about keeping his body in shape for sports to dabble in drugs. And even drinking, a rite of passage for adolescent boys, didn't hold much allure. Perhaps because he had grown up in a house where alcohol was freely available and handled wisely.

But sex…hell, he'd had a lot of sex. Money equals power…even sixteen-year-old girls could figure that out. So Luc was never without female companionship, unless he chose to hang with his buddies.

When Hattie came into his life, everything changed. She was different. She liked him, but his money didn't interest her. At first, he thought her attitude might be a ploy to snag his attention. But as they got to know each other, he realized that she really didn't give a damn that he was loaded.

She expected thoughtfulness from him, attention to her likes and dislikes. She wanted him to *know* her. And that was something money couldn't buy.

It was only much, much later that he realized his money was actually a stumbling block.

A faint noise made him turn his head. Hattie hovered in the doorway, her sun-streaked blond hair pulled back into a short ponytail, her feet bare. She was dressed as casually as he was.

He patted the seat beside him. "Would you like more wine?" The upcoming conversation might flow more easily if she relaxed.

She shook her head as she perched gingerly on the far end of the couch, tucking her legs beneath her. "No, thanks. Water would be nice." Her toenails were painted pale pink. The sight of them did odd things to his gut.

He went to the fridge behind the bar, extracted two Perriers and handed her one. As he sat back down, he allowed the careful distance she had created to remain between them. It meant she was nervous, and that gave him an edge. He handed her a slim white envelope. "We'll start with this." Inside were three credit cards with her soon-to-be name, Hattie Parker Cavallo, already imprinted.

She extracted them with patent reluctance. "What are these?"

He stretched an arm along the back of the sofa. "As my wife, you'll need a large wardrobe. I entertain frequently, and I also travel often. When it's feasible, I'd like you and Deedee to accompany me. In addition, I want you to outfit the nursery up-stairs. I've put a selection of baby furniture catalogs in the desk drawer in your bedroom. Ana will show you the suite I picked out for Deedee. If it doesn't meet with your approval, we'll decide on another."

She paled, her eyes dark and haunted.

He ground his teeth. "What's wrong?"

She shrugged helplessly. "I…I feel like you're taking over my life. Like I've lost all control."

His fists clenched instinctively, and he had to force himself to relax. "I understood there was some sense of urgency to the situation…that we needed to back up your lie quickly."

"There is…and we do…but…"

"But what? Do you disagree with any of the ar-rangements I've made thus far?"

"No, of course not."

"Then I don't understand the problem."

She jumped to her feet and paced. With her back to him, he could see the way the soft, worn jeans cupped her butt. It was a very nice butt. With an effort, he dragged his attention back to the cur-rent crisis.

She whirled to face him. "I'm used to taking care of myself." The words were almost a shout.

Something inside him went still…crouched like a tiger in waiting. He feigned a disinterest he didn't feel. "We don't have to get married at all, Hattie.

My team of lawyers loves going for the kill. Custody situations aren't their usual fare, but with Eddie in self-destruct mode, it shouldn't be too hard to convince a judge that you're the obvious choice to raise Deedee." He paused, risking everything on a gamble, a single toss of the dice. "Is that what you want?"

Hattie pressed two fingers to the center of the forehead, clearly in pain. Her entire body language projected misery. "I want my sister back," she said…and as he watched, tears spilled down her wan cheeks.

He tried to leave her alone, he really did. But her heartbreak twisted something inside his chest. She didn't protest when he took her in his arms, when he pulled the elastic band from her ponytail and stroked her hair, careful not to further hurt her injury.

She felt fragile in his embrace, but he knew better. Her backbone was steel, her moral compass a straight arrow.

The quiet sobs didn't last long. He felt and sensed the moment she pulled herself together. She stiffened in his embrace. Though it went against his every inclination, he released her and returned to his seat on the sofa. He took a swig of sparkling water and waited her out.

She studied a painting on the wall. It was a Vermeer he'd picked up at an auction in New York last year. The obscure work immortalized a young woman in her tiny boudoir as she bent at the waist to fasten her small shoe. The play of light on the girl's graceful frame fascinated Luc. He'd bought it on a whim, but it had quickly become one of his favorite pieces. Impulse drove him at times—witness the way he'd agreed so quickly to this sham marriage.

But in the end, his impulses usually served him well.

He grew impatient. "I asked you a question, Hattie. Do you want this marriage? Tell me."

She turned at last, her fists clenched at her sides. "If I don't go through with this, Eddie's family will know I lied. And they'll use it against me. I don't have a choice."

Her fatalistic attitude nicked his pride. His heart hardened, words tumbling out like cold stones. "Then we'll do this my way. You can't run out on me this time, Hattie. I love irony, don't you?"

His sarcasm scraped her nerves. She was being so unfair. Luc had done everything she had asked of him and more. He didn't deserve her angst and criticism. She owed him more than she could ever calculate.

The fact that her body still ached for his only complicated matters.

Swallowing her aversion to the feeling that she was being bought and paid for, she sat back down and summoned a faint smile. "Giving a woman that much plastic is dangerous. Should we discuss a budget?"

His expression was inscrutable. "I know you pretty well, Hattie Parker. I doubt seriously if you'll bankrupt me." He reached in his pocket and pulled out a small velvet box, laying it on the cushion between them. "This is next on the agenda. I thought it was customary to make such things a surprise, but given your current mood, perhaps I should return it and let you choose your own."

She picked up the box and flipped back the lid. *This* was a flawless diamond solitaire. Clearly he understood her style, because the setting was simple in the extreme. But the rectangular stone that flashed and sparkled was easily four carats.

She bit her lip. "It's lovely," she said, squeezing the words from a tight throat. He made no attempt to take her hand and do the honors. She told herself she was glad. When she slid the ring onto her left hand, the brilliant stone seemed to take on a life of its own.

"So you don't want to exchange it? I wouldn't want to be accused of controlling your life."

His tone was bland, but she felt shame, nevertheless. "I love it, Luc. Thank you."

It was his turn to get up and pace. "I've made some preliminary wedding inquiries. Do you need or want a church wedding?"

Disappointment made her stomach leaden. Like most girls she had dreamed of her wedding day. "No. That's not necessary."

"Our family owns a small private island off the coast, near Savannah. If you're agreeable, we can have the ceremony there. The location precludes the possibility of Eddie or any of his relatives showing up to make a scene. Do you have someone you'd like to stand up with you?"

She picked at a stray thread on the knee of her jeans, her mind in a whirl of conflicting thoughts. "My best friend, Jodi, would have been my choice, but her husband is in the military, and they were transferred to Japan two months ago. With Angela gone, well, I…"

"I'm sure Ana would be honored to help us out."

It was a good choice, and a logical one given the circumstances. "I'll ask her tomorrow."

"A honeymoon will be important," he said, bending to turn on the gas logs in the fireplace. The spring evening had turned cool and damp.

"I'm not sure what you mean."

He turned to face her, his expression blank. "We

can't risk any accusation that our marriage isn't real. I know you'll protest, but I really think we should go away for at least a week. Ana's niece is a college student working on her early childhood certification. I've already spoken to her, and she's willing to stay here at the house with Ana and Sherman while we're gone, to help with the baby."

Hattie gnawed her bottom lip. He'd neatly cut the ground from beneath her feet. Every argument anticipated and countered. It all made perfect sense. And it scared the heck out of her. "You seem to have thought of everything."

He shrugged. "It's what I do. As far as the wedding dress and the ceremony itself, I'll leave that to you. I have a good friend who is a justice of the peace. He's prepared to fly down with us and officiate."

"Who's going to be your best man?"

"Leo."

"Does he know about me…about Deedee?"

"I told him I was marrying someone he knew, but I left it at that. Leo will be there. But as far as he is concerned right now, this is a normal marriage. You and I will be the only people who will know the truth."

"You'd lie to your own brother?"

"I'll tell him the situation later…when it's a done deal."

"And your grandfather?"

"He's flying over for his big birthday party in the fall. I won't encourage him to come this time."

"I wonder if Leo will even remember me."

Luc chuckled. "My brother never forgets a beautiful woman. We'll get together with him for dinner when we come back from our honeymoon, and you can reminisce."

Hattie winced inwardly. Leo probably thought she was the worst kind of tease. Leading Luc on back in college and then dumping him. Leo would side with his brother, of course. Just one more thing to look forward to in her new, surreal life.

She took a deep breath. "When are we going to do this?"

"May 14 works for my schedule. I've cleared the week following for our honeymoon. Is there anywhere in particular you'd like to go? The company has a top-notch travel agent."

She smiled faintly. "Since I've never really *been* anywhere, I'll let you choose."

"I thought Key West might be nice…a luxurious villa on a quiet street. A private pool."

Her mouth dried. "Um, sure. Sounds lovely." Why did she suddenly have a vision of the two of them naked and…cavorting in the moonlight? *Dear heaven.* May 14 was two and a half weeks away. This was happening. This was real.

She couldn't wait any longer to address the elephant in the room. Or perhaps she was the only one who was worrying about it. Luc was a guy. Sex came as naturally to him as breathing. He probably thought nature would take its course.

But she needed to have things spelled out. "Luc?"

He rejoined her on the sofa, this time sitting so close to her that their hips nearly touched. Deliberately, he lifted her hand nearest him and linked their fingers. "What, Hattie? Permission to speak freely."

His light humor did nothing to alleviate her nerves. She squeezed his hand briefly and stood up again, unable to bear being so close to him when she was on edge. "I had a feeling earlier this evening…at dinner…that one of the things you wanted to discuss in private was sex. It makes sense…to talk about it, I mean. You're a virile man, and I assume you'll be faithful to our wedding vows. So no one can question the validity of our marriage. For the baby's sake."

His face darkened. "For the baby's sake…right. Because I assume that otherwise you could care less if I went to another woman for satisfaction."

He was angry, and she wasn't sure why. She picked up the elastic band he'd removed from her hair. With swift, jerky movements she put her ponytail back in place. She didn't want to think about how it felt to have his fingers combing through her hair, his hard, warm palms caressing her back.

"I'm trying to explain, Luc, that I'm okay with it."

"Okay with what?"

His black scowl terrified her. If she handled this wrong, he might back out entirely. "I understand that it makes sense for us to be intimate…while we're together. A man and a woman living in the same house…married. I'm willing.… That's all I wanted to say."

His lip curled. His dark eyes were impenetrable. "Well, you were right about one thing."

"I was?"

"I did want to talk about sex."

"I thought so."

"But while I am deeply touched by your desire to throw yourself on the sacrificial altar, I don't need your penance."

"I don't understand."

His legs were outstretched, propped on the coffee table. He feigned relaxation, but his entire body vibrated with intense emotion. "It's simple, Hattie. All I wanted to say was that it seems somewhat degrading to both of us to exchange *physical pleasure* for money."

The way he drawled the words *physical pleasure* made her belly tighten. "You're confusing me."

"Sex has nothing to do with this marriage agreement. Is that clear enough? If we end up in bed together, it will be because we both want it. I'm attracted to you, Hattie…just as I would be to any beautiful woman. And I have a normal man's needs. I'll welcome you to my bed anytime. But you'll have to come to me. Your body is not on the bargaining table."

He was being deliberately cruel. Perhaps she deserved it. But humiliation swept through her in burning waves. She had offered herself up in all sincerity, and he had reduced the possibility of marital intimacy to scratching an itch.

Dimly, apprehensively, she began to understand what Luc was going to get out of this marriage. He was going to make her dance to his tune. He was going to make her beg.

And what scared her even more than being totally at his mercy was the inescapable knowledge that she would be the one to crack. And she might not make it through the honeymoon.

Chapter 6

The days before the wedding flew by. Hattie was consumed with setting up the nursery and shopping for an appropriate dress in which to become Mrs. Luc Cavallo.

After the embarrassing scene with Luc in the den, Hattie saw little of him. He spent four days in Milan at a conference, and when he returned to Atlanta, he worked long days, ostensibly getting caught up so he could be away for a week's vacation. No one at his office knew anything about a wedding.

Deedee was thriving. There had been no further word from Eddie, and on the surface, life seemed normal.… Or at least as normal as it could be given the current situation.

Sherman and Ana adored Deedee and spoiled her with toys and other gifts. Hattie relished being part of that circle. She had never known her own grandparents, and the new relationships she was building helped fill the emotional hole in her soul. Things might become awkward when the marriage ended, but she would worry about that when the time came.

The wedding was only four days away when trouble showed up. Not Eddie this time. A loud knock sounded at the front door midday, and Hattie answered it. Sherman was out back washing the cars, and Ana was making dinner preparations.

The man standing on the doorstep was familiar. "Leo," she said, her heart sinking. "Please come in."

"Well, isn't this nice," he sneered. "Playing lady of the manor, are we?"

She ignored his sarcasm. Clearly, he *did* remember her…and not fondly. "Luc's not home."

Leo folded his arms across his broad chest. "I came to see you." He was a physically intimidating man, and his brains more than equaled his brawn. Back in college he had played at flirting with her. Not seriously, just to get his brother's goat. But the look on his face at the moment said he'd just as soon toss her in the river as look at her.

"How did you know I was here?"

"I didn't. But I knew *something* was going on. My brother's been acting damn strangely. And now I know why."

Ana appeared, wiping her hands on a dishcloth. "Mr. Leo. How nice to see you." She turned to Hattie. "If you would like to step out back to the patio, I'd be happy to bring you a snack."

Leo smiled at the housekeeper, a warm, I'm-really-a-nice-guy smile. "Sounds wonderful, Ana. I've been running all day and missed lunch." He eyed Hattie blandly. "What a treat."

Hattie felt Leo's eyes boring into her back as they made their way through the house. She hadn't expected a warm welcome from Luc's brother, but she also hadn't anticipated this degree of antipathy from him. They sat down in wrought-iron chairs, and moments later Ana brought out a tray of oatmeal cookies and fresh coffee.

The older woman poured two cups and stepped back. "I'll put the monitor in the kitchen, Hattie, so I'll be able to hear the baby if she wakes up."

Leo paled. As soon as the housekeeper was out of earshot, he swallowed half a cup of coffee and glared at Hattie over the rim of a bone china cup. His big hand dwarfed it. "Luc's a daddy?"

"No, of course not. Or not in the way you're thinking. Has he told you anything about my situation?" It was difficult to believe that Luc would cling to his intent of keeping Leo uninformed.

"Luc didn't tell me diddly squat. All he mentioned was that I should show up on the fourteenth wearing my tux when and where he said."

"Oh."

"Perhaps you'd like to fill me in." It wasn't a request.

"I'm sorry he's been keeping secrets from you. It's my fault." She quickly gave him the shortened version of the last two months. "I think that until the lawyers get a handle on this custody thing, Luc thinks the less said the better."

Leo ate two more cookies, eyeing her with a laserlike stare as he chewed slowly. "That's not why he didn't tell me. Luc knows I can keep my mouth shut. But he knew I would try to talk him out of this ridiculous sham of a marriage."

Hattie's heart sank. The two brothers were close. Could Leo, even now, derail what Luc and Hattie had set in motion?

She set down her cup so he wouldn't see her hand shaking. "Why would you do that? If you're worried about the money, or the company...you needn't be. I've already signed a prenup."

Leo snorted. "You may be a lot of things, Hattie, but even I know you're not a gold digger."

"Then why is this any of your business?" She

heard the snap in her own voice and didn't care. What did Leo Cavallo have to gain by sticking his big Roman nose into her affairs?

He pulled his chair closer to the table, his knees almost touching hers beneath the glass. His accusatory mood made her want to run, but she refused to give him the satisfaction. He spoke softly, with menace. "Ten years ago, you almost destroyed my brother. You let him fall in love with you, encouraged it even. And then when he proposed, the first and only time he's ever done that by the way, you shut him down. A man has his pride, Hattie. You let things go too far. If you weren't going to love him back, why in the hell did you sleep with him? Why did you let him think you were his girl, his future?"

She bent her head, staring down at the crumbs on her plate. "That's just it, Leo. I did love him. I was sick with loving him."

"That's bull." He lifted her chin, his gaze boring into hers. "Women in love don't do what you did to Luc."

"That's not true," she cried. "We never would have worked out in the long term. I wasn't the right person to be his wife. I did the right thing by breaking it off. You know I did."

He let go of her and sat back, brooding, surly. "Then how do you explain this?" He waved a hand.

"You damn sure appear to be enjoying the fancy house and the hired help."

"Don't be hateful."

"Not hateful, honey. Just stating the facts."

"This is all temporary."

"Does Luc know that?"

"Of course he does. When enough time has passed to make our marriage appear to be the real thing, we'll separate quietly. And I'll raise Deedee on my own."

"And what happens when my softhearted baby brother falls in love with the little girl sleeping upstairs? Will you tear his heart out again by taking her away?"

Hattie closed her eyes, regret raking her with sharp claws. "That won't happen," she said weakly.

"How do you know?" Leo asked quietly. "And how do you know he won't fall in love with *you* again?"

She laughed without amusement. "I can assure you *that* is not a possibility. Luc's helping me because he's a good man. But he's made it very clear that this is strictly business."

"And you believe him?"

"Why would he lie?"

"To protect himself perhaps?"

"From what?"

"The correct answer is *from whom*. You, Hattie. A man never forgets his first love. Why else would he turn his entire life upside down in a matter of days?"

"I think he's hoping for some payback, if you want to know the truth. I know I hurt him. I'm not stupid. This is his chance to be in control. To make me fall in line, not in love."

"How so?"

"He made it very clear that he has no feelings for me anymore."

Leo shook his head. "You don't know anything at all about men, sweetheart. If that's what he said, he's kidding himself. He sounds like a man who knows his own limits and is covering his ass."

Hattie mulled over Leo's words, torn between embarrassment and hope.

She was on the bed playing with Deedee when the master of the house came home. It surprised her that he sought her out. They had barely spoken a dozen words in the last week.

He looked tired. Not for the first time, she pondered the unfairness of what she had asked him to do. But what choice did she have? On her own, Eddie's family would have eaten her alive. And Luc had jumped at the opportunity to throw his weight around. So why did she feel guilty?

He sat down on the corner of the bed and grinned

at Deedee. She wriggled her way across the mattress toward him in a sort of commando crawl. He scooped her up and held her toward the ceiling. "Hey, kiddo. What mischief have you been up to today?"

Deedee squealed with laughter, her round cheeks pink with exertion. Luc nuzzled her tummy and lowered her to blow raspberries against her belly button.

Hattie watched them, her heart warmed by the budding connection man and infant shared. "She really likes you."

Luc glanced at Hattie. "The feeling is mutual."

His obvious enjoyment of something as simple as playing with a baby brought Leo's words rushing back. In all the time Hattie had thought about what would happen when the marriage ended, she had never considered the toll on Luc and her niece. Deedee would still be young. She wouldn't even remember Luc after a few months. But would Luc grieve?

Damn Leo for planting doubts.

Luc let the baby loose to roam the mattress again. Hattie had surrounded the edge with pillows, so Deedee couldn't go far. When the child latched on to one of her favorite toys, Luc finally spoke directly to Hattie. "How was your day?"

The prosaic question surprised her somehow.

She leaned back on her elbows. "They delivered the nursery furniture early this morning. Deedee has already napped twice in the new bed and pronounced it quite satisfactory."

"Good." Long awkward silence. "Are you ready for the weekend? Do you need anything?"

She sat up. "I'm pretty much packed. Ana has been helping me."

"And the dress?"

"I finally found what I wanted yesterday. I hope it will be appropriate."

"I'm sure it's fine."

Hattie sighed inwardly. Next thing you know, they'd be discussing the weather. She grabbed Deedee's ankle and pulled her toward the center of the bed. "Leo came by today."

That got Luc's attention. His eyes narrowed. "What did he want?"

"Well, apparently you neglected to mention that you were marrying me...or that I came with a baby. He wasn't happy."

Luc shrugged, his expression dangerous. "I don't make decisions based on Leo's likes and dislikes. If he doesn't want to come to the wedding, Sherman can do the honors."

"Don't be so pigheaded. Leo loves you."

"Leo believes his fourteen-month head start gives him the obligation to run my life."

"I think you should call him."

Luc's face went blank, wiped clean of all emotion. "I'll see him soon enough."

"Fine. Be an arrogant jerk. See if I care."

Luc stood up, gazing down at Hattie with an odd expression. "Sherman and Ana have the night off."

"I know. Did you want me to fix you something for dinner?"

"I thought we could take the baby on a picnic."

"It's kind of late."

"It won't hurt her to stay up just this once. Will it?"

"I guess not. I'll need to change, though."

He eyed her snug yellow T-shirt and khaki shorts. "You're fine. Let's go. I'm starving."

Luc had a garage full of expensive cars for every occasion. They took one of the more sedate sedans, a sporty Cadillac, and Luc moved the car seat. On the way, he dialed his favorite Chinese restaurant for takeout. Ten minutes later a helpful employee ran three bags out to the curb. The young man smiled hugely when Luc handed over a hundred and told the kid to keep the change.

Hattie wasn't prepared for their destination. Atlanta had many lovely spots for al fresco dining, but Piedmont Park brought back too many memories. Had Luc chosen the location on purpose?

As Hattie freed Deedee from her seat, Luc gathered the food, a blanket from the trunk, a bottle of chilled wine and a corkscrew he'd added before they left the house. It was a perfect spring evening. The park was crowded, but after a few minutes' walk, they found a quiet spot away from Frisbees and footballs.

Deedee had eaten earlier, so Hattie buckled her into a small, portable seat with a tray and fed her Cheerios while Luc opened containers. The smells made Hattie's stomach growl.

She snagged an egg roll. "This looks heavenly. I'm probably going to make a pig of myself."

Luc ran his gaze from her long legs all the way up past her waist to her modest breasts. "A few extra pounds wouldn't do you any harm."

The intimacy in his voice caught her off guard. What kind of game was he playing?

They ate leisurely, rarely speaking, content to watch the action all around them. Hattie remembered their college days with wistfulness. Back then, Luc would already have had his head in her lap. She'd be stroking his hair, touching his chest.

She trembled inwardly as arousal made her weak with longing. Deedee was no help. Her little head slumped to the side as she succumbed to sleep. Hattie unbuckled her and lifted her free. Luc moved the seat, and together they tucked the baby between them.

Luc reclined on his side facing Hattie. "I heard from the lawyers today. They've spoken to their counterparts, and it seems that Eddie's trying to claim it was really your sister at the wheel that night. That he was confused by the impact and that was why he left the scene."

Hattie clenched her fists. "Please tell me that won't fly."

He propped up one knee. "The police report is pretty clear. But that doesn't mean the case won't drag on. I don't know what they're getting paid, but my guys said the other team doesn't seem to have trouble with Eddie committing perjury if it will get him off."

Hattie was stunned. Since when could a man literally murder other people by driving under the influence and not end up in prison?

Luc was attuned to her distress. He stroked the sleeping infant's back. "Try not to worry. I'm only keeping you informed. But I don't want you to obsess about this. Our bottom line is keeping Eddie away from Deedee. Some judges side with a biological parent automatically, but if it comes to a hearing—and it may not—we'll show proof that Eddie would be a danger to his own child."

Hattie shivered. "I hope you're right. Judges can be bought."

Luc's grin was feral. "Good thing I have deep pockets."

Moments later he surprised the heck out of her by falling asleep. As Hattie looked at man and baby, she realized an unpalatable truth. It would be dangerously easy to fall in love with Luc Cavallo again. The few men she had dated seriously in the last decade were shadows when held up against Luc's vibrant personality.

Hesitantly, she reached out and barely touched his hair. It was soft and thick and springy with the waviness he hated. Usually, he kept his cut conservatively short, but perhaps he'd been too busy for his customary barber visit, because she could see the beginnings of a curl at the back of his ear.

Something hot and urgent twisted in her belly. She wanted to lie down beside him, whisper in his ear, pull him on top of her and feel his powerful body mate with hers. Her hand shook as she pulled it back. She would go to him eventually. It was inevitable. And he would have the satisfaction of knowing that she had made a mistake in leaving him. He would taste her regret and know the scales had been evened.

Luc held all the power. She was helpless to stem the tide of the burgeoning desire she felt. It had only been lying dormant, waiting to be resurrected.

And no matter how much pain she would have

to endure when the marriage ended, she would not be able to walk away from the temptation to once again be Luc Cavallo's lover.

Chapter 7

The morning of May 14 dawned bright and clear. The entire household was up at first light. Ana brought Hattie breakfast in bed, toast and jam and half a grapefruit.

Hattie, who had been awake for some time, sat up, shoving the hair from her eyes. "You didn't have to do this."

Ana sat down on the edge of the bed. "A bride deserves special treatment on her wedding day. Sherman and Mr. Leo have taken Deedee outside for a walk in the stroller. All you need to do is relax and let the rest of us pamper you."

Hattie took a bite of toast and had trouble swallowing. Even the freshly brewed hot tea didn't help. Fear choked her. Panic hovered just offstage. She wiped her hands on a soft damask napkin and looked at Ana. "Am I doing the right thing?"

A few nights ago, Luc and Hattie had decided the older couple needed to know the truth. Luc had hired round-the-clock security to be in place during the honeymoon, but it wasn't fair to leave Deedee's caregivers out of the loop.

Ana smoothed the embroidered bedspread absently. "Did I tell you that Mr. Luc offered Sherman and me an embarrassing amount of money if we wanted to retire?"

It seemed an odd answer to Hattie's question.

"I knew he gave you the option. But he told me you loved the house and didn't want to leave."

"As it was, he almost doubled our salaries. We're taking our first cruise this fall, nothing too fancy, but it will be a change of pace."

"Sounds like fun."

"The thing is, Hattie, I've worked my whole life. I wouldn't know what to do if I had to sit around all day. The previous owners of this grand old property were both in their nineties when they passed. They never had a family, and Sherman and I weren't able to have children, either. This is a big, wonderful house with all kinds of interesting history. But until you and Deedee moved in, it was missing something." She paused and smiled softly. "Mr. Luc wants to help you and that precious baby. What could be wrong with that?"

"But it isn't a real marriage. We're not a family."

Ana shrugged. "That may be true at the moment, but things happen for a reason. I've seen it too many times in my life not to believe that. Take it a day at a time. You'll be fine, Hattie dear. Now eat your breakfast and get in the shower. Mr. Luc's not one for running late."

Luc had chartered a private plane, and at ten-thirty sharp, it was wheels up. The short flight from Atlanta to the southeast coast of the state was a source of constant fascination for Deedee. She sat with Ana and Sherman, stuck her nose to the window and was uncustomarily still as she watched the clouds drift by.

Leo and Luc huddled together in the front row talking business and who knows what else. Luc's friend, who was to do the ceremony, sat with them. Hattie was left to chat with Ana's niece, Patti. The young woman's eyes were almost as big as Deedee's.

She took a Coke from the flight attendant and turned to Hattie with a grin. "I've never been on a plane before, and especially not one like this. I could get used to the lifestyle. Did you know the bathroom has *real* hand towels…not paper?"

Hattie smiled at the girl's enthusiasm. "I can't thank you enough for helping out while we're gone on our honeymoon."

Patti wrinkled her nose. "Well, I love kids, and when Mr. Cavallo offered to pay my fall tuition in exchange for the week, I wasn't about to say no. My aunt and uncle and I will take such good care of Deedee. You won't have to worry about a thing."

Hattie gulped inwardly. Her debts to Luc were piling up more quickly than she could calculate.

Before Hattie could catch her breath and gird herself for what was to come, the plane landed smoothly on a small strip of tarmac. Three large SUVs sat waiting for the wedding party. Once in the cars, they were all whisked away to a nearby dock where they boarded a sleek black cabin cruiser.

At first, Luc's island was nothing more than a speck against the horizon, but as the boat cut through the choppy waves, land came into view. Down at the water's edge, a large wooden pier had been festooned with white ribbons. Uniformed staff secured a metal ramp and soon everyone stood on dry land.

Hattie looked around with wonder. They were too far north in latitude for the island to have a tropical flavor, but it was enchanting in other ways.

Ancient trees graced the windswept contours of the land, and birds of every color and size nested in limbs overhead and left dainty footprints in the wet sand.

Luc appeared at her side. "What do you think?"

She smiled up at him. "It's amazing…so peaceful. I love it, Luc. It's perfect."

"We're trying to get the state to designate it as a wildlife refuge. Leo and I have no plans to develop this place. But one day, when we're gone, we want it to be protected." He took her arm. "Let's go. There's more to see."

Hattie's skin tingled where he touched her. Their hands were linked…perhaps he didn't notice. But the intimacy, intentional or not, was poignant to Hattie.

Dune buggies took the group up and over a crest to the far side of the island where a weathered but genteel guesthouse stood, built to blend into the landscape.

Luc helped her out of the fiberglass vehicle. "There's plenty of room inside for everyone to change. Will thirty minutes give you long enough? There's no real rush." He paused, and stared down at her, his expression pensive. "This is your day, Hattie. I know the circumstances aren't ideal, but you're doing a wonderful thing for Deedee."

For one brief moment, wistfulness crushed her

chest as she wondered what it would have been like to marry Luc when she was twenty-one. Determinedly, she thrust aside regret. This was not the same situation at all. She lifted a hand and cupped his cheek. "Thank you, Luc. I don't know what I would have done if you had turned me away."

The space around them was ionized suddenly, the hot, sticky air heavy with unspoken emotions. She went up on her tiptoes and found his mouth with hers. Someone groaned. Maybe both of them. He tasted like all her memories combined, hot and sweet and dangerous.

But they were not alone.

Luc took a step backward, and her hand fell away. Something akin to pain flashed across his face. "We both want what's best for the baby," he said, his voice gruff. "That's the important thing."

Sherman and Patti tended to Deedee while Ana helped Hattie get dressed. Hattie disappeared into a well-appointed bathroom to freshen up and slip into an ivory bustier and matching silk panties. Ana stepped in briefly to help with buttons and then tactfully left Hattie alone.

The day was warm and humid, and Hattie was glad she had decided to wear her hair up. She tweaked the lace trim at her breasts, adjusted the deliberately casual knot of hair at the back of her head and looked into the mirror. Too bad Luc wouldn't get a chance to see her in the delicate garments. They made her feel feminine and desirable, and she had charged them to one of the new credit cards without a qualm.

Ana waited in the bedroom, the wedding dress draped over her arms. In a small exclusive boutique in Buckhead, Hattie had found exactly what she wanted. The off-white dress was made of watered silk fabric and chiffon. The halter neckline flattered her bust and the fitted drop waist fluffed out into several filmy layers that ended in handkerchief points. The ecru kid slippers she'd bought to match were trimmed in satin ribbons that laced at her ankles.

Both women blinked away tears when Ana zipped up the dress and turned Hattie to face the mirror. It was fairy-tale perfect for a beach wedding—definitely bridal, but spritely and whimsical. Truth be told, it was not really a "Hattie" sort of dress. But it was her wedding day, damn it, and she wanted to be beautiful for Luc.

Ana picked up the narrow tiara and pinned it carefully to the top of Hattie's head. It was the appropriate finishing touch.

The older woman fluffed the skirt and stepped back. "You look like an angel." Her expression sobered. "I'm so sorry your mother and sister aren't here with you."

Hattie hiccupped a sob. "Me, too."

Ana looked alarmed. "No crying, for heaven's sake. My fault. Shouldn't have said anything. Let's touch up your makeup and get outside. I'll bet good money you have an eager groom waiting for you."

Ana left to take her place, and for a moment, Hattie was alone with her thoughts. She couldn't say in all honesty that she had no doubts. But perhaps a lot of brides felt this way. Scared and hopeful.

There was a brief knock at the door. When Hattie opened it, Leo's large frame took up the entrance. He looked her over, head to toe. A tiny smile lifted a corner of his mouth. "You'll do, Parker." He handed her a beautiful bouquet of lilies and eucalyptus. "These are from my brother. He's impatient."

He held out his arm, and she put her hand on it, her palm damp. "I care about him, Leo…a lot."

"I know you do…which is the only reason I'm here. But God help me, Hattie…if you hurt him again, I'll make you pay."

Not exactly auspicious words to start a new life.

Leo escorted her to the corner of the house, just out of sight of the water's edge where the ceremony would take place. He bent and kissed her cheek, then stepped back. Perhaps he saw the sheer panic in her eyes, because he smiled again, a real smile this time. "Break a leg, princess." And then he was gone.

Hattie's cue was to be the opening notes of "Pachelbel's Canon." A sturdy boardwalk led from the porch of the house out over a small dune to the temporary platform and the wooden latticed archway where she and Luc would stand.

The music started. She clenched her fists and then deliberately relaxed them. One huge breath. Several small prayers. One foot in front of the other.

Afterward, she could not remember the exact details of her solitary journey to the altar. In keeping with the unorthodox nature of the marriage and the ceremony, she had decided to walk to Luc on her own. This was her decision, her gamble.

When she first caught sight of the groom, her breath lodged in her throat and she stumbled slightly. Though there were three other people framed against the vibrant blue-green of the ocean, she only had eyes for Luc. He was wearing a black tux…a formal morning coat and tails over a crisp white shirt and a gray vest.

His gaze locked on hers and stayed there as she traversed the final fifty feet. As she stepped beneath the arch and took her place by his side, she saw something hot and predatory flash in his dark eyes before he turned to face the justice of the peace.

Without looking at Hattie again, Luc reached out and took her right hand, squeezing it tightly. The officiant smiled at both of them. "We are gathered here today to witness the union of Luc Cavallo and Hattie Parker. Marriage is a…"

Hattie tried to listen…she really did. But her thoughts scattered in a million directions. Too many stimuli. The feel of Luc's hard, warm fingers twined with hers. The familiar tang of his aftershave, mingling with the scent of her bouquet. The muted roar of the nearby surf as waves tumbled onto shore.

If she had the power, she would freeze this moment. To take out later in the quiet of her bedroom and savor everything she missed the first time around.

Out of the corner of her eye, she could see the giant live oaks that cast shade and respite on this hot, windy day. Sherman and Patti stood guard over the stroller, which was draped in mosquito netting. Apparently, Deedee had decided to cooperate and sleep through it all.

Closer to hand, Ana smiled, her cheeks damp. She was wearing a moss-green designer suit that flattered her stocky frame and shaved ten years off her age. Hattie had no doubt that Luc had financed the expensive wedding finery.

For a split second Hattie caught Leo's eye. The resemblance between the two brothers was striking, but where Luc was classically handsome, quieter and more reserved, Leo was larger than life. He winked at her deliberately, and she blushed, turning her attention back to the words that would make her Luc's wife.

"May I have the rings?"

Ana commandeered the bouquet, Hattie and Leo complied, and moments later, Hattie slid a plain gold band onto Luc's left hand. He returned the favor, placing a narrow circlet of platinum beside the beautiful engagement ring to which Hattie had yet to grow accustomed.

More words, a pronouncement and then the moment she had unconsciously been waiting for. "You may kiss the bride."

In unison, she and Luc turned. The breeze ruffled his hair. His expression was solemn, though his eyes danced. He took Hattie's hands in his. Time stood still.

Ten years…ten long years since she had been free to kiss him whenever she wanted.

He bent his head. His mouth brushed hers, lingered, pressed more insistently. His tongue coaxed.

His arms tightened around her as her skirt tangled capriciously with his pant legs.

Her heart lodged in her throat, tears stung her eyes, and she moved her mouth against his.

Aeons later it seemed, a chorus of unison laughter broke them apart. Luc appeared as dazed as Hattie felt.

Suddenly, hugs and congratulations separated them, but every moment, Luc's eyes followed her.

They led their small parade back to the house. Hattie had only seen one of the bedrooms, but now they all entered the great room on the opposite side of the building. The ambience was rustic but elegant. Exposed beams of warmly-hued wood were strung with tiny white lights. Dozens of blush-pink roses in crystal vases decorated every available surface.

A single table covered in pale pink linen was set with exquisite china, crystal and silver. When they were all seated, with Luc and Hattie at the head, Leo stood up.

As a waiter deftly poured champagne for everyone, Leo raised his glass. "Luc here, my baby brother, is and will always be my best friend. When Mom and Dad drowned, out on that damned boat they loved so much, Luc and I were shipped off to Italy to live for three years with a grandfather we barely knew. The language was strange, we were a mess, but we had each other."

He paused, and Hattie saw the muscles in his throat work with emotion. He moved to stand between and behind the bride and groom, laying a hand on each of their shoulders. "To Luc and his beautiful bride. May they always be as happy as they are today."

Applause and cheers filled the room, and moments later, the unobtrusive waitstaff began serving lunch.

Hattie knew the food was delicious. And wine flowed like water. But she couldn't taste any of it.

She was married to Luc. For some undefined period of time in order to protect the baby she had grown to love. But at what price?

When Luc put his arm around her bare shoulders, her heartbeat wobbled and sped up. He leaned over to whisper in her ear. "Are you doing okay, Mrs. Cavallo?" Gently, he tucked a wayward wisp of her hair into place.

She nodded mutely.

Luc laughed beneath his breath. "It might help if you quit looking like a scared rabbit."

She shrugged helplessly. "I'm in over my head," she admitted quietly. "What have we done, Luc?"

He stroked her back as he answered a cheerful question from across the table. "Forget reality," he murmured. "Pretend we're on Fantasy Island. Maybe this is all a dream."

Beneath the table, his hand played with hers.

The silly, childish game restored her equilibrium. Moments later their intimate circle was broken as Deedee demanded, in a loud string of nonsense syllables, to be recognized.

Luc chuckled as he stood to take the baby from Sherman and handed her to Hattie. Immediately, Deedee reached for the tiara. She yanked on it before Luc could stop her, and soon Hattie's hair was askew.

Amidst shrieks of infant temper, the tiara was rescued, the baby given one of her toys and the two at the head table became three. Luc tickled one chubby thigh, making Deedee chortle with laughter. He growled at her playfully and reached to take her in his arms.

Deedee's eyes went wide. She clung to Hattie's neck, burying her little face. And in a soft, childish, unmistakably clear voice, she said, *"Mama."*

Chapter 8

Luc had known Hattie for a very long time. And he saw the mix of feelings that showed so clearly on her face. Shock. Fierce pride. Joy. Sorrow. Almost too much for one woman to bear, particularly on a day already filled with strong emotion.

He stood and addressed the small group. "Hattie and I are going to slip away for a few moments to spend some time with Deedee before we have to say goodbye. We'll cut the cake when we return. In the meantime, please relax and enjoy the rest of your meal."

He coaxed Hattie out of her seat, witnessing the

way she held the baby so tightly to her chest. A crisis was brewing.

In the bedroom where Hattie had changed clothes, his brand-new bride faced him mutinously. "I can't leave her. It's cruel. We'll have to change our plans."

At that moment, Deedee spotted a carry-all stuffed with her favorite toys on the floor in a corner. She wiggled and squirmed and insisted on being put down. Hattie did so with patent reluctance.

Luc tugged Hattie toward the bed and sat her down. "Deedee will be fine. You know it in your heart. Aside from the fact that we need to make our marriage look absolutely real, you need a break, Hattie. Badly. This past year has been one crisis after another. You desperately need to rest and recharge your batteries."

Hattie looked up at him, her lips trembling, her big, brown eyes suspiciously shiny. "She called me *Mama*."

"She certainly did." Luc smoothed her hair where the baby had disheveled it. "And that's what you are."

Hattie bit her lip, not seeming to notice that he was touching her. "I feel guilty," she whispered.

"Why on earth would you say that?"

"I'm happy that Deedee is growing closer to me.

I know that's a good thing in the long run. But does that make me disloyal to Angela? How can I be so thrilled that the baby called me *Mama* when she won't even remember Angela, her real mother..."

Luc struggled for wisdom, though he didn't have a good track record when it came to Hattie. "As Deedee grows older you'll show her pictures of your sister.... And later still, you'll explain what happened, when the time is right. Angela will live in your heart, and by your actions, in Deedee's."

"And what about Eddie? What do I tell her about him?"

Luc ground his teeth, unused to feeling helpless in any situation. Did he want to replace Eddie as the baby's father? The temptation was there—he felt it. But he had no desire to be a family man, and Hattie had made it painfully clear that his help was only needed on a temporary basis.

He tried to swallow his frustration. "None of us knows how that situation will work out, but I doubt seriously if Eddie has any interest in being a father. That truth will be hurtful when she's old enough to understand it. But if you've filled her life with love and happiness, Deedee will get through it."

"I hope so," she said softly, her gaze pensive.

He reached out with one hand and touched her bare shoulder, resisting the urge to stroke the satiny skin. "You look beautiful today." The words felt like razor blades in his throat.

Finally, he regained her attention.

A pale pink blush stained her cheeks, and she lowered her head. Her long eyelashes hid her thoughts. "Thank you. I thought this was a better choice than a traditional wedding dress."

Something in her voice made him frown. "Do you regret missing out on a church wedding?"

She shrugged. "I thought I would. It's what many women dream about. But today was..."

"Was what?" he prompted.

She touched his hand briefly, not linking their fingers...more of a butterfly brush. "It was...meaningful."

Her answer disappointed him. He'd hoped for more enthusiasm, more feminine effusiveness. But it hadn't escaped his notice that she'd been careful with the wording of the ceremony. He'd left that portion of the day in her capable hands. The printed order of service she'd handed over on the plane had notably omitted any reference to "till death do us part" or even the more modern "as long as we both shall live."

He turned his attention toward the baby, trying not to notice the way Hattie's rounded breasts filled the bodice of her gown. She hadn't worn the pearl necklace today, and the omission hurt him, though he'd chew glass before he'd admit it. The only reason he cared was because it was an outward symbol of the fact that she belonged to him. She relied on him. She needed him. No other reason.

He bent and picked up Deedee. "We'd better get back to our guests. They'll be waiting for cake."

Though the day and the room were plenty warm, Luc realized that Hattie's fingers were cold when he put his hand over hers and pressed down firmly with the knife. Hattie had insisted, in private, that having a photographer document their faux wedding was unnecessary. So at the official cake cutting, only Sherman's digital camera was available to record the moment.

Hattie's smile toward Luc was apologetic as she picked up a small square and pressed it into his mouth. He wasn't sure which he wanted to eat more: the almond-flavored dessert, or her slender, frosting-covered fingertips.

He returned the favor, being careful not to mess up Hattie's makeup or dress. He fed her a tiny piece of cake and then deliberately lifted her hand and licked each of her fingers clean. The guests and servers signaled their approval with a cheer, and Hattie's red-faced embarrassment was worth every penny Luc had spent to make his bride's day special.

Ana stepped forward with a smile. "Shall I help you change clothes, *Mrs. Cavallo?*"

Luc put an arm around Hattie's waist, drawing her closer. He kissed her cheek. "I think we can handle that," he said, his voice low and suggestive.

Once in the bedroom, an irate Hattie rounded on him. "What was that show about? Ana and Sherman know the truth. You embarrassed me."

He shrugged, his hands in his pockets to keep from stripping the deliberately tantalizing dress from her in short order. "The waitstaff and the drivers are outsiders. They may talk, and if they do…I want them to believe that you and I are so much in love we can't keep our hands off each other. Any gossip will help us, not hurt us if they think we're a normal bride and groom."

Hattie stood in the middle of the room, her expression troubled.

He lost his temper. "Oh, for God's sake. I'm not going to jump you when your back is turned. Take off that damned dress and put some clothes on."

She blanched. He felt like a heel. Sexual frustration was riding him hard, and he wondered with bleak mirth what in hell had possessed him to insist on a honeymoon. If his brand-new bride didn't soon admit she wanted him the way he wanted her, he'd be a raving, slobbering lunatic by the time they got back home.

But he couldn't let her think he was affected by the day and the ceremony. The softer, gentler Luc she had known back in college was a phantom. The real Luc was cynical to a fault. What he was feeling was lust, pure and simple. Hattie would be in his bed. Soon. But he wouldn't be weak. Never again. He had his emotions on lockdown.

He turned his back on her and looked out the window blindly, the ocean nothing but a blur. All of his senses were attuned to Hattie's movements. Even when he heard the bathroom door shut, he remained where he was. It was impossible not to imagine her nudity as she stepped out of her bridal attire.

His hands were clammy, and his gut churned.

The bathroom door opened again, and he sighed inwardly. But still he didn't turn around. It was only when Hattie appeared at his elbow that he finally spoke. "Are you ready to go?"

He turned and inhaled sharply. The tiara was gone, her hair was down, but she was still dressed.

She raised a shoulder, her face rueful. "I'm sorry. I can't unzip it. Will you help me?"

God in heaven. She turned her back to him with innocent trust. His hands shook. Inch by inch, as he lowered the zipper, the dress gaped, revealing a sexy piece of fantasy-fueling lingerie. He cleared his throat. "Do you…uh…"

Hattie nodded. "Yeah. The bustier, too."

A million tiny buttons held the confection in place. God knows how long it took him, but he finally succeeded in revealing the pale skin and delicate spine he remembered with such painful clarity. He also remembered running his tongue down that very spine, not stopping until he reached the curve of her ass. And sometimes not even then.

The exercise in torture lasted for what seemed like hours rather than minutes. At last he was finished.

Hattie held the dress to her front with a death grip.

He made himself step back. "All done," he croaked.

She nodded jerkily and scooted toward safety. But just as she reached the bathroom, her toe caught on a scatter rug, she stumbled, and Luc grabbed for her instinctively. His arms went around her from behind and his hands landed in dangerous territory.

Lush, soft breasts. Pert nipples begging to be stroked. He sucked in a breath, sucker punched by the slug of hunger. Hattie froze on the spot like an animal hoping not to be noticed by a hunter.

He nuzzled the nape of her neck. "Your skin is so soft," he muttered. He squeezed gently, cupping the mounds of flesh that he remembered in his dreams.

Her head fell back against his shoulder. "Luc..."

That was all. Just his name. But the single word fraught with what he hoped like hell was longing made him hard as stone and ready for action. He tugged the dress and undergarment from her death-like grasp and tossed them aside. He couldn't see her face, and he didn't want to.

He continued to play with her breasts slowly. "Tell me you want me, Hattie."

"I want you, Luc...but..."

The last word made him frown. He slid one hand down her belly, between her legs. Hattie gasped audibly.

He bit gently at her earlobe. "But?"

"I don't think we're ready." Her whispered protest barely registered on his consciousness.

He pressed his aching erection against her, her beautiful round butt covered in less than nothing. "Oh, I'm ready, Hattie. Trust me."

The choked laugh she managed made him smile.

At that precise moment, when he felt paradise within his grasp, a loud shout of nearby laughter shattered the moment. They weren't alone. And they had guests waiting.

He cursed in frustration and released her abruptly, wanting to howl at the moon. His timing sucked. "Damn it.... I'm sorry."

Hattie didn't even turn around. He suspected her face was one huge blush. He reached for the discarded clothing and handed it to her. "Go," he said curtly. "We'll deal with this later."

Hattie huddled in the bathroom, her blood running hot and cold in dizzying, equal measure. She had come within inches of shoving her new husband onto the bed and pouncing on him. Feeling his hands on her bare skin had been more arousing than anything she had experienced in the last ten years.

She hadn't been celibate. But still...*holy cow.*

It took her three tries to button her lavender silk blouse. The cream linen trousers she stepped into were part of the outrageously expensive new wardrobe that now filled two large Louis Vuitton suitcases and a garment bag.

She looked in the mirror, wincing at her crazy tousled hair. Nothing to do but to put it up again. Ana had promised to collect the wedding finery and make sure it got back to the house. So all that was left for Hattie to do was to slip into low-heeled, gold leather sandals and wash her face.

She added fresh lip gloss, took the shine off her nose with a dash of powder, and spritzed her favorite perfume at her throat. What had Luc been thinking as he undressed her? Did he have any feelings left for her at all? Or was it only sex? What if she had turned in his arms and kissed him? Would she have been able to read his face?

He might feel the tug of attraction, but he was no green kid unable to control his body. Hell would probably freeze over before Luc would ever think about having a real relationship with Hattie, whether he saw her naked or not. He liked having her at his mercy. She had invited that with her artless marriage proposal. But Luc was thinking about sex…not a wistful reunion of lovers.

Luc had gained a heck of a lot of sexual experience since they parted. Hattie was old news.

Thinking of the women Luc had probably invited into his bed over the years was a bad thing to do on her wedding day. It only increased her misery. She'd had her chance. And being with Luc again made her rethink her youthful decision for the umpteenth time. Luc's money gave him power. No doubt about it. But from the perspective of ten years down the road, she admitted ruefully that he wouldn't have used the inequality in their bank accounts to control her, no matter what her mother said.

Her mother's take on life had always been hard-edged. Early disappointments had made her suspicious of people and their motives. Hattie had tried not to follow suit. But perhaps unconsciously that inherent attitude of distrust had been largely to blame for Hattie's breakup with Luc.

When she could procrastinate no longer, she slowly opened the bathroom door. Luc looked up and stared. Something arced across the room between them.

He cleared his throat. "I'll go change now. Why don't you play with the baby? I won't be long."

Before she could respond, he was gone.

Twenty minutes later, amidst the chaos of getting everything and everyone packed up for the return trip, she finally saw her husband again. He was wearing dark slacks and a pale blue dress shirt with the sleeves rolled up. His casual, masculine elegance took her breath away.

It shocked her to realize that she and Luc were not returning on the plane with the rest of the group. And Luc didn't take the time to explain, leaving Hattie to build scenarios in her head, each more unlikely than the next.

Ana stood by as Hattie said one last goodbye to the baby who had become so dear. When Angela was still alive, Hattie had been extremely fond of her tiny niece…as any doting aunt would. But now…now that Hattie played the role of mother, the bond was fierce and unbreakable. She couldn't pinpoint a single instant when it had happened. But the connection was substantial. As much as she was looking forward to spending time with Luc, it pained her to say goodbye to Deedee.

So much was still uncertain. And the baby was so helpless.

Ana patted Hattie's shoulder. "Don't worry... please. We'll watch over her as if she were our own."

Hattie handed over the sleepy child and forced a smile. "I know you will. She adores you and Sherman already. I wouldn't trust her with anyone else." The captain signaled Luc, and Luc began ushering everyone toward the boat.

Leo lingered to speak to Hattie. "I hope you know what you're doing."

She smiled wryly. "Do any of us ever really know what we're doing? I'm trying my best, Leo. It's all I can do."

He hesitated. "Call me if you need anything," he said gruffly. "And be good to my brother."

Before she could respond, he loped toward the end of the dock and boarded the cabin cruiser.

A mournful toot of the horn heralded departure. Luc rejoined Hattie, and they both watched and waved as the vessel moved away from the pilings, picked up speed and slowly skimmed out of sight.

Hattie shifted her feet restlessly. The sun was lower in the sky now, and a breeze had picked up, alleviating some of the heat. "Why didn't we go with them?"

Luc took her arm, leading her back toward the house. "It's been a long, stressful day. I thought it might be nice to relax here for the night. I've ordered a helicopter to pick us up at ten in the morning. He'll take us to the Atlanta airport, and we'll catch our flight to Key West from there."

"Oh."

He must have misread her quiet syllable as lack of enthusiasm, because he frowned. "I'm sorry I'm not taking you somewhere more exotic…like Paris, or St. Moritz. But with Eddie still a loose cannon, I thought it would be wiser to stay where we could get home quickly if need be."

"I think you're right."

Conversation evaporated as they neared the house. Hattie's heart was pounding in her breast. Two people alone on the proverbial deserted island. What happened next?

The truth was anticlimactic. Luc paused on the porch, running a hand through his hair, and for the first time that day, looking uncertain. "Are you hungry at all? We have leftovers."

Hattie had been too nervous earlier to eat much at their wedding meal. "Well, I…"

"It might be nice to sit out on the beach and watch the water while we eat."

Was that a note of coaxing in his voice? She indicated her clothes. "I dressed to travel. Do you mind if I change?"

"Roll up your pants legs. We'll go barefoot and pretend we're teenagers again."

This time there was definitely self-mockery in his words, but she was easily persuaded. They raided the kitchen, and in short order cobbled together a light meal. Luc found a large-handled tote, and they loaded it. Leaving Hattie to carry nothing but two bottles of water, Luc scooped up an old, faded tarp and swung the bag over his shoulder.

She laughed when he kicked off his shoes and rolled his trousers to his knees before they left the house. Following suit, she joined him outside, smiling when she felt the still warm boards beneath her feet.

It was her wedding day. Perhaps an unorthodox one at best, but still deserving of at least a jot of ceremony.

What had happened earlier lingered between them…unspoken, unacknowledged. But it was there, filling her veins with heady anticipation.

Luc managed to spread the ground cloth with her help, though the stiff wind made it necessary to quickly secure the corners with food containers. They sat down side by side. With no baby to act as a shield between them, either literally or figuratively, the mood was much different than it had been during the evening at the park.

Here, on an island far from land, removed from any other humans, it was more difficult to ignore the past.

Luc leaned back on his elbows, his expression pensive. "I wondered about you over the years... what you were doing...if you were happy." He turned his head suddenly and looked straight at her. "Were you?"

"Happy, you mean?"

He nodded.

"It's hard to pin down happiness, isn't it? I had a job that I liked. Friends. Family. So yes, I guess I was happy."

He frowned slightly. "I was an idiot back then. When we were in college. Confusing lust with love. I'm not sure love exists."

Her chest hurt. "How can you not believe in love?"

His gaze returned to the sea. "I understand loving a child, a parent. Those emotions are real. But between men and women?" His lips twisted. "Mostly hormones, I think. Makes the world go round."

The deliberate cynicism scraped at her guilt. Was that his intention? She curled her legs beneath her, poking at a small crab scurrying in the nearby sand. "You've never come close to marrying before now?"

He smiled faintly. "You mean after the debacle with you? No. Once was enough."

"I'm sorry."

"Don't be. It was a lesson well learned."

She hated his current mood. He was spoiling whatever pleasure she had managed to squeeze from today's events.

Her temper sizzled. Abruptly, she stood up. "I can only apologize so many times. You hate me. I get it. But I can't change the past."

Chapter 9

Luc cursed beneath his breath as Hattie ran from him. Had that been his subconscious intent? To make her angry? So there would be no question of appeasing the ache in his groin?

To say he was conflicted was an understatement. He wanted Hattie with a raw intensity that only increased day by day. But he wasn't willing to give up his position of power. He wouldn't let her see him as a supplicant. It was up to her to come to him. God help him.

He reached into the food bag and found a block of aged cheddar. Not bothering with a knife, he ripped off a hunk and bit into it. The cheese tasted bitter in his mouth. And since he knew all the food at the wedding was top-notch, the problem must be him.

He tossed the uneaten portion back in the bag and went to stand at the water's edge.

Until now, he hadn't allowed himself to think about the men who had shared her life in the intervening years. His fists curled, and he wished violently that he was at the gym so he could beat the crap out of a punching bag.

A swim in the rough surf might appease the beast inside him, but he couldn't take the chance. He wasn't worried about his own safety, but leaving Hattie alone if something happened to him would be the ultimate mark of irresponsibility.

And he was nothing if not responsible.

Damn it. He took off in his bare feet, running full-out, dragging air into his lungs, ignoring the shell fragments that pierced his skin. He kept up the brutal pace, rounding the point and covering mile after mile until he came full circle to where the uneaten picnic lay.

With his chest burning, his feet aching and his skin wind-burned, he stopped suddenly, bent at the waist and rested his hands on his knees. He was used up, worn-out, ready to stop.

But still he wanted Hattie.

Inquisitive gulls had found the bag of food.

Much of it would have to be tossed. He waved them away and packed up what he and Hattie had brought to the beach.

The house was quiet and dark when he slipped through the door. He dumped everything in the kitchen and went to his own bedroom, acutely aware that Hattie's was only a few yards away. It was only nine o'clock, but he couldn't see any light from beneath her door.

He stripped off his clothes and took a blisteringly hot shower. The water felt good on his tight, salty skin, but if he had been hoping for a soothing experience, he was out of luck.

His recalcitrant imagination brought Hattie into the glass stall with him. Her generous breasts glistened with soapy water as he washed her from head to toe. His erection was painful. As he stroked himself, he imagined lifting her and filling her, wrapping her long legs around his hips.

Ah.... He came with a muffled groan, slumping at last to sit on the narrow seat and catch his breath. He ran his hands through his wet hair, massaging the pain in his temples.

He was ninety-nine percent sure that Hattie was still sexually attracted to him. And he wanted her in his bed again. But on his terms. She had nearly destroyed him once upon a time. He'd be a fool to let it happen twice. So he'd be on his guard.

Sleep was elusive. Though he'd been up before dawn, he tossed and turned until he finally gave up the pretense of reading and turned out the light. He left the window open, relishing the humid night air. It suited his mood.

The nocturnal sounds were vastly different from back home. Birds and other wildlife filled the night with muted chirps and rustles and clicks. The sea created a hushed backdrop.

At 2:00 a.m. he tossed the tangled covers aside and padded to the kitchen in his boxers to get a drink. The house was dark and silent. He might as well have been the only person on the planet.

He drained the tumbler of water and stepped outside, tempted to run on the beach again. As he moved forward on the boardwalk, his heart stopped. A slender figure in white stood silhouetted against the dark horizon. Hattie. As he closed the distance between them, unconsciously treading as silently as possible, he saw that her back was to him. Her head was lifted to the stars. Her hair danced in the breeze. That same wind plastered her satin nightgown to her shapely body, leaving little to the imagination.

He should have turned back. It was the wise choice. But retreat had never been an option for him. Jump in the deep end, full steam ahead, onward and upward. Pick your cliché—that was how he lived his life. Perhaps if he had handled things differently a decade ago, he might never have lost her.

Something in her posture screamed sadness. And loneliness. An artist would have painted her and titled the canvas *Melancholy*. Seeing Hattie like this cracked something inside him. It hurt.

She didn't flinch when he joined her. Was she as attuned to him as he was to her?

He stood beside her, their shoulders almost touching. Her freshly washed hair was a tangle of damp waves, the light scent of shampoo mingling with the faint fragrance of her perfume.

"Are you okay, Hattie?"

Her chin lowered a bit, her gaze now on the water. She shrugged, not answering in words.

"I was being an ass earlier. I'm sorry."

Her lips twisted. "I should be the one apologizing. I was painfully young and immature back then. I know I hurt you, and I regret it more than you realize. I should have done things differently."

He winced inwardly. She wasn't apologizing for the breakup…only for the way she did it. The distinction was telling.

"I think we're going to have to agree to leave the past where it belongs. We're different people now."

"Leo remembers."

"Leo?"

"He threatened to tear me limb from limb if I hurt his baby brother again. He's very loyal."

Luc snorted. "Leo's a pain in the butt when he wants to be. Forget anything he said to you. I don't need his protection. And he's hardly in a position to be giving relationship advice."

"Maybe not, but he loves you very much."

They fell silent. Luc tried to steady his breathing, but the longer he stood beside her, so close that her warmth radiated to him, the more he became aroused.

"You're sad," he accused softly. "Tell me why."

She shifted restlessly from one foot to the other. "It's not exactly the wedding night I dreamed of."

Dangerous territory. "I'm sorry, Hattie. But, hey." He forced a dry chuckle from his throat. "At least there's moonlight, a romantic beach, a million stars. Could be worse."

"Could be raining." She shot back with the famous line from *Young Frankenstein,* and they both burst into laughter.

He couldn't help himself. He touched her. It was a matter of utmost urgency to find out which was softer—the satin, or her skin. At first, all he did was take her chin in his hand. He turned her so that they were face-to-face, their pose and position mimicking that of the wedding ceremony.

Hattie moved restlessly and he dropped his hand. He sighed. "I take it you couldn't sleep?"

"No."

"Me, either. I've never had a wedding night before. Turns out this stuff is pretty stressful."

That coaxed a small smile from her. "At least you didn't have to contend with a receiving line and five hundred guests."

"Why do people do that? Sounds exhausting."

"I imagine they want to share their happiness with as many people as possible, and they want to express their appreciation to those who made the effort to show up."

"You apparently have given this some thought."

"It's a typical teenage girl fantasy."

"I wish you could have had your dream wedding."

"Can we talk about something else?" The hint of fatigued petulance made him smile. It was so unlike her.

"I could tell you that when I first looked out here, I thought I was seeing a ghost."

She touched his cheek, making him tremble. "I suppose this must seem like a bad dream to you, your whole world turned upside down. And no end in sight. I owe you, Luc."

He put his hand on hers, keeping the connection. "Perhaps I could collect an installment right now."

He'd be kidding himself if he didn't admit that this had been his intent all along. Otherwise, he'd have stayed in the house. But he wouldn't force her. "I'm not the groom you would have chosen, and this sure as hell isn't what you expected from a wedding day. But at least we deserve a kiss…don't we?"

His free hand settled at her waist, caressing the satin-covered curve that led to her hip. As far as he could tell, she was bare beneath the seductive piece of lingerie.

Her eyes searched his, and she moved her hand away. Now both of his palms cupped her hips, inexorably pulling her closer. Her breasts brushed his bare chest. Someone moaned. Was it him?

He leaned his forehead on hers. "Do you want me to stop?"

Small white teeth mutilated her bottom lip. "What I want and what is wise are two different things."

He pushed his hips against hers, letting her feel the evidence of his arousal. He was going to pay like hell for this, but he couldn't stop. "I don't really give a damn about what's wise right at this moment."

They were pressed together now, and they might as well have been naked for all the modesty their thin garments afforded. Every hill and plane of her body fit with his like the most exquisite puzzle. Yin to yang. Positive to negative. Male to female.

She slid her arms around his neck.

He shuddered, struggling to keep a rein on his passion. Sexual attraction. That's all it was. Natural male urgency after a stretch of celibacy.

At first, their lips barely met, hardly touched. Some innate caution they both recognized pretended to slow the dance. But the cataclysm was building and nothing could hold it back.

When her small tongue hesitantly traced his bottom lip, he growled and lifted her off her feet. Their mouths dueled, fumbled, smashed together again in reckless, breathless pleasure.

He had never forgotten her taste…sweet, but with a tart bite like an October apple. The month they first met. The time he'd fallen hard.

And speaking of hard. He rubbed his shaft against her soft belly, making her whimper. That sound of feminine longing went straight to his gut, destroying all semblance of sanity.

Again and again he kissed her…throat, cheeks, eyelids, and back to her soft, puffy-lipped mouth. He dropped to his knees and tongued her navel, wetting the fabric and gripping her hips so tightly he feared bruising her.

Her hands fisted in his hair. But she was holding him close, not pushing him away.

The tsunami crashed over him, an unimagined, unexpected wave of yearning so endless, his eyes stung.

But the aftermath was devastation.

He stumbled to his feet when Hattie tore herself from his embrace, her hair wild, her eyes dark and wide.

She held out a hand when he would have taken her in his arms again. "You've got to give me time," she whispered, her voice hoarse. "It's not just me anymore. I have the baby to think about. I can't afford to make another mistake."

"A mistake." He repeated it dumbly, his control in shreds. His soul froze with a whoosh of unbearable coldness. He shrugged, the studied nonchalance taking every ounce of acting skill he possessed. "You'll have to forgive me. I got carried away by the ambience. But you're right. We're both adults. We should be using our heads, not succumbing to moonlight madness. Let's chalk this up to a long day and leave it at that."

Her arms wrapped around her waist. For a moment he could swear she was going to say something of import.

But she didn't. And for the second time that day, she left him.

If Hattie slept at all, it was only in bits and snatches. Her eyes were gritty when the alarm went off at eight-thirty. And the fact that she had set an alarm for the first morning of her honeymoon made her want to laugh hysterically. She bit down on the macabre humor, afraid that if she let loose of the tight hold she had on her emotions that she would dissolve into a total mess.

She was dressed, packed and sitting on the bed by nine-fifteen. There was plenty of food in the kitchen, but the prospect of eating made her nauseous. Her stomach was tightly knotted, her mouth dry with despair.

When Luc knocked on her door just before ten, she opened it with pseudo calm. "Good morning."

He didn't return her greeting, but merely held out a cup of coffee. It was black and lightly sweet, just the way she liked it. Luc's expression was shuttered, dark smudges beneath his eyes emphasizing his lack of sleep.

As he picked up two of her bags, he spoke quietly. "I can hear the chopper. The pilot and I will load the luggage. Why don't you wait on the porch until we're ready?"

It was all accomplished in minutes. The man flying the helicopter was polite and deferential as he handed Hattie up into the large doorway. Luc followed. They buckled in, the rotors roared to life and moments later they were airborne.

Hattie gazed down at the island and had to blink

back tears. It had been a fairy-tale wedding. Too bad she knew that fairy tales were nothing more than pleasant fiction.

The noise in the chopper made conversation impossible. Which was fine by Hattie. She kept her nose glued to the glass and watched the shoreline recede as they cruised across central Georgia. Ignoring Luc at the moment equaled self-preservation.

Landing at Atlanta's enormous airport was frantic. Chaos reigned in controlled waves. Luc gave her a sardonic look as they made their way into the terminal followed by their luggage. "We're flying commercial today," he said, scanning the departure board for their gate. "I know your Puritan soul would have balked if I had chartered a jet for just the two of us."

The security lines were long and slow. But finally, they were able to board. Hattie had never flown first-class. The width of the seat was generous, but still dangerously close to Luc's. She closed her eyes and pretended to sleep as the jet gathered speed and took off.

Pretense became reality. She woke up only when they touched down in Miami. Luc must have slept, as well, because his usual sartorial perfection was definitely rumpled.

Their connecting flight to Key West was a small

plane with only two seats on either side of a narrow aisle. Now she and Luc were wedged hip to hip. After her long nap, it was hard to fake sleep again. So she pretended an intense interest in watching the commotion outside her window.

When they were airborne for the short flight, Luc pulled out a business magazine and buried his head in it.

Hattie and her new groom had barely spoken the entire day.

She was travel-weary, depressed and missing Deedee.

The Key West airport was as tiny as Atlanta's was huge. Nothing more than a handful of plastic chairs and a few car rental counters. Luc had taken care of every detail. Their leased vehicle, a bright, cherry-red convertible, was waiting for them.

The first humorous moment of the day arrived when they struggled to fit their luggage into the car's small trunk. A disgruntled Luc finally conceded defeat and went inside to swap the car for a roomier sedan.

While he was gone, Hattie made a decision. They couldn't ignore each other forever. Last night was a bad mistake. He knew it, and she knew it. So it was best to start over and go from here.

She managed a smile when he returned with the

new set of keys. "Sorry that didn't work out. I liked the convertible."

He thrust the last bag into the backseat and motioned for her to get in. "I'd buy you one, but it's not a great car for a mom."

His casual generosity was one thing, but hearing herself called a "mom" shocked her. It was true. She was a mother. The knowledge still had a hard time sinking into her befuddled brain.

Luc had apparently been here before or had at least memorized the route, because he drove with confidence, not bothering to consult the navigation system. When they pulled up in front of a charming two-story structure that looked like a sea captain's home from the nineteenth century, Hattie was surprised and delighted. This was so much better than an impersonal hotel.

The wooden building was painted mint-green with white trim. Neatly trimmed bougainvillea, and other flowers Hattie couldn't name, bloomed in profusion, emphasizing the tropical ambience.

Luc and Hattie had barely stepped from the car when a distinguished gentleman, perhaps in his early sixties, came out to meet them. He extended a hand to each of them. "Welcome to Flamingo's Rest. I'm the innkeeper, Marcel. We have the honeymoon suite all ready for you."

Marcel opened the weathered oak door and ushered them inside.

He grinned at Hattie, clearly happy to be welcoming guests. "You've come at a beautiful time of year."

Marcel led them up carpeted stairs and flung open the door to an apartment that took up half of the second floor. Before Hattie could do more than glance inside, their host smiled broadly. "Key West is the perfect spot for a romantic getaway. Let me know if you need anything at all."

Chapter 10

In the wake of the innkeeper's departure, Hattie watched as Luc prowled the elegant quarters. The bedroom boasted an enormous four-poster king-size bed. Just looking at it through the doorway made Hattie tremble.

At the moment, she was ensconced in less volatile territory. The living area was furnished luxuriously, including a sofa and several chairs, a flat-screen TV, a wet bar and plush carpet underfoot.

Hattie curled up in one of the leather chairs. "This is very nice," she said, her words carefully neutral.

A brief knock at the door heralded the arrival of their luggage. Marcel and a younger employee stowed everything in the generous closets, accepted Luc's tip with pleased smiles and exited quietly.

In the subsequent silence, awkwardness grew.

Hattie waved a hand, doing her best to seem unconcerned. "I'll sleep out here. The couch is big and comfortable. I'll be fine." She tried changing the subject. "I'm going to call Ana now and see if I can talk to Deedee." She stopped and grinned wryly. "Well, you know what I mean. Do you want to say anything?"

Luc grabbed a beer from the fridge, his movements jerky. "Not right now. I have some business calls I need to make. I'll be in the bedroom if you need me."

Hattie choked on a sound that wasn't quite a giggle. She couldn't help it. After last night, his careless comment struck her as darkly funny.

Luc grimaced, his gaze flinty. "Give Ana and Sherman my regards."

Hattie sighed as he disappeared. Luc was definitely disgruntled. She didn't really blame him. Men didn't do well with sexual frustration, and Hattie herself was feeling out of sorts. What would it take to coax him back into a less confrontational mood?

Deedee chortled and babbled when Ana held the

phone to the baby's ear. But Hattie couldn't really tell if Deedee recognized her voice. When the call ended, she had to wipe her eyes, but she knew that this separation wouldn't harm her niece. It was Hattie who was having a hard time.

The sitting room actually had its own bathroom, so Hattie decided to freshen up. Fortunately, she had kept her personal bag with her, so she didn't have to invade the bedroom. Knowing how airlines could lose luggage, she'd packed a pair of khaki walking shorts and a teal blouse in her carry-on. She changed out of her dress into the more casual clothes, breathing a sigh of relief.

Being Luc Cavallo's wife was going to take some adjustment. Hattie was accustomed to traveling in jeans and sneakers, not haute couture.

Her shoes were in one of the big suitcases, so she padded barefoot to the window and looked out into the courtyard. Two small pools, one behind the other, glowed like jewels in the late afternoon sun. It struck her as she glanced at her watch that she had been married an entire day already.

It was a full hour before Luc reappeared. He, too, had changed, but only into a fresh dress shirt. He had his briefcase in hand and a jacket slung over his shoulder.

Hattie's eyes widened. "What's going on?"

"I have to leave." He didn't quite manage to meet

her gaze as he fiddled with his watch strap. "There's a crisis in the Miami office, and I'm the closest man on the ground. Our VP there is supposed to be signing a hot new Latin designer, and apparently things aren't going well."

"You're going to Miami?" She was stunned.

He shrugged into his jacket. "I'll talk to Marcel on the way out. Everyone understands business emergencies. He'll look out for you while I'm gone. Shouldn't be more than twenty-four hours at the most, not enough time for anyone to question our marriage. You'll enjoy the shopping here. And order dinner in if you don't feel like getting out tonight."

"You're leaving me on our honeymoon?" The reality was sinking in. She couldn't decide if she was more angry or hurt.

Luc strode to the door, opened it and looked back, his eyes empty of any emotion. "My life didn't suddenly stop when you came back, Hattie. I've done everything you asked. Deedee is safe. We both know this marriage is temporary. You'll have to make some allowances. I sure the hell am."

She curled up on the massive bed and cried for an hour. Insulting, that's what it was. So what if this wasn't a real marriage? Didn't she deserve at least a *pretend* honeymoon?

And did Luc care so little for her feelings that he could simply desert her after last night?

Her eyes were red and puffy, but she was calm when her cell phone rang at nine o'clock. She didn't recognize the number, though she knew it was an Atlanta area code.

Leo's deep voice echoed on the other end. "I need to talk to my brother. He's not answering his damn phone."

Hattie tucked a strand of hair behind her ear and scooted up on the down pillows. "He's not here, Leo."

"What do you mean he's not there?"

"He left. He's gone. Kaput. Some commotion in the Miami office about a new designer and an important contract."

"What the hell?"

Hattie winced. "I don't know what to say, Leo. He's not here."

Muffled profanity on the other end of the line was followed by Leo's long, audible sigh. "I'm sorry, Hattie. I should have gone to Miami. But I've been tied up with another deal."

"It's not your fault. I'm pretty sure this is his way of showing me he's the boss. Or maybe he's dishing out a bit of payback. He still harbors a lot of anger toward me. And I can't really blame him."

"I'm sure the Miami crisis is real."

"It probably is," she said, her voice dull. "But how many brides do you know who would put up with this? Me? I don't have a choice. He holds all the cards. Good night, Leo."

Luc stood on his balcony, staring out at the ocean and cursing his own stubbornness. He'd handled the business crisis in record time and had been ready to speed back to his lovely wife. But at the last moment he decided to stay gone overnight. It was important that Hattie understand he wouldn't be swayed by his lust.

They were going to have sex…and soon. But he wasn't a slave to his libido. And he wasn't going to fall at her knees and beg.

The irony didn't escape him. He'd been on his knees on his wedding night. But Hattie's indecision had saved him from making a fool of himself. He was back in the driver's seat.

He wondered what Hattie was doing right now. Was she at a restaurant, where available men were hitting on her? He slammed his fist on the railing and welcomed the pain. Maybe it would clear his head.

In business, he knew that the key to success was always, always keeping the upper hand. Last night had been a bad mistake. He'd allowed Hattie to see how much he still wanted her. And that knowledge was power.

She was supposed to beg *him* for sex, not the other way around. He wasn't in love with her. This gnawing ache in his gut was simple male lust. His last relationship had ended several months ago, and since then work had been all-consuming.

When Hattie showed up on his doorstep, it made sense that he would respond to her strongly, given their past and his recent stretch of celibacy. And it made sense for them to enjoy each other physically as long as they were legally man and wife. But when Deedee's situation was secure, Luc would make it clear that it was time for the two females to go.

Hattie fell into an exhausted slumber somewhere around two in the morning. So she was peeved when Marcel knocked at her suite before nine. But when she opened the door, the man standing there was not Marcel. It was Leo Cavallo. Her brand-new brother-in-law.

She ran a hand through her hair, ruefully aware that she looked a mess. "What are you doing here?"

He seemed unusually somber. "May I come in?"

Her knees went weak. "Oh, God. Is it Luc?" She grabbed his shirt. "Tell me. Is he okay?" Little yellow dots danced in front of her eyes and the world went black.

When she came to, she was lying flat on her back on the sofa with Leo hovering nearby. He patted her hand. "I'm sorry I scared you. Luc is fine." His gaze was accusatory. "You still love him."

She sat up carefully. "Of course I don't."

"Are you pregnant? Is that why you fainted?"

"Leo. For God's sake. I didn't eat dinner and I haven't had breakfast. I got woozy. End of story."

She stood up carefully and went to the mini-bar for a Coke. She needed caffeine badly, and she wasn't prepared to wait for coffee to brew. "You still haven't told me why you're here." She shot him a bewildered look.

He shrugged, dwarfing the armchair in which he sat. "When you told me Luc had gone to Miami, it got me to thinking. At the wedding, only a blind man could have missed the fact that Luc still has strong feelings for you...and vice versa. I wasn't the only one who noticed."

"Your imagination is impressive."

"Deny it if you want. But regardless, it's a crappy thing to do to you...abandoning you on your honeymoon."

"And you've come to tell him that?"

"No. I'm here to get him to sign some papers.

They're important, but I wouldn't have bothered him on his honeymoon except for the fact that he apparently doesn't see anything wrong with mixing business with pleasure." He held up his hands. "I'll hang out with you until he gets back."

She shook her head, smiling. "I thought I was the villainess of the piece."

"I've been known to be wrong on occasion." He shrugged, his boyish grin equally as appealing as her husband's. But Leo's smile didn't stir her heartbeat in the least.

"That's sweet of you, but not necessary. I can entertain myself."

"Quit arguing. Go put your swimsuit on. I'll do a quick change myself and get Marcel to roust us up some brunch."

Leo was as good as his word. When Hattie made her way down to the pool in silver slides and an emerald-green maillot, her brother-in-law was already stretched out on a chaise lounge, apparently content to while away a few hours.

As she sat down beside him, she heard a quiet snore. He must have taken the red-eye. Poor guy. She'd let him sleep.

When the sun warmed her through and through, she slipped into the pool with a sigh of pleasure. Being rich definitely had its advantages. She did some laps and then floated lazily, feeling the hot rays beating down on her.

It was nice of Leo to keep her company, but Hattie wanted her husband…stripped down to nothing but his swim trunks so she could ogle his body to her heart's content.

If Marcel thought it odd that a new bride was frolicking poolside with a man who wasn't her husband, he made no sign. He was polite and unobtrusive when he brought out a tray laden with everything from scrambled eggs and bacon to fresh mangoes and homemade croissants filled with dark chocolate.

Leo roused in time to devour his share of the repast. "I was hungry," he said sheepishly as he snitched a lone strawberry.

Hattie lay back, her cup and saucer balanced on her tummy. "This coffee is to die for. I'll have to find out what brand it is." She finished her drink and turned on her stomach…drifting, half-awake, listening to birdsong and the gentle sough of the wind in the palm fronds.

Leo poked her knee. "You're turning pink, princess. Better put some sunscreen on."

Without opening her eyes, she reached for the bottle of lotion under her chair. "Will you do my back, please? I'll throw a towel over my legs, so don't bother with that."

* * *

Luc parked the car in front of the B and B and sat for ten seconds, giving himself a lecture. He was calm. He was in control. Hattie would dance to his tune.

He had a plan. One that would satisfy the hunger riding him and at the same time make it clear to his new wife that nothing had changed. Their marriage was still temporary.

It was an unpleasant shock to find their suite empty. But then he took a deep breath. Hattie was shopping, that was all. Women loved to shop. The tourist district of Key West wasn't all that big. Maybe he would take the car and drive around for a bit, see if he spotted her.

As he hurried back down the stairs, keys in hand, Marcel intercepted him. "Welcome back, Mr. Cavallo. I hope your business was transacted successfully."

"Yeah," Luc muttered, unaccountably embarrassed. "Do you happen to know if Hattie has gone to town?"

Marcel shook his head. "Your wife is out by the pool with her friend. I served them a meal not long ago. Shall I bring more food?"

"No thanks. Not hungry."

Luc's hackles rose. *Her friend?* No doubt, some

handsome surfer type had taken advantage of Luc's short absence to make a move.

Well, not for long, buddy.

Luc walked outside, keeping behind the bushes until he got a clear shot of the pool. Hattie was stretched out, facedown, in a suit that made his mouth water. But the sight that took his breath away was the large man rubbing lotion into Hattie's shoulders.

Damn and double damn. The guy had his back to Luc, and at this distance, Luc couldn't really tell much about him...except that he was getting way too chummy with Luc's wife.

The man murmured something to Hattie that made her laugh. Luc's vision blurred with rage and indignation.

He burst through the shrubbery and advanced on the couple by the pool. "What in the hell is going on?"

The man turned his head and smiled...a wicked, *look what I'm up to* smile. Leo stood up. "Well, hello, Luc. It's about damn time you got here."

Though he was stunned, Luc didn't let on. "Why are you here, Leo? If you're dying for a honeymoon, find your own damn wife."

Leo mocked him deliberately. "When I heard that you were willing to transact business this week, I brought some contracts that need your John Hancock ASAP."

By this time, Hattie had scrambled to her feet. Her sweat-sheened breasts revealed by the relatively modest décolletage of her suit gave Luc pause for a second or two, but he dragged his eyes away from his wife's erotic body and faced off with his sibling.

Luc looked pointedly at Leo's casual attire. "But nothing so urgent that you couldn't chill out by the pool," he said, irritated beyond belief. It had been years since he and Leo had tangled in a fistfight, but Luc was spoiling for a rematch.

Hattie grabbed his arm. "Sit down, Luc. You're being rude."

Leo egged him on. "It's your fault, little bro. I wouldn't be here if you hadn't been such a Type A jerk."

That was it. Luc lunged at Leo, determined to pummel him into the ground. Their bodies collided and the fight was on.

But Luc hadn't counted on Hattie.

She grabbed his shirt and clung to him. "Stop this. Right now. You're both insane."

He shrugged her off. "Get out of the way." He rammed his shoulder into Leo's chest. Leo fired back with a punch to Luc's solar plexus.

Hattie jumped on Luc's back this time, her arms

around his neck in a stranglehold. "I mean it," she pleaded, her voice shaking. "He's your brother."

A second time Luc shook her off. "He's a pain in the ass."

Leo was momentarily distracted by Hattie's distress. Luc used the brief advantage to land another right to Leo's chin, this time splitting his own knuckles.

Hattie tried a third intervention, grabbing Luc's belt with two hands. But both men were in motion and when she lost her grasp, she slipped on the wet surface of the pool deck and fell sideways, her cheek raking the edge of the glass-topped table as she went down.

Luc and Leo froze. Luc was down on his knees in seconds, scooping her into his arms. "Oh, God, Hattie. Are you okay?"

She struggled to a sitting position and said, "Yes."

But she was lying. Blood oozed down her cheek from a nasty gash.

Leo crouched with them, cursing beneath his breath. "Is it bad?"

"I can't tell," Luc said, his hands shaky. "We need to get her checked out."

Hattie waved a hand. "Hellooo. I'm right here. If you two doofuses would kiss and make up, I'll be fine."

Luc eyes his brother sheepishly. "Sorry, man."

Leo grinned. "I deserved it."

Hattie rolled her eyes. "Morons." Luc heard rueful affection in the two syllables.

He motioned to his brother. "Grab one of those cloth napkins."

Leo complied, wetting the fabric in a water glass.

When Luc pressed gently at the wound, Hattie winced. "That hurts. Let me do it."

He surrendered the makeshift swab reluctantly, watching in dismay as Hattie removed more of the blood. It was an odd cut, and one that stitches wouldn't necessarily help.

The unflappable Marcel appeared, handing over a first aid kit. He glanced quickly at Hattie's cheek. "A butterfly bandage should do the trick, I think."

Luc applied antibiotic ointment and pressed the plaster in place as tenderly as he could. He and Leo helped her to her feet.

Now that the immediate crisis was over, Hattie was clearly flustered. She reached for her sheer cover-up and slid her arms into it. "I'm going upstairs to take a shower," she said, her eyes daring him to protest. "I suggest you two get your act together while I'm gone."

She turned with dignity to Marcel. "Thank you for your help. It's nice to know that someone around here has good sense."

As she flounced her way into the house, Leo shook his head and smiled. "Your wife is one tough cookie."

Luc nodded, sobered by what might have been. "For once, I agree with you completely."

Chapter 11

When Hattie stepped into the sitting room, she saw Luc ensconced on the sofa, elbows on his knees, waiting for her.

He stood and faced her. "You look nice."

She picked up her purse, fiddling with the contents. "Thanks." She was wearing a gauzy ankle-length dress in shades of taupe and gold. It was sleeveless, and the V neck dipped low front and back. A necklace and bracelet in chunky amber stones complemented the outfit.

The small bandage on her cheekbone made her self-conscious, but that was mostly vanity talking.

Her ensemble was dressy but comfortable. After the last few days, relaxation was high on Hattie's list.

She bit her lip, not wanting to resurrect any bad feelings. "Where's Leo?"

Luc made a face. "Don't worry. I signed the damn papers. He's changing downstairs to give us some privacy. I thought we'd go out for a late lunch somewhere nice, and afterward, he'll head home."

Leaving us all alone on our "it-has-to-get-better-than-this" honeymoon. The thought swept through Hattie's brain like wildfire, singeing neurons and making her legs weak. "Sounds good."

But when they got downstairs, Leo was gone. Marcel handed over a note. Luc read it, his expression blank and then passed it over to Hattie.

Don't want to intrude. Have a good week. See you in Hotlanta.

Hattie tossed the little piece of paper in a nearby trash can, her palms damp. "I guess it's just us."

Luc's gaze was hooded. "Guess so."

He ushered her out to the car, and they drove the short distance to the historic district. After squeezing into a tiny parking space on a street curb, Luc shut off the engine and came around to open Hattie's door. His hand on her elbow did amazing things to her heart rate.

She told herself not to expect too much. Nothing had changed. They weren't a normal couple by any means.

But it was hard to remember such mundane considerations amidst the tropical atmosphere of Key West. Everyone was in a good mood, it seemed. And no wonder. The view from Mallory Square was filled with cerulean seas, colorful watercraft and white, billowing triangles atop sailboats that zigged and zagged across the open waves.

Just offshore lay a palm-fringed island that looked so perfect Hattie wondered if the Chamber of Commerce had painted it against the sky to frame the sunsets.

When she said as much, Luc responded. "One of the large hotel chains owns it. You can rent one-, two- or three-bedroom cottages, and they even have their own man-made beach."

Hattie had already realized that Key West was not a typical "beach" destination. The coastline was rocky or coral-built. The Conch Republic, as it was called, was literally the last stop before Cuba, a mere ninety miles southwest.

At a marina adjacent to one of the fabulous hotels, Luc took Hattie's hand and helped her down into a sleek speedboat. Moments later, they were cutting across the waves, bound for the island.

In minutes, they pulled up to a well-kept dock and stepped out of the boat. A uniformed attendant directed them to the restaurant. It was open air on three sides, with huge rattan ceiling fans rotating overhead as an adjunct to the natural sea breezes. Delicate potted orchids bloomed on each table. China, silver and crystal gleamed.

The food was amazing...fresh shrimp gumbo and homemade corn bread. Hattie chewed automatically.

She was ready for a showdown, but if she initiated what might turn out to be a shouting match, would it be worth it? Hattie's mother had made a life's work out of tiptoeing around Hattie's stepfather. She always acted as if he might desert her at any moment.

The truth was that the guy loved Hattie's mother and would have given her anything. But early lessons are hard to unlearn. Hattie wasn't proficient at confrontation, but then again, she was no pushover. Luc was doing her a favor, yes. But that didn't mean he could dominate her.

She waited until the server put a piece of key lime pie in front of each of them before she fired the first shot. "How was your business trip?"

Luc choked on a bite of dessert. "Fine," he muttered. "This pie is great."

She wouldn't be deterred. If she had been clearer about her feelings a decade ago, she and Luc might possibly have worked things out. Her jaw tightened. "There was no excuse for you to leave on the first day of our honeymoon. Not only was it disrespectful to me, it also endangered our pretense of a happy marriage. I think you were trying to teach me a lesson, but it backfired."

Luc set down his fork and leaned back in his chair, his face sober. He exhaled slowly, his lips twisted. "You're right, of course. And I do apologize."

She cocked her head, studying him, trying to see inside his brain. "I've never said this, but my leaving you wasn't really about money. It was about control."

Luc jerked as if she had slapped him. "I don't understand."

"As a young woman, my mother had an affair with her boss, a wealthy, powerful man. When she told him she was pregnant, he cast her off without a second thought. That shining example of a man was my father. My biological father."

Shock creased his face. "I wasn't your boss, Hattie. What does that have to do with anything? I feel sorry for your mother, but you're certainly not the kind to do something so reckless."

"You're missing the point. My whole childhood revolved around this missing mystery man. This terrible person who didn't want me. And to hear my mother tell it, money was what gave him all the power. Leaving her power*less* and alone. From the time I was old enough to understand, she drilled into me the importance of making my own way in the world and not letting any man control my destiny."

"And you thought I would do something like that to you?" He looked haunted.

"Of course not. But I was so head over heels in love with you, I was afraid I'd lose myself in your life. It's very easy to be taken care of, very addictive. And I wasn't brave enough to stick with you. In hindsight, I believe I was stronger than I realized at the time. But as a kid of twenty, all I could see was that you had the money and power to do anything you wanted. And I felt lost in your shadow."

"Despite the fact that I wanted you so badly I followed you around like a puppy."

"You were a young man at the mercy of his hormones. Sex makes men do crazy things."

They were sitting at adjoining corners of a table for four. Beneath the linen cloth, Luc took her hand and deliberately pushed it against his erection. "I'm not so young now," he growled, releasing her fingers and eating his pie as if nothing had happened.

The imprint of his rigid flesh was burned into Hattie's palm. She took a reckless swallow of wine. "Don't be crass."

He shrugged, his eyes a dangerous flash of obsidian. "What do you want from me, Hattie?"

She hesitated, torn between fascinated curiosity about his response to her and a healthy sense of caution. "Do you really think we can be intimate and then walk away?"

Luc shrugged again. "I can if you can."

Hattie frowned, licking whipped cream from her spoon. His nonchalance could be an act. Her heart beat faster.

She cocked her head and stared at him, trying to read his mind. He was as inscrutable as the great and powerful wizard of Oz. If Hattie could click her heels in ruby slippers, she'd be able to go back to that innocent time in college.

Did she want to? Or did she want to move ahead as an adult woman with adult needs? She'd be taking an enormous risk. What if she fell in love with Luc again? What if she never had really *stopped* loving him? What if they had sex and it was ho-hum?

Not likely.

She scraped one last bite of topping from her plate and ate it absently. Luc's hungry gaze followed every motion she made. Her throat dried. It was now or never.

When the waiter moved to a safe distance, Hattie rested her arms on the table and moved in close to

Luc. She put her hand over his. "You said I had to be the one to say yes or no. But you have to know that my answer has nothing to do with protecting a baby…nothing to do with mistakes we made in the past. No feelings of obligation. This is about us… you and me. And I say—"

Luc put his hand over her mouth, his expression violent. "Not another word."

Luc was burning up. The tropical heat and Hattie's proximity made him sweat. Her gaze seemed to dissect him like a bug. To burrow inside his brain and discern his secrets. He lifted an impatient hand for the check, deliberately breaking their physical connection. He was too close to the edge. Hearing Hattie acquiesce to their mutual desire for sexual intimacy could push him over. And it wouldn't be smart to let her realize how desperate he was to have her. Talking about sex in a public venue had not helped in the least when it came to controlling his baser urges.

After he shoved two large bills into the folio, he took Hattie by the wrist, dragging her toward the exit. "We're going back to the house," he said. "I think you have sunstroke."

She laughed softly. They reached the dock, and it was all he could do not to crush her against one of the wooden posts and ravage her mouth with his. He damned the surroundings that forced him to act like a gentleman. He'd never felt less civilized in his life.

Other tourists joined them beneath the awning, and soon the return boat arrived. Hattie's hip and thigh were glued to Luc's in the small, crowded craft. Back on dry land, she followed him meekly to the car. Her honey-blond hair gleamed in the unforgiving sun.

Seeing her pink shoulders made him think of Leo again. Which made him think of doing the lotion thing for Hattie, covering every inch of her creamy skin with fragrant moisture.

He knew what she was going to say, and his body said a resounding *"hell, yeah!"* But in addition to his need to remain in control, it occurred to him that he owed her some romance…to make up for his less than stellar behavior as a new groom. They had eight or nine hours to kill before bedtime. It was far too hot to walk the streets in the midday heat.

Fortunately, their rental was parked beneath a huge shade tree. Luc leaned his elbows on the top of the car and faced Hattie with the vehicle between them. "What would you like to do now?" he asked, wishing he could supply the answer.

She lifted the hair from the back of her neck and sighed. "I love the pool," she said. "Do you mind too much if we go back and swim? We can play tourist tomorrow."

"Whatever you want," he croaked, his mind racing ahead. Swimming as foreplay made as much sense as anything else to his testosterone fuddled brain.

In the bedroom there was an awkward moment when they both reached into suitcases with plans to change clothes. Luc held up his hands, gripping a pair of black swim trunks. "I'll use the other bathroom."

He was ready in four minutes. It took Hattie an extra twenty. But when she reappeared, he wasn't about to complain. Her hair was swept up on top of her head, leaving recalcitrant tendrils to cling to her damp neck. The white terry robe she wore covered her from throat to knee, but it molded to her breasts and hips with just enough cling to encourage his imagination.

He thought he had himself under control. But all bets were off when they reached the pool and Hattie ditched the cover-up. She wore a different suit this time, and he was damned glad Leo hadn't been around to see this one.

It was a neon-blue bikini. Luc was stunned. She was a sexual goddess, even more lovely than she had been in college. The bikini bottom fastened at the hips with a large gold circlet on either side.

The two tiny triangles of fabric that made up the top barely met decency standards.

Luc looked around suspiciously to see if anyone else was enjoying the show, but their privacy was absolute. Nothing but flowers and water and a mermaid just for his entertainment. If there were other guests at the small inn, they were not around at the moment.

Luc made a show of selecting a chaise lounge and flipping out his towel. "I'm going to nap."

Hattie gazed at him over her shoulder, her eyes hidden behind tortoiseshell sunglasses. "Will you do me first?"

His body went rigid in shock until he saw the bottle of sunscreen she held out. "Sure."

When she was situated, he perched on his hip beside her and unscrewed the lid. Immediately, the scent of coconut assailed his nostrils. Hattie pillowed her head on her arms, a small smile tilting her lips.

Luc groaned inwardly. Giving her a taste of romance before the main event might drive him mad.

When his hands touched her back, she flinched. "It's cold."

He ran his fingers across her shoulder blades. "It won't be. Relax."

Too bad he couldn't take his own advice. Every one of his muscles was tight enough to snap. He exhaled slowly and concentrated on Hattie. His fingertips still remembered the hills and valleys of her body. His thumbs pressed on either side of her spine.

Hattie moaned.

Dear Lord.

When he hesitated, she lifted a hand and waved it lazily, her eyes closed. "Don't stop."

He smoothed one final spot of lotion into her skin and capped the bottle. "All done."

Hattie didn't answer. She was so still he suspected she had drifted off. Which irked him, because sleep was the furthest thing from his mind. He stood up and went to the deep end of the pool. After one last glance at Hattie, he dove in and started a series of punishing laps. Harder and faster, pushing his body to exhaustion.

He swam until his legs began to feel like spaghetti. And then he swam some more. When spots of light began to dance behind his eyelids, he dragged himself out of the pool and collapsed onto his lounger facedown. Hattie lay where he had left her, her almost naked body lax and limp, her skin glistening with a dewy sheen of lotion and perspiration.

Luc closed his eyes, his heart pounding in his chest. He had a painful erection. His body was clenched with desire, despite the brutal workout.

He was a man, not a eunuch. He might not be in love with Hattie like he'd been as a stupid kid of twenty, but he had normal male needs. If she didn't come to him soon, he'd never be able to keep up the pretense that he was in control of the situation.

It was a shock to feel hands on his back. He'd been so caught up in his own turmoil, he never heard Hattie move. She mimicked his earlier position and was now preparing to rub sunscreen into his burning skin. Thankfully, his Italian heritage made him able to endure the sun without painful consequences, but he knew he needed the protection.

The question was—who or what would protect him from Hattie?

Her hands were small, but strong. Despite the ostensible point of the exercise, this was foreplay. And Luc was strung so tightly, he wasn't sure he could bear it.

Five minutes later, his body aching with the need to roll over and pull Hattie down into his arms, she finished. He felt her touch on his hair, her fingers ruffling the wet strands.

She leaned in closer, her breast brushing his side. "I'm getting in the water. Why don't you join me?"

It was a dare. He recognized it as such and knew that this game of cat and mouse had only one possible conclusion. But it was up to him to write the script and make sure Hattie knew who was in control.

He swung to a sitting position. Now they were so close, he could have leaned forward a scant two inches and kissed her. But he didn't. Not yet.

He smiled grimly, cursing his body's weakness. "After you."

She didn't try to dive in, but instead used the ladder to lower herself into the pool. The water was only chest high where she stood. He executed a show-off dive from the opposite direction and came up beside her, shoving the hair from his face. Her eyes were wide.

He touched her shoulder. "Want a ride in the deep end?"

Hattie nodded, not speaking.

He took her hand. "Get on my back."

When she complied, her legs wrapping around his waist and her arms encircling his shoulders, he shuddered. "Hang on."

He walked forward, feeling the bottom of the pool fall away beneath his feet. When he could barely touch bottom, he tugged her off his back and around until she faced him. The slightly surprised look in her eyes when she realized she was out of her depth made him smile inwardly.

Her hands clenched his shoulders, her finger-nails leaving marks in his skin. Their legs drifted together and apart. He knew she felt the evidence of what she did to him.

Hattie nibbled her bottom lip. "The water feels great."

She was nervous. He liked that. "A lot of things feel great," he said, deliberately taunting her.

"You didn't let me give you my answer earlier," she said, her eyes alight with mischief.

He kissed her softly, a bare brush of mouth to mouth. She tasted like warm summer fruit. "It will keep," he muttered. "No need to rush."

Need swam between them. His. Hers. It might have been a decade, but some pleasures the body never forgets.

Her eyes drifted shut.

"No. Look at me." He cupped one breast.

Hattie's eyelids fluttered open, her gaze unfocused, her cheeks flushed despite the cool water. Her soft cry went straight to his gut.

He kicked his legs rhythmically, keeping them afloat. Now he took the other breast. Two handfuls...warm, seductive, feminine bounty. He massaged gently, moving the barely-there bikini top aside to find naked flesh.

The pleasure flooding him from touching her so intimately blurred his vision. His hands settled at her waist as he took her mouth in a ravaging kiss.

They were in danger of losing all rational thought. And he was sinking fast.

As fact matched thought, they slipped beneath the surface of the water. He kissed her again, and this time, he slid his hand into the bottom of her bikini and cupped her, pressing a finger into her tight passage and probing…stroking.

It lasted no more than a few seconds. He dragged them both back up for air. Hattie wrapped her legs around his waist, her ragged breathing matching his. She had a death grip on his shoulders, her breasts mashezd to his chest.

She initiated the kiss this time, her small teeth nipping his bottom lip, her tongue sliding between his teeth, dazing him with an ache so intense, his head hurt. Hunger raged like a wild animal, one that hadn't been fed in a decade.

She whimpered when he cupped her bottom, pulling her closer. "Luc…Luc."

Hearing his name on her lips almost unmanned him. "What, Hattie?"

"Please," she groaned. "My answer is yes. Please, please, please make love to me."

Exultation filled his chest. That was what he needed to hear. "Ask me again," he demanded.

Her gaze filled with frustration. "No games. Take me. Now."

Chapter 12

Hattie stumbled as Luc dragged her toward the house, their few belongings left behind in his haste. His grip on her wrist allowed no protest. But then why would she…protest, that is?

She wanted Luc—the sooner the better.

If she had expected awkwardness in the bedroom, she was wrong. Luc was smooth, determined. He stripped off his trunks, grinning tightly when she looked her fill.

His erection was magnificent. Thick, long and ready for her…only her. His broad chest and strong arms rippled with muscles. He cupped her face in his hands. "Take it off."

His adamant tone brooked no refusal.

She trembled inside and out as she unfastened the knot at the back of her neck and reached behind to undo the clasp. For seconds, the bikini top clung damply to her breasts as she clutched it in sudden, belated hesitation.

The corner of Luc's beautiful mouth quirked in a half smile. "Don't go all shy on me now, Hattie."

She gulped inwardly and let the scraps of fabric fall. Luc inhaled sharply. The look in his eyes made her weak. In college, he had been her first love, her first lover. Now he was a mature man in his sexual prime. She felt the heat of his desire, not as quiet warmth, but as a flashpoint poised to explode.

There was the problem of what to do with her hands. She wanted to cover her breasts instinctively. But she knew Luc would have none of that. So her arms hung at her sides as she shifted from one foot to the other.

He lifted an eyebrow. "You're not finished."

She might have taken umbrage at his arrogant tone had she not been as eager as he was for the next act. Removing her last barrier of modesty proved harder than she expected.

Luc lost patience. He gripped her hips. "Too slow," he growled. He kissed her wildly, his mouth everywhere…her lips, her throat, and finally, her bare breasts. The sensation was an electric shock.

Her entire body melted into him, closer and closer still.

His hard shaft bruised her hipbone. The soft, wiry hair on his chest tickled her sensitive skin. Breath by gasping breath they relearned the taste of each other—the touch, the sound, the smell. It was a smorgasbord of sensual delight. A cornucopia of excess.

He tangled his fingers in the rings at her hips and jerked hard, ripping the thin fabric from the metal. The remnants that he tossed aside represented Hattie's last resistance, if indeed she had any.

She was drunk on memories laced with present passion.

A nanosecond later he lifted her. Her legs wrapped around his waist instinctively. The intimate position made her limp with longing. He backed her up to the nearest wall and buried his face in her neck. Tremors shook his large frame. His chest heaved.

Slowly, as if giving her time to protest, he aligned their bodies and entered her with one forceful upward thrust. He was big, but she was ready for him. When he was buried inside her, he went still.

"Hattie?" His voice was hoarse.

"Hmmm?" She bit his earlobe and heard him curse.

"You okay?"

The four-letter word didn't come close to describing what she was. "Don't stop."

"Whatever the lady wants."

The last words were barely audible as he directed all his energy toward driving them both insane. Her bare butt slapped against the door as Luc pounded into her over and over.

A searing heat built inside her, coalesced at the spot where their bodies were joined. Higher. Stronger. The world ceased to exist. Her arms tightened around his neck as she felt the storm begin to break. "Luc…" Stars cartwheeled inside her head and tumbled downward to reignite when Luc's own release sent him rigid and straining against her.

When it was over at last, Luc staggered into their bedroom, still carrying her, and dropped her onto the mattress. He came down beside her and rested his head on her chest.

Her heart stopped. A perfect cocoon of intimacy enveloped them.

She might have slept for a few minutes—she wasn't sure. Luc was out, his body a heavy weight half on top of her. She wanted so badly to stroke his hair, but she resisted. A black hole of self-destruction yawned at her feet. She was far too close to the edge.

Awkwardly, she slid from beneath him and tiptoed to the bathroom. After quickly freshening up, she put on one of the soft luxurious robes that hung on the back of the door. Belting it tightly, she peeked out into the bedroom.

Luc's speculative gaze met hers. "You won't need the robe."

Five simple words. That's all he needed to make the moisture bloom between her legs. She grasped the door frame to steady herself. "I won't?" All the starch had left her legs. She was melting, body and soul.

He crooked a finger. "Come back to bed."

Removing the robe was even more difficult than shedding her swimsuit. In the heat of the moment, her inhibitions had gone on vacation. But now they were back.

As she padded into the room, shivering, she noticed for the first time that the AC had been kicked up a notch. Luc held a string of condom packets in his hand. "We skipped a step. I'm sorry, Hattie. That was my fault."

She shrugged with what she hoped was blasé sophistication. "It's the wrong part of the month. I'm not worried."

His grin was tight. "Then let's not waste any more time."

The robe fell at her feet. Luc's amusement faded visibly to be replaced by sheer male determination. When she shivered now, it had nothing to do with the temperature in the room and everything to do with the man stretched out on his back like a sleek, not-quite-satisfied predator.

Nothing this older, more experienced Luc did was predictable. Instead of covering her with his aroused body, he pulled her on top. It was a position she had never really liked, because it made her feel too vulnerable. But when she tried to protest, Luc took care of that by lightly touching the small bud of nerves at her center.

She braced her hands on her thighs and tried not to flinch as he explored her most private recesses. In an embarrassingly short amount of time, she moaned and climaxed, the second event no less powerful than the first.

He held her close and stroked her hair, though she could feel the strength of his unappeased desire. Tears clogged her throat. "Luc, I…" *love you.* No, she didn't. It was just the sex talking. Shades of auld lang syne. An overabundance of postcoital hormones.

He kissed her cheek. "You what?"

"I wonder if we made a mistake." She felt him go still.

"Regrets already?"

Something in his tone made her cringe. She shouldn't have introduced reality into their bed. Not now. But she was compelled to answer. "This makes things complicated. When we go our separate ways."

His hands moved from her hair, her shoulders. He shifted her until they lay side by side. Already she missed his warmth.

His tone was perfectly calm when he answered. "You're making too much of nothing. There's no harm in enjoying each other. Divorces are simple nowadays. We'll deal with any complications when we have to. It's nothing to worry about."

She winced inwardly, her lovely moment shattered by her own bad timing and Luc's carelessly callous comment. No more pretending. This wasn't a honeymoon. This was sex for the sake of scratching an itch. No use dressing it up with romantic frills.

No reason for tears to sting her eyes and a painful lump to clog her throat.

She swallowed, her mouth dry. "I want to take a shower."

Luc pounced verbally. "No, Hattie. I don't think so."

He hardly noticed that she didn't answer. He'd been kicked in the gut and was left reeling. The sweat was barely dry on their bodies and she was already talking about leaving him. Damn it to hell.

He would be the one to end this relationship…not Hattie.

He was hard as a pike, his erection painfully stiff. With jerky motions, he ripped open a packet and rolled on a rubber. A split second later he groaned aloud as he penetrated Hattie's tight, wet warmth. She lay passive beneath him, and it pissed him off.

He took her chin in his hand. "Look at me, Mrs. Cavallo." She obeyed. He had to grit his teeth to keep from coming right then. "What we do in the privacy of our bed is our own business. We're good together. Don't fight it. Don't fight me. Let yourself go, Hattie."

Big brown eyes looked up at him with a mixture of emotions he couldn't decipher even if he wasn't being driven by his baser needs. She whispered the single word. "Okay."

It was enough. He felt her hands touch his hips, recognized the moment when she arched her back and matched her rhythm to his. A red haze clouded his vision. His hips pistoned in agonized yearning for release. It was good…so good.

Hattie gave a small shocked cry as he felt her inner muscles squeeze him. Her release triggered his, and he bore down, losing himself in her welcome embrace and finding momentary oblivion.

* * *

Sometime later, sanity returned. He could hear his own jerky breathing in the silence of the room. Hattie was still and quiet again. Had he hurt her? He moved aside with a muttered apology, relieving her of his considerable weight.

Sweet mother of God. He hadn't had sex that good in he didn't know when. *Oh, yes, you do. It was back in college when Hattie was warm and willing and you were both blissfully happy.*

He shook off the memories. No need for those when he had the real thing in his arms. What was she thinking? He was too tired to pry it out of her. He'd barely slept the night before.

His eyes closed involuntarily.

Aeons later it seemed, he felt her try to escape. His fingers closed around her wrist. "Stay."

"I need a shower."

He scrubbed his hands over his face, yawning, his head muzzy. "I'll join you."

The look on her face made him laugh as he got to his feet. "Don't be so modest. It's the green thing to do."

After turning the water to a comfortable temperature, he dragged a clearly reluctant Hattie into the luxurious shower enclosure. His lovely new wife huddled in a tiled corner, her arms wrapped around her waist.

Everything about her screamed innocent seduction...from her long slender legs to her hourglass waist, to her plump, shapely breasts. If he could paint, he'd commit her to canvas exactly like this.

He picked up a bar of soap shaped like a shell. "Turn around."

Hattie was drowning in her own need. In her wildest imagination she had never invented a scenario like this. "Why?" she muttered.

His grin was lethal. "I thought you wanted to get clean."

"You're a dirty old man."

"Not old," he deadpanned.

She gave him her back reluctantly, hyperaware that she was at his sexual mercy. The first touch of the washcloth made her jump. But it was Luc's chuckle that made her blush.

As he washed from her neck down her spine, she braced her hands on the wall and hung her head. Luc had turned the spray so that it cascaded between them. The water was cool on Hattie's hot skin.

Luc moved the rag slowly, more of a massage than a simple exercise in cleanliness. He reached her bottom and squeezed. "Turn around."

She obeyed instinctively, their gazes colliding amidst the steamy air. "I can do the rest," she said.

He shook his head. "Why bother? I'm off to a hell of a good start." He took her hands and tucked them behind her butt. "Don't move."

The hot water was enervating, draining Hattie of any will to challenge Luc's control. This time he made no pretense of using the washcloth. He took the bar of soap and ran it in circles around her breasts. Then he pressed gently over her nipples, decorating them with tiny bubbles.

When he was satisfied, he paused to kiss her... slow and deep. With one hand, he manacled her wrists behind her back with a firm grip. Now their bodies were touching chest to chest. She felt his erection throbbing between them.

He nuzzled her nose with his and ground his hips into hers. "More work to do," he muttered.

His hand holding the soap found its way south to the middle of her thighs. Her legs parted instinctively to give him access.

When the soap glided over a certain sensitive spot, Hattie cried out and struggled. But Luc kept his tight hold on her wrists as he moved the soap between her legs.

Hattie rested her forehead on his chest, panting. "Enough," she whispered. "I'm clean." She was close to the edge, but she didn't want to make the journey alone. She wanted Luc inside her, filling her, making her his.

Without warning, he dropped the soap and released her wrists. The shower boasted a roomy stone seat. Luc reached for the condom he'd tucked on a ledge, sheathed himself, and then pulled Hattie down to sit astride his lap.

Their bodies were slick and wet, and the moment when they joined was seamless…easy. Hattie threw back her head, the water still streaming over them. Her eyes were closed, intensifying the sensation of having Luc inside her.

He was strong. He lifted her up and down in a gentle rhythm, teasing them both.

Longing crescendoed, hunger peaked. Luc's hands bruised her bare butt as he gave a muffled shout and found his release. Hattie still lingered on the knife edge of pleasure. She could stay there forever.

Luc bit her neck, ran his tongue over her tightly furled nipples. It was enough. It was too much. She arched her back and gave a choked sob as everything inside her splintered and fanned out through her veins in cascading ripples of pure joy.

Afterward, she was weak as a baby. Luc dried her tenderly and scooped her up in his arms to carry her to their bed. Hattie had lost all sense of time. And didn't really care.

Luc muttered an apology as he slid beneath the covers and moved over her and into her. She had nothing left, but this coupling was warm and lazy. He rode her forever, it seemed, pausing each time he came close to the end and making himself wait, stretching out the incredible connection, the deep, undulating eroticism.

He enveloped her, overwhelmed her. His scent, his touch, his powerful domination.

Somewhere in the deep recesses of her consciousness lingered the knowledge that she would have to pay for this day. That down the line her heart would face pain equal to the present elation.

But she refused to let such maudlin considerations ruin the present.

She put a hand to his cheek, loving him with her eyes. "You're amazing," she whispered. "I haven't felt like this in a very long time."

His cheeks were ruddy, his eyes hooded, his chin shadowed with late-day stubble. Everything about him reeked of uncivilized, ravenous male. Little was left of the suave businessman, the wealthy CEO.

And Hattie loved it...loved him. God help her, she did. This was a man she could live with...share a life with.

But the other Luc still existed outside this room. And that was the problem. Just as it had always been.

He groaned and his whole body shook as his

mighty control finally snapped. "Hattie…" He climaxed in a series of long, rapid thrusts.

Despite her exhaustion, echoes of pleasure teased her once again.

In the aftermath, they slept. And as the tropical sun sank low in the sky, coaxing the stars out to play in the gathering dusk, Mr. and Mrs. Luc Cavallo were in perfect accord for one fleeting moment.

Chapter 13

Luc rolled over and looked at the clock sometime around 9:00 p.m. His stomach was growling, and no wonder. Their late brunch was the last meal he had eaten.

He slung an arm above his head and yawned, his somber gaze noting that Hattie slept peacefully. Too bad he wasn't as relaxed. The sex had been nothing short of spectacular, but now that his head was in control and not his libido, he was able to think clearly. And the conclusions he drew were unsettling.

He was in danger of falling in love with Hattie all over again. Perhaps in some ways he had never fallen *out* of love...which might explain why the many women he had dated in the last ten years never quite seemed to measure up to some unknown standard. His grandfather had accused him of being too picky...of expecting a paragon of a woman to fill his bed and his life.

Turned out...his grandfather was right.

And that woman was Hattie Parker.

He watched her sleep for a long time, mulling over his options. Right now she needed him because of the baby. Which gave him an advantage for the moment. But what happened when the kid's father was no longer a threat? What then?

Would Hattie try to bid Luc a pleasant good-bye and walk away? The possibility made his chest tight. He was no longer a naive and vulnerable kid. He'd learned his lesson well. Loving someone too much only opened the way for hurt.

Losing both of his parents at the same time had sent him and Leo into a tailspin. Only their grandfather's gruff, tough affection had rescued them. Perhaps way back in college Luc had fallen hard for Hattie because he needed so badly to fill a void in his life.

He was more self-sufficient now, able to enjoy a physical relationship without involving messy emotions. And besides, the barrier between Hattie and him remained the same: his need for control. He had let her too close once upon a time and suffered the consequences. And if his money gave him power, did she expect him to give it all away and live in a shack?

Perhaps since his embarrassment of riches was currently saving her niece, she might decide that being with a wealthy man wasn't exactly a ticket to purgatory.

He touched her arm…he couldn't help himself. The need to keep her close was all-consuming. She had come to him for help…for protection. He would keep Hattie and Deedee safe at all costs. It was the honorable thing to do. And he'd given his word.

Hattie was grateful to him…and she was attracted to him. But that wasn't enough. He wanted her to need him, to depend on him, to beg him to let her stay. How or why she initially came to him didn't really matter in the end. She was vulnerable now. And God help him, he liked it. His course was clear: enjoy the physical side of their marriage as long as it lasted, maintain his emotional distance… and then…

He refused to contemplate the future. Not now when life was close to perfect. He would keep her as long as it suited him.

The next time he awoke, it was morning; dawn to be exact. Clear, liquid light filtered into the bedroom. He stroked his wife's shoulder. She was sleeping on her stomach, her face turned away from him. "Wake up, sleepyhead. I'm starving."

She blinked her eyes and struggled up onto her elbows. One brief glance at her warm, pink breasts was all he got before she rolled onto her back and clutched the sheet to her chest.

Her eyes were wide, her honey-blond hair tousled. "What time is it?"

"Early. We slept through the night. But missing dinner was definitely worth it."

A deep blush painted her face crimson.

He took pity on her. "I'll use the other bathroom to get ready."

"Ready?"

"I thought we'd go snorkeling this morning. Out to the reef. Are you game?"

She frowned. "I've never done it. Is it difficult?"

He patted her leg. "Not really. You'll love it, I promise." Her expression was unconvinced, so he grinned at her. "Or...we could stay in bed all day."

Hattie stumbled to her feet, almost tripping over her bed-sheet toga. "Snorkeling sounds great," she said, the words breathless as she struggled to maintain her modesty. "If you'll order breakfast, I'll be dressed in a jiff." She disappeared into the bathroom.

He chuckled aloud at her discomfiture. Teasing

Hattie had always been fun. Too bad she agreed to the snorkeling. He could have been persuaded to follow option two.

Just thinking about the night before made him hard. With an inward groan, he picked up the phone and called for sustenance. It was going to be a long day, and he needed some serious calories.

Hattie dressed in a modest coral one-piece and covered it with a crisp, white poplin top and khaki walking shorts. A new pair of taupe leather sandals completed the outfit.

When she looked in the mirror, she winced. Going to bed with damp hair meant that she looked like a wild woman. It took a hairbrush and patient determination to tame the mess. Finally, she tucked it up into a ponytail, donned an Atlanta Braves cap and smoothed sheer sunscreen onto her face, neck and arms.

In addition to her new wardrobe, Luc had gifted her with an array of expensive cosmetics. Though most of it was products she would only use for fancy occasions, she had already come to appreciate the many wonderful skin-care creams and lotions.

Breakfast was just arriving when she stepped out of the bathroom. Luc, freshly shaven, his hair damp, tipped the young woman who brought up the largesse.

He spread a hand. "Let's eat."

They consumed an embarrassingly large amount of food in record time. Hattie hadn't realized how hungry she was.

Luc watched her bite into a huge strawberry. "You've got juice all over your chin. Let me..." He dabbed her sticky skin with a cloth napkin, his face close to hers. His expression was shuttered, and she wanted badly to know what he was thinking.

Her head was filled with memories of last night...experiences that were life-changing.

But men were far more cavalier about sex and intimacy. When it was over it was over. Luc might want to be with her again, but that didn't mean he'd be doodling a heart with both their names on scrap paper.

Sex was only physical as far as Luc was concerned. She'd do well to keep that fact firmly planted in the front of her brain. And that meant staying out of this suite as much as possible.

She scooted back from the table. "Let's go. I'm excited about this."

Luc had not chartered a private boat. And for that Hattie was glad. Having other people around diffused the natural awkwardness she was experiencing. She couldn't even look at Luc without remembering how his powerful body had joined with hers, how their skin had been damp with exertion, their muscles lax with pleasure.

If she let herself, she could imagine that they were like any normal newlyweds. Deeply in love, and ravenous for each other.

Luc didn't help her resolve to be sensible. He was in turns tender, affectionate and teasing. More and more she saw glimpses of the young man she had fallen in love with. Away from the pressure of business and responsibilities, Luc laughed often, was more relaxed and carefree.

He handed her a pair of flippers. "Put these on, and I'll help you with your mask." All around them, fellow passengers were doing the same thing. The large catamaran had cut its engines and was bobbing in clear blue-green water over the reef below.

Hattie and Luc had already shed their outer clothing and tucked all of it into a big raffia tote bag. She tried not to drool over her new husband. His black swim trunks were plain, but it was his sculpted torso and powerful arms that drew attention. Hattie didn't miss the fact that she wasn't the only one eyeing Luc's masculine beauty.

He wore expensive, reflective sunglasses that made him look like a movie star. It didn't seem fair for one man to have everything—looks, character and money to burn.

She sighed inwardly as he handed her a mask and snorkel tube. "What happens if I swallow water?"

"You'll be fine. I'll be right beside you."

The boat captain gave some basic instructions, including a warning to listen for the whistle that signaled time to return to the boat. Hattie was very glad she had a reliable partner.

She had assumed they would jump over the side like in the movies, but the catamaran had a ladder that could be lowered into the water between the two large hulls. Backing down the steps was a little claustrophobic, but Luc went first and was waiting for her as she descended. He took her arm, his face almost unrecognizable behind his mask. "Come on, little mermaid. We don't want to waste any time."

Hattie was not a superconfident swimmer. And learning to breathe through the tube was challenging. But Luc's patience and support, along with a life vest, erased much of her fear, and soon she was moving through the water, head down, discovering the wonders of the reef.

The colors were muted and not as dramatic as Discovery Channel specials she had seen about the Great Barrier Reef, but the experience was enchanting nevertheless. Corals bobbed and swayed in eerie dances. Multicolored fish, large and small, moved with unconcern in and around the landlubber visitors.

Much of the necessary communication involved pointing and arm touches. But when Hattie spotted a familiar shape, she gasped, swallowed water, and had to come up to catch her breath. "It was a shark," she cried, coughing as she cleared her throat.

Luc shoved his mask on top of his head and laughed. "I've never seen anyone's eyes get that big. I thought you were going to faint dead in the water."

She shuddered. "Don't say dead. I wanted to take some pictures, but he was too fast." The snorkeling package included disposable waterproof cameras. "He wasn't very big though."

Luc tugged her ponytail. "You were hoping for *Jaws?*"

She giggled, feeling happier than she had been in a long time. "Well, not really, but it would have made a great Facebook post."

He glanced at his diver's watch. "We'd better get back to it. Time's almost up."

By the time the whistle sounded, Hattie was ready to quit. The experience was amazing, but the unaccustomed exercise, combined with learning how to manipulate the equipment, had exhausted her.

Back onboard everyone dried off and deposited their gear in large barrels for cleaning. Young crew members passed out lemonade and cookies. Luc and Hattie sat side by side, the wind in their faces as the boat cut rapidly through the waves on the home journey. Their swimsuits dried rapidly in the heat.

Luc put his arm around her back. "Was it what you expected?"

She glanced up at him, controlling a shiver at the delicious feel of his warm skin on hers. "Even better," she said. The sun was making her drowsy. Her head lolled against his shoulder, and she let herself lean into his body.

As they docked in Key West, she roused. It was the work of minutes to slip back into shorts, shoes and top. Luc followed suit, and soon they disembarked with the other passengers.

They lingered at the dock for a few minutes watching parasail enthusiasts go airborne. Hattie shaded her eyes with a hand. "That looks fun, too."

Luc took her arm. "Maybe tomorrow. Let's find a restaurant."

She punched him softly. "Is that all you ever want to do?"

He paused in the middle of the road and kissed her—hard. He brushed a stray hair from her cheek. "Actually, it's way down on the list, but I'm trying to be a considerate husband."

That shut her up. What would Luc say if she demanded to go back to the guesthouse and spend the afternoon and evening as they had the day before?

Sadly, she didn't have the guts to propose what she really wanted to do. Instead, she pretended interest in the fried plantains at the Cuban restaurant they found near the harbor. She ate mechanically. Every moment that passed brought them closer to the evening hours. When they would go to bed... together?

The uncertainty made her crazy. Was last night a one-time faux pas on their parts, or was Luc assuming they would continue to have sex for the duration of the marriage?

Hattie hated the idea of divorce, but what choice did they have? They had allowed sexual hunger and curiosity to lead them down a dangerous path, and she knew what happened to that proverbial cat.

Luc nudged her elbow. "I thought you'd be hungry. Swimming always gives me an appetite."

She shrugged. "I think it's the heat getting to me. Do you mind if we go back to our place? I'd love to take a shower and wash the seawater off my skin."

His fork stilled in midair, and his cheekbones went dark. He cleared his throat. "Of course. Whatever you want."

Hattie cursed her own artless stupidity. Did that sound like an open invitation for sex? She hadn't meant it that way.

Or had she?

Luc finished his meal and summoned the waiter

for their check. Shortly after, they made their way through the crowded streets. Apparently, many tourists had arrived early to celebrate the Memorial Day holiday. Hattie barely noticed the commotion. All she could think about was how to handle the return to their luxurious bridal quarters.

The leather seats in the car were hot…no shade trees this time. She wriggled uncomfortably, and rolled down her window to let the steamy air escape. Luc was silent, his face impossible to read.

The ride was brief and silent. They exited the car. Marcel welcomed them as they strolled through the courtyard. "Are you enjoying your stay in Key West?"

Luc shook his hand, but Hattie answered. "It's lovely. So vibrant and colorful. You're lucky to live here year-round."

Marcel nodded as he trimmed an overgrown bougainvillea. "The only time I rethink my address is during hurricane season, but we are lucky here in the Keys…very few major hits."

Luc frowned. "Have you heard a forecast for tonight and tomorrow?"

"Nothing but calm, clear skies. Perfect vacation weather."

Hattie preceded Luc up the stairs, wondering what was up. Luc seemed focused on some unknown objective. And once in their room, instead of throwing her on the bed as she had hoped or expected, he seemed to be preoccupied...or at least avoiding sex at the moment. "Why were you concerned about the weather?" she asked him.

He tossed the car keys and his sunglasses on the dresser. "I have an idea."

"Uh-oh," she teased. "Should I be worried?"

He sprawled on the sofa. "Do you remember those camping trips we took in college?"

"Of course." They had journeyed to the north Georgia mountains a number of times, spending several chilly spring and autumn nights curled together in a double sleeping bag...just the two of them. Those had been magical times, and Hattie had loved them even more because the outings were inexpensive.

His arms stretched along the back of the couch, his fingers drumming restlessly. "I thought it might be fun to do that again."

In this heat? Was Luc so spooked by the intense emotion of the night before that he was going to keep them busy, nonstop? "Umm, well..."

"There's an island with an old fort. We can camp there. It would be an adventure. What do you say?"

The boyish eagerness on his face was irresistible. Despite her better judgment, she managed an enthusiastic smile. "Sounds like fun."

Chapter 14

While Luc was on the phone making arrangements for their impromptu trip, Hattie showered and then checked in with Ana.

The baby is fine. No problem. Enjoy yourselves.

Hattie ended her call and surveyed the room. Luc was paying who knew how much money for this wonderful suite, and yet he wanted to abandon it for parts unknown. Men… She found him in the sitting room, still on the phone, but now she could tell it was business. Knowing what she did of his work ethic and his drive and determination, it really surprised her that he had been willing and able to get away for a honeymoon, pretend or otherwise.

He hung up and turned to face her, jubilation on his face. "I got us two spots. They only allow a small number of campers each night. But there's one catch."

"Oh?"

He winced, gauging her reaction. "We have to leave right now."

"Seriously?"

"Yeah. Everything for the week was full except for tonight."

Gulp. "Okay. What do I need to pack?"

"Anything that's comfortable and cool. Plus a swimsuit. We'll be able to snorkel in the shallow water around the fort."

And at night? What would happen then?

Hattie pondered that question. And how did one prepare for possible seduction on a remote, uninhabited island? After dithering in the bedroom for several minutes, she dumped out her carry-on bag and began filling it methodically. One set of clean clothes and underwear. Swimsuit. A long T-shirt to sleep in. Sunscreen.

She picked up a lilac silk nightgown and held it to her cheek for a wistful moment. Not exactly camping attire. But what the heck. This was her honeymoon. She stuffed it in.

It was easy to see why Luc was so successful. In barely an hour, he had secured bags of food, all sorts of camping gear, two coolers and transportation. They found parking near the dock and unloaded. Hattie was stunned to see Luc walk toward a stylish, powerful speedboat.

He held out a hand. "Come aboard, my lady."

The vessel must have been wickedly expensive, even as a rental. Everything about it gleamed, from the hardwood deck to the shiny chrome trim. Luc stowed their supplies and tossed Hattie a yellow life jacket.

She wrinkled her nose. "Do I have to?"

He slid his arms into a navy one. "Captain's orders."

"How far are we going?"

"About seventy miles."

Her apprehension must have shown on her face, because he sobered. "It's perfectly safe, Hattie. Leo and I learned to pilot boats before we could drive cars. Grandfather's villa is on the shores of Lake Como, and as teenage boys, we spent all the time we could in and on the water. I'll take care of you, I promise."

He was as good as his word, and in his competent hands, the sleek craft ate up the miles effortlessly. Hattie had donned her baseball cap back at the dock, and she was glad, because the wind whipped and slapped them in joyous abandon.

At times, dolphins leaped beside the boat, gamboling playfully, their beautiful skin glistening in the sun. Hattie laughed in delight and sat back finally, her eyes closed, her face tilted toward the sun. If she and Luc could keep going forever into the next sunset, life would be perfect.

Or almost. She couldn't bear the thought of giving up her niece. Deedee wasn't a burden. The baby was a joy.

Hattie shook off reality with a deliberate toss of her head. She took advantage of Luc's concentration to watch him unobserved. He controlled the boat with a relaxed stance that gave testament to his comfort being on the water. When several dark shapes began growing ahead of them, she scooted up beside him. "Is that it?"

He gave her a sideways grin. "Yep. We're in Dry Tortugas National Park."

"Never heard of it."

"Well it's only been a national park since 1992, so that's not so surprising."

"Why the name?"

"*Tortugas* because they look like a group of turtles, and *Dry* because there's no fresh water on any of them."

As they neared their destination, she stared, incredulous. She and Luc were miles from civilization, literally in the middle of nowhere. Yet perched on a handkerchief-size piece of land sat a sturdy brick fort, its hexagonal walls enclosing a large grassy area, and its perimeter surrounded by a water-filled moat. Even at a distance, the evidence of crumbling decay was visible.

Luc waved a hand as he throttled back the engine. "Fort Jefferson."

Hattie leaned her hands on the railing and absorbed it all. "I can't believe this."

"You know the expression 'Your name is mud'?"

She nodded as Luc tied up to the dock. "Of course."

"Some people attribute that remark to Dr. Samuel Mudd who was incarcerated here in the 1860s."

"What did he do that was so terrible?"

"He had the misfortune to set the broken leg of John Wilkes Booth after Booth assassinated President Lincoln."

"Wow."

"Exactly. Mudd was convicted of treason and sent here to serve a life sentence."

Hattie shuddered. Knowing there was no possibility of escape must have been mentally anguishing. "How dreadful."

"The story does have a bit of a happy ending," Luc said. "As you can imagine, disease was rampant in the fort. Dysentery, malaria, smallpox... and, at one time, a terrible outbreak of yellow fever. It was so bad, the entire medical staff died."

"And that's where Dr. Mudd comes to the rescue?"

"Right. Even knowing as he did that the disease was a killer, he stepped in and began caring for the soldiers, saving dozens of lives. For his heroism, he ultimately received a full pardon and was allowed to return home."

Hattie pondered the sad story. She wasn't a superstitious person, but the island, beautiful though it was, carried an aura of past suffering. Dr. Mudd had earned a second chance. Would Hattie and Luc be as lucky?

Luc had arranged for one of the park ranger's sons to unload all their supplies and set up camp. Luc lent a hand, but even so, it took several loads to carry everything to the designated camping area, a small sandy strip of land lightly dotted with grass and shrubs. At the far end, a young family with two kids had already erected a red-and-white tent.

Luc handled the minimal paperwork with the ranger on duty and then turned to Hattie. "You ready for a swim?"

Disappointment colored her words. "I thought we were going to explore the fort."

He held up his hands and laughed. "Okay. Fine. Maybe it will be a little cooler in there."

They grabbed cameras and water bottles and headed out. The empty silent rooms in the fort almost reeked of despair. The thick walls blocked out some of the afternoon heat, but at the same time contributed to the oppressive dungeonlike atmosphere. There were no furnishings. The stark, barren chambers seemed to echo with the voices of long-ago inmates.

After wandering through several sections of the fort, Luc pointed out the entrance to Dr. Mudd's cell. Hattie read aloud the inscription over the arch. *"Whoso entereth here leaveth all hopes behind."* She shuddered. "Gruesome. But it sounds familiar."

Luc nodded. "It's from Dante's *Inferno*."

"I need to see the sky," she muttered. She stepped back out into the sunshine, noting again the way the bricks were slowly disintegrating as time took its toll. "Can we climb the lighthouse?"

Luc took her arm. "It's about a thousand degrees today. The lighthouse is inactive. And I need a swim."

"Wimp," she teased. But she allowed herself to be persuaded. Back at the tent, there was an awkward moment.

Luc avoided her gaze. "Not much room in there," he said gruffly. "You go first."

It didn't take her long. Later, while she waited for Luc to change, she shaded her eyes and watched the numerous boats anchored offshore. Divers were taking advantage of the opportunity to explore the reef and other items of interest on the ocean floor.

When Luc emerged from the tent, she swallowed. He was wearing black nylon racing trunks that left little to the imagination. She smiled weakly, her temples perspiring, as he tossed her a towel.

Luc slung an arm around her shoulders, his own towel around his neck. "Let's go."

The water felt blissfully cool. Hattie paddled happily in the shallow water near the fort, finding it a lot easier than her first experience, since she could occasionally stand up. Some of the boaters were snorkeling as well, but they stayed mostly to the back of the fort.

She noticed that the family with the two children was also taking advantage of an afternoon swim. It suddenly occurred to her to wonder how far sound carried on the night air. Her breathing hitched, and she shivered despite the blazing sun. Anticipation and anxiety mingled in her stomach, making her feel slightly faint. If she got in over her head tonight, she'd have no one to blame but herself.

Luc had been swimming in deeper water, but he reappeared suddenly by her side, tugging off his mask and running a hand through his hair, flinging drops of water everywhere.

He smiled lazily. "Having fun?"

She nodded. "It's amazing."

He glanced at his high tech waterproof watch. "I thought I'd go on back and set up the grill, get the fire started. Will you be okay?"

She motioned him away. "By all means. I'm working up an appetite."

Without warning, he lifted her against his wet chest, her feet dangling in the water. His head lowered. "So am I, Hattie. So am I."

His mouth found hers, and the raw sensuality of his kiss made her dizzy. She closed her eyes, her other senses intensifying. He tasted salty, with a hint of coconut from the sunscreen he'd used. She pulled his lower lip between her teeth and bit gently.

His entire body quaked. He released her slowly, allowing her to slide the length of his virtually nude form. By the time her feet touched the sandy bottom once again, she could barely stand.

He laughed shakily. "Well, hell. I don't know if I have the strength to climb out of the water." He rested his chin on the top of her head, his arms wrapped around her waist. "You know what's going to happen tonight."

She nodded, mute, her face pressed to the muscular flesh just above his nipple.

He released her and stepped back. "Okay, then."

An hour later, they ate dinner in style. Hattie should have known that a Cavallo wouldn't prepare anything as plebian as hamburgers or hot dogs. Luc grilled T-bones and fresh shrimp over mesquite charcoal and then produced corn on the cob and potato salad to go with it.

She looked at him wryly over her heaping plate. "This isn't how I remember camping."

He shrugged. "My tastes have matured."

They lingered over their al fresco meal. Hattie was relaxed and yet keenly aware of the tension humming between them. Luc offered fresh chocolate-dipped strawberries for dessert. She bit into one carefully, licking the sweet juice from her lower lip.

He watched her constantly until she swatted his arm. "Stop it."

His wide, rakish grin was all innocence. "I don't know what you mean."

Moments later, the teenager showed up to do KP. He would be leaving soon when his father went off duty. There was no official presence at the fort overnight.

Luc suggested a boat ride. The sun was beginning its slow decline. Hattie prepared her camera. Luc steered the boat to a perfect vantage point to get shots of the fort washed in the beautiful evening light.

Afterward they anchored in deep water and dropped the ladder over the side. Hattie climbed over the rail, but Luc made a neat dive off the rear of the boat.

They swam and played for a long time, until the light began to fade. Back on the boat, they dried off and Hattie put on a T-shirt over her suit. As they picked up speed, the stiff breeze raised goose bumps on her arms and legs.

While they were tying up once again at the boat dock, the young father from the family across the way approached them.

He shook Luc's hand and smiled ruefully. "Our youngest son has developed an earache, and we know from past experience that we'll need medicine, so we're going back to Key West. We wanted to tell someone, because the park service occasionally does a head count out here."

Luc grimaced. "That's too bad. It's going to be a beautiful night. But I'll help you load up."

Hattie walked back to the tent and stretched out on a sleeping bag. Daylight was fading fast. It was a half hour before Luc returned. Out the tent flap she could see the family pull away from the dock. The other boats she had watched offshore earlier in the day had long since lifted anchor and sailed or motored away.

For the first time since their arrival, she and Luc were completely, irrevocably alone.

He crouched and held out a hand. "Let's take a walk."

While she stretched her arms over her head and then donned a windbreaker, Luc retrieved a flashlight from his pack and zipped up the tent. They approached the fort and skirted the edge until they could step onto the sea wall. For most of the perimeter of the fort, the barrier separated the moat from the sea.

Hattie didn't need Luc's warning to watch her step. Although the wall wasn't particularly narrow, the thought of falling into the mysterious ocean was daunting.

On the far side of the fort they sat down, crosslegged, and surveyed the vast expanse of sky and sea. A tiny sliver of new moon did little to illuminate the night. As their eyes became accustomed to the dark, they could just make out the faint line of demarcation separating the silvery pewter of the ocean from the midnight-blue of the sky. Several miles away, a working lighthouse flashed a periodic caution to boats, warning of the reefs and small rocky islands.

They sat in silence for several minutes. Hattie finally whispered, "It's like we're the only two people in the entire world. I'm not sure I like the feeling."

He took her hand and squeezed it. "Do you want to go back?"

"No." She leaned her head on his shoulder. "It's beautiful and awe-inspiring, and a little frightening to be honest, but I wouldn't have missed this for anything. Can you imagine what it must be like here during a hurricane?"

Luc chuckled. "I don't even want to think about it."

They sat hand in hand for a long time, wrapped in a cocoon of darkness and the intimacy of complete isolation. Far out across the waves, traces of phosphorescence lent a ghostly aura to the night.

Eventually, by unspoken consent, they made their way back around to the campsite. After a quick visit to the Spartan toilet facilities near the dock, they met back at the tent and stood facing each other.

Luc lifted a hand and traced her chin with his thumb. "It's not too late to change your mind. We have a perfectly good king-size bed back at the hotel. I can wait if you'd rather."

She took a step closer, leaning into his chest. "I want you, Luc…tonight."

Chapter 15

She felt his chest lift and fall as a shuddering breath escaped his lungs. He wrapped his arms around her. "Do you need a few minutes in the tent to get ready?"

"Yes," she muttered, her throat tight with nervousness. He handed her the small flashlight. She unzipped the tent and knelt to climb in, carefully removing her shoes and leaving them in a corner so no sand would find its way into their comfy sleeping space.

Luc had spread thick, soft sleeping bags on top of a single, large, cushiony air mattress. Since it was too hot to sleep inside the bags, he had also procured crisp cotton sheets complete with small pillows tucked inside lace-edged cases. The resulting effect was one part *Out of Africa* and two parts *Pretty Woman,* a stage unmistakably set for seduction.

Earlier, Hattie had regarded the tent as pleasantly roomy. Now, with Luc standing somewhere outside, it felt surprisingly claustrophobic, especially when she imagined Luc's large frame dominating the enclosed space.

She picked up her overnight case and found her toiletry bag. After quickly cleaning her face, she stripped off her clothes, thankful that the evening swim had left her skin feeling cool, if a bit salty. Luc had thought to bring a small container of fresh water, so she dampened a cloth and used it to further freshen up.

At Luc's murmured request, she passed the water container and a clean towel out to him. While he was presumably taking care of his ablutions, she found a tube of scented lotion and applied it to her elbows and legs and one or two other interesting spots.

She pulled out the lilac gown and slipped it over her head, relishing the feel of the silk against her bare skin. When she was done, she tucked the flashlight under Luc's pillow, leaving only the smallest beam of light to illuminate the tent.

Taking a deep breath and smoothing her hair, she called out. "I'm ready."

The tent flap peeled back instantly, and she saw him place his shoes and the water canister inside at the foot of the tent before he crawled in, immediately dwarfing the tiny space. He had already undressed.

Hattie's heart stopped for a split second, and then lurched back into service with an unsteady beat. Even her ploy with the flashlight didn't disguise his impressive attributes. She put a hand against her breastbone, feeling a bit like a Regency virgin in need of smelling salts.

Luc zipped the tent flap shut, tossed a few foil packets beside his pillow, and then stretched out with a sigh onto the comfortable bedding. He lay on his side facing her, leaning on his elbow with one leg propped up, looking like a centerfold.

Only, he was real. Here. In the flesh.

Hattie remained seated, her spine stiff as a poker, her legs paralyzed in a pretzel position. He patted the space beside him, and she saw him smile. "You're too far away," he complained.

She uncurled her legs and scooted closer, still leaving a healthy distance between them.

He reached out and smoothed a hand over her thigh covered in lilac silk. "I'm betting you didn't order this little number from L.L. Bean," he said, the words laced with amusement.

Suddenly, he reached behind him and picked up the flashlight, momentarily blinding her when he pointed it in her direction. He focused the tiny beam of light on her left shoulder.

His voice came out of the darkness. "Ditch the gown, Hattie, starting with that strap."

She couldn't see his face, only the outline of his body. Her fingers went to the slim strap he'd indicated, and she lowered it, slipping her arm free, but keeping her breast covered.

The beam of light moved to her other shoulder. "Now that one."

The second strap fell. She put a hand against her chest to hold the gown in place.

The light slipped down to her abdomen. He spoke again, his tone hoarse and rough. "Now all of it."

She rose to her knees, trembling, and let the fabric fall to her hips, and then, with a little shimmy, to the sleeping bag. Luc's indrawn breath was audible. The beam of light rose slowly to circle one breast and then the other. Her nipples tightened painfully. The light slid over the taut plane of her stomach to rest in the shadowed valley between her thighs.

His voice this time was barely a whisper. "Hand me the gown."

She lifted her knees, an awkward maneuver given the situation, and pulled the silk free, tossing it to him.

He buried his face in the cloth momentarily. Then the light went out. He called her name. "Hattie...come here."

She tumbled forward, her eagerness assisted by his firm grasp on her forearm. She landed half-sprawled across his chest, and one of her hands lodged in an interesting position between his legs. She found the hot, smooth length of him and stroked gently.

Luc groaned, covering her lips with his, the kiss ravenous and demanding. His tongue plundered the recesses of her mouth, exploring every crevice, nibbling and biting until she was breathless and whimpering with need.

Seconds later she sensed him trying to slow things down, but it was too late. While he fumbled for a condom, she rubbed her breasts against his chest, savoring the delicious friction. She felt his hands settle on her bottom. He lifted her until she sat astride him, and she tensed.

On and off during the last decade she had dreamed about being with him. But those fleeting fantasies didn't come close to approximating the reality of Luc Cavallo, naked, nudging with barely concealed impatience at the heart of her feminine passage.

She arched her back and felt him enter her, stretching her to an almost painful fullness. "Oh, Luc..." The sensation was incredible.

He froze, not moving an inch, his body taut and trembling. "Am I hurting you?"

She choked out a laugh, wriggling, forcing him centimeters deeper. "No." It was all she could manage. She raked his nipples with her fingernails. He heaved beneath her, burying himself to the hilt. The connection was stunning—her, adjusting to the sensation of his possession, him, clearly struggling for control.

He lifted his hands to cup her sensitive breasts. She cried out, nearing a peak so intense, she could feel it hovering just out of reach. He withdrew almost completely, but before she could voice a protest, he thrust even deeper, initiating a rhythm that sent them both tumbling into a fiery release. Somewhere in the fringes of her consciousness, she heard him shout as he emptied himself into her body, but her orgasm washed over her with such power, she was unable to focus on anything but her own pleasure.

Luc lay perfectly still, trying to recover from the effects of Hurricane Hattie. Her slender body lay draped over his in sensual abandon that filled him with a fierce masculine satisfaction overlaid by the terrifying realization that he had fallen in love with her…again. Far away from the familiar trappings of his daily life, it was all so clear. He didn't need *things* to be happy…not money or electronic toys or even the adrenaline-producing challenge of his job.

His arms tightened around her. A time machine couldn't have taken him back any more successfully than this sham marriage and this ill-conceived honeymoon. Hattie filled his life with an exhilaration he had experienced only once before. She brought *fun* into his days, joy into his home, passion into his bed.

But nothing had changed. He was still rich, and she was still wary about ceding power and control to a man like him.

The baby was the fragile glue holding this house of cards together. Unless he could convince Hattie that great sex covered a multitude of sins, it was only a matter of time until she left him.

He sighed as he felt her tongue trace his collarbone. The slightly rough caress sent trickles of heat down his torso straight to his groin. He smoothed his fingers over her bottom, guiltily aware that he might have bruised her pale skin.

She leaned on her elbow and kissed him briefly. "I think I've developed a whole new appreciation for roughing it…if I can say that with a straight face while lying on 800 thread count sheets."

He chuckled. "I never knew you liked it rough."

She punched his arm. "You're so bad. But I like that about you…" Her head found its way to his shoulder.

As her voice trailed off, he shifted her to one side. Not that he didn't enjoy having her body glued to his like wallpaper, but her proximity made it difficult to form a coherent thought. He hoped that if he handled this interlude correctly, he might be able to bind Hattie to him in such a way that she couldn't escape.

Women, unlike most men, had a hard time separating sex from emotional ties. All he had to do was convince Hattie that the compatibility they experienced in bed could carry over to life in general. That the incredible sex was only a sign of their overall rightness for each other…that they had more in common than she realized.

When Hattie slipped a hand across his thigh, he lost all interest in thinking. Her curious fingers found his partially erect shaft and began exploring. He shuddered, giving himself up to the heady pleasure of having Hattie map his body with an eagerness that was as flattering as it was arousing.

Her questing hands feathered over him like butterfly wings, brushing, touching. He clenched his teeth against a surge of lust as she found a particularly sensitive spot. "Hattie…"

She nipped his hipbone with her teeth. "Hmmm?"

His hands tangled in her hair, and he pulled her up for a hard kiss. This time, it was her tongue that demanded entrance, taunting his mouth with sweet little licks and strokes that made him groan with hunger.

Almost…almost he lifted her astride him as he had earlier, craving the sensation of filling her with one swift thrust. But at the last second, he broke the kiss and pushed her to her back, determined this time to give her the tenderness and attention she deserved.

She reached for him, but he eluded her, sliding down the length of her body to concentrate on the source of her pleasure. His hands glided over her skin, skin softer than any silk nightgown. He traced her navel and abdomen with his tongue. She twisted restlessly.

Gripping her hips and holding her down, he bent his head lower, ignoring her incoherent protests. She stiffened at the first touch of his lips, her back arching off the sleeping bag. A panting cry escaped her. He licked gently, and seconds later she shattered in a moaning climax.

He scooped her into his arms, holding her tightly

as the last tremors racked her body. She was his. He was familiar with sexual satisfaction, but this need to claim, to possess, was something he had experienced only one other time in his life.

When she stirred in his embrace, he stroked the hair from her face with an unsteady hand. He kissed her softly, tenderly, trying to tell her with his touch what he knew she wasn't ready to hear in words.

The kiss lengthened. Deepened. His own unappeased arousal clawed to the surface, reminding him that making Hattie fly moments ago was only a prelude. He rose over her, trapping both her hands in one of his and raising them above her head. His maneuver lifted her breasts in silent invitation. With his free hand, he caressed them, stroking the petal-soft curves, avoiding her nipples, deliberately building her need once again.

When her pleading whispers and writhing hips told him she was ready for his possession, he abandoned her breasts and slid his hand between her legs, testing her heat and dampness with one finger.

She turned her head and bit the tender flesh of his inner arm, silently demanding. He released her hands, scarcely noticing when they grasped his shoulders. His need had become a roaring torrent, a driving urgency toward completion. Damning the necessity, he sheathed his rock-hard erection in a condom.

With one knee, he spread her legs and settled between her thighs, positioning himself. He looked down at her, inwardly cursing the darkness, needing desperately to see her face. "Tell me you want me, Hattie," he said huskily. "Beg me."

She spread her legs even wider, seeking to join their bodies, but he held back, driven by some Neanderthal impulse. "Say it, Hattie."

Her voice, a rasping, air-starved whisper reached his ear. "Please Luc. Take me…please."

He surged forward, shuddering as her body gripped him. She was tight and hot, and her long, slender legs wrapped around his waist. He knew in an instant that once more there would be no slow, sweet loving. He drove into her again and again until the tide swept over him, pulled him under, erasing every thought but one. Hattie was his.

He tried to hold back, to prolong the exquisite sensations for a few moments more, but it was hopeless. With a hoarse shout, he came inside her for long, agonizing seconds, conscious of nothing but searing pleasure and blinding release.

In the aftermath, they clung together, breathing fractured, skin damp, hearts pounding in unison. With his last ounce of energy, he reached for the top sheet, pulled it over them. Hattie's limp body curled spoon fashion against his, her bare bottom pressed to the cradle of his thighs.

Luc surrendered to the oblivion of sleep.

Chapter 16

Hattie slipped from Luc's arms and donned a long T-shirt and panties before quietly exiting the tent. Her body was stiff and sore in some interesting places, and she felt at once exhausted and exhilarated.

After a necessary trip to the bathroom, she stood in the eerie gray light of predawn, her arms clasped around her middle. Just a few hundred feet offshore, a tiny strip of land, hardly big enough to merit the designation *island,* was covered with a teeming mass of flapping, squawking birds.

Their raucous calls and noisy confusion mirrored the turmoil in her heart. What in the heck was she going to do? There was no longer any doubt about her feelings for Luc. Having sex with him last night in such an erotic and abandoned way had been at once the most perfect and the most stupid thing she had ever done in her life.

She might one day find another man as intelligent as Luc. As kind, as handsome, as funny... perhaps. But there was no doubt in her mind that the lovemaking they had shared was unique. He'd been a good lover in college, no question. But this time around, the sex was even better. She hadn't expected the intensity, the shattering intimacy, the feeling that she had bound herself to him body and soul.

He was also better at reading her. Some internal radar seemed to pick up her moods, to see inside her head and know what she was thinking. Which made him very dangerous to her peace of mind.

And his empathy was a huge problem given that this relationship was temporary and supposedly pragmatic. She didn't want to feel so connected to him. What a mess. As much as she longed to enjoy this surprising honeymoon all the way to its conclusion, another smarter Hattie said, *Go home.*

She looked over her shoulder at the small blue tent, its outline shrouded in the misty morning fog. In a short while, the cozy housing would be dismantled, much like her short-lived marriage. The campsite would be cleared, leaving no trace of the spot where Hattie Parker had given her heart to Luc Cavallo.

But hearts healed, didn't they? And life went on. She would go back to her job perhaps, settle into a new place, learn to play the role of single mom. And perhaps this ending wouldn't be as painful as the one ten years ago. Maybe Deedee's chortling smiles would be a distraction.

Hattie and Luc might remain friends…or, if not, she'd have memories.… And if she was lucky, someday a lover who didn't know that he was second best.

Luc knew the instant Hattie stirred from his embrace and left the tent. Even in his sleep he'd been aware of her warmth and softness twined in his arms, their legs tangled, her head tucked beneath his chin. Twice more during the night they had come together in exquisite lovemaking, the first a slow gentle mating, the second a hard, fast, almost desperate race to the finish.

But Hattie's recent stealthy departure said louder than words that she needed some time alone. That she hadn't wanted to face him. He understood her motivation. He just didn't like it.

The warm pillows still retained a remnant of her fragrance. He climbed out and put on his shorts. As he ran a hand over the stubble on his chin, he grimaced. Perhaps spending the night on a deserted island wasn't the greatest way to win over a woman. But Hattie had been a good sport about it all, and something about the isolation had deepened the intimacy of their lovemaking.

He exited the tent and walked over to where she stood looking out to sea. Looping his arms around her waist from behind, he rested his chin on the top of her head. "Good morning."

She turned slightly, enough for him to see that she was smiling. "Good morning, Luc."

He squeezed her gently. "You ready for some breakfast?"

She nodded. "At the risk of sounding unladylike, I could eat the proverbial horse."

They fixed the meal together, Hattie cutting up fresh fruit while he toasted bread on the grill. He had hoped to make love to her once more before they left, but it wasn't going to happen. Hattie had retreated to some distant place, and the invisible line in the sand was one he couldn't cross.

By ten o'clock everything was packed up and loaded in the boat. He suggested climbing the lighthouse, but Hattie shook her head, saying she was tired and ready to go back. He wanted to tease her about her fatigue. Lord knew neither of them had gotten much sleep, but his courage failed him. He had just experienced one of the most incredible nights of his life, but the lady involved was treating him like a favorite brother.

It was hell on a man's self-esteem.

They made the return trip to Key West mostly in silence. Hattie sat in the back of the boat on a bench seat wearing her baseball cap pulled low over her eyes and with her arms curled around her knees. Clouds had rolled in during the morning, making the sky sullen and angry. He had to keep both hands on the wheel to handle the choppy waves.

Docking, unloading and getting back to the hotel were interminable chores. He was determined to have his say, strangely afraid that if he didn't mend some unknown rift, she would slip away from him altogether.

Hattie unlocked the door to their room. He followed her in. She dumped her things on the sofa and turned to face him, a forced smile on her lips. "Thanks for taking me to the fort. It was wonderful."

His jaw clenched. "And what about us? Were we wonderful, too?"

He watched as shock followed by what could only be described as a flash of pain crossed her face.

As she took off her cap and ran her hands

through her hair, she glanced at him. "What do *you* think?"

He jammed his hands in his pockets to keep from reaching for her. "I think we were pretty damn fabulous.... Wouldn't you agree?"

A rosy flush climbed from her throat to her cheeks. She nodded slowly. "We never had trouble in that department."

He laughed softly. "Hell, no." He sensed a softening in her, so he pressed his advantage. "Imagine what we could do in that big bed with wine and clean sheets and candles."

Her blush deepened. He stepped toward her, smiling inwardly as she backed up until her legs hit the sofa and she fell backward. He leaned over her, bracing his hands on the back of the couch, bracketing her with his arms. "Kiss me, Hattie."

Her dark eyes looking up at him were filled with secrets. "Do you really think we'll stop with a kiss?"

He bent to nuzzle her neck. "Does it matter?"

"We're both pretty grungy." She twisted her lips. "I could use a shower."

He nibbled the skin behind her ear, coming down beside her and scooping her into his lap. "I hadn't noticed."

She sighed as he kissed his way around to her collarbone, pushing aside the neckline of her

T-shirt to gain easier access. He slid a hand beneath the hem and stroked her breast through her bra, lightly pinching the nipple. She groaned. "Luc…"

The flush on her cheeks deepened when he slipped a hand inside her shorts, finding the soft fluff between her legs. She arched into his caress, her breathing ragged.

He'd been teasing earlier. He had every intention of giving her a quick kiss and then getting some business done while she was in the shower. But Hattie was smarter than he was. Clearly a kiss wasn't enough.

He ripped at the zipper on her shorts, jerking it down and removing those and her panties in one quick maneuver. Seconds later, he had her beneath him as he settled between her legs. Hearing her chant his name in soft whispers went straight to his gut. Somewhere deep in the recesses of his brain he realized this was dangerous. This mindless, desperate urge to take her. But he couldn't stop. Didn't want to.

He entered her a bare inch and hesitated, his body racked with tremors. Her eyes fluttered shut. He touched her cheek. "Look at me, Hattie."

She complied, her eyes cloudy and unfocused. He went an inch deeper, and they groaned in unison. She panted, her chest rising and falling rapidly, but she held his gaze.

Struggling for almost nonexistent control, he stroked her cheekbone. "We have to deal with this."

Her head moved slowly in a gesture that could have been agreement or denial. "You talk too much." She grabbed a handful of his hair, pulling his head down for a kiss. "Just get on with it."

The breathless demand snapped his feeble efforts to maintain any kind of sanity. If she wanted it, he'd give it to her. No questions asked. He drove deeper into the hot, tight warmth of her, wanting desperately to make it last longer, but realizing with a sort of incredulous despair that he was losing the battle.

He gritted his teeth, holding back the scalding rush of pleasure. But Hattie's sudden cry and his own body defeated him. He surged harder, blindly emptying himself until he felt blackness close in around him.

A long time later he rolled off of her and flopped onto his back on the plush carpet, staring at the ceiling fan rotating overhead. He felt Hattie's fingers twine with his, and heard her voice, filled with unmistakable amusement. "Now I *really* need a shower."

He laughed, stung by chagrin at his emotionally reckless behavior but filled with a deep, boneless contentment. He glanced at his watch and swore.

"I have to make two quick calls. But I won't be long, I promise."

She leaned over to kiss him. "It's okay, Luc. Really."

"And was it okay that I took you like a wild man?"

"You *were* pretty intense."

Remorse rode him for not even fully undressing her. "What can I say? You're a temptress."

She looked down at her rumpled clothes and rolled her eyes. "Oh, yeah…that's it."

He stood up, and she followed suit as they each adjusted their clothing. Though he wanted nothing more than to drag her into the bedroom, he resisted the urge. Unless he knew for sure that Hattie was falling for him, he'd be well-advised to rein in his sexual enthusiasm.

But he couldn't resist the urge to woo her. "Why don't we go somewhere fancy for dinner? We can talk about your situation, maybe dance a little…"

Her expression was difficult to read. "That would be nice."

"And we can relax by the pool this afternoon. I'll get Marcel to serve us lunch out there."

"Sure."

He watched her turn toward the bedroom. "I could join you in the shower," he said, consigning his phone calls to the devil.

Hattie shook her head. "Do what you have to do. We've got plenty of time."

Luc let her go for the moment. She was his, body and soul. Perhaps she didn't know it yet, but he would fight dirty if he had to. He wouldn't lose her.... Not again.

Hattie stepped under the strong, stinging spray of the shower and luxuriated in the hot, steamy flow of water. It was amazing what twenty-four hours of deprivation could accomplish. She would never have made it on that TV survivor show. Never mind eating bugs; she would have begged to be voted off after the second day just so she could be clean again.

She dried off with one of the inn's sinfully thick towels. A nap sounded appealing, but she wasn't prepared to give up a day of sunbathing. Donning a robe, she returned to the bedroom and rummaged in her suitcase for the only swimsuit she had not yet worn. It wasn't at all skimpy by today's standards, but the shiny gold fabric clung to her body like a second skin. When Luc appeared in the doorway, his jaw actually dropped. "Tell me you're not wearing that thing outside our room."

She grinned, and then summoned a pout. "I thought you would love it."

He strode toward her. "Love it, hell. When a suit looks like that on a woman, the designer's only motivation is to drive men insane." He skimmed his hands over her body. "Good Lord. It feels like you're naked." He smoothed her bottom. "Are you sure you want to go to the pool? It's nice and quiet and cool up here in our room."

Though the coaxing note in his voice made her knees weak, Hattie held him at arm's length. "I want to go home with at least a semblance of a tan. So I refuse to be distracted by your masculine charms."

He lifted an eyebrow. "You think I'm charming?"

"I think I've made that pretty obvious this week."

He laughed, and for a brief second, she wondered if he felt anything more for her than lust. His actions seemed to indicate affection, but nothing he had said in any context contradicted his earlier plan to make their marriage temporary.

She wanted so badly to say the words swelling in her heart, but she chickened out. It was still too soon.

When Luc's cell phone rang she headed for the door. "You get that if you want to. I'll be out at the pool."

The concern in his words when he spoke with the caller stopped Hattie dead in her tracks.

The conversation was brief. Luc hung up, his expression serious.

Her skin chilled. "What's wrong?"

"The baby's running a temperature."

Hattie sank onto the sofa. "How bad?"

"A hundred and three. It's probably just a virus. They're on the way to a pediatrician right now. Ana wasn't unduly concerned, but she was sure you'd want to know."

"I do. Of course."

Luc eyed her. "What are you thinking?"

She winced, feeling ungrateful for all he had done. "Do you mind if we go home? I need to be with her...to make sure she's okay."

He nodded. "I thought as much. Start packing, and I'll see what kind of flights I can find."

Chapter 17

It was almost midnight when they made it back to Atlanta and drove from the airport to the house. Leo was on hand to pick them up since they didn't have a car. He and Luc sat in the front. Hattie in the back.

Leo looked over his shoulder. "How was Key West?"

"Very nice," she replied, refusing to be baited.

The two brothers chuckled in unison. Hattie pretended a sudden interest in the passing scenery.

Leo helped unload the luggage into the foyer, shook Luc's hand and kissed Hattie on the cheek. "Let me know how Deedee is. I'll be at the office in the morning."

As he drove off, Hattie yawned. Ana met them in the hallway, not waiting to be asked for an update. "She's sleeping. The doctor says it's a bad ear infection. She may need surgery to have tubes put in."

Tears sprang to Hattie's eyes, a reaction to fatigue and the thought of having her small baby put to sleep.

Luc put his arm around her. "We'll deal with that when the time comes. Thank you, Ana. Hattie and I will take it from here. You go get some rest."

"If you're sure. I wrote down her medication schedule on the nightstand in her room and the two bottles are there, too."

In the nursery, Hattie approached the crib on tiptoe. But Deedee was sleeping peacefully, her bottom in the air as she crouched in a ball on the mattress.

Luc touched Hattie's arm. "I'll bring our bags up. Why don't you get ready for bed?"

Hattie couldn't resist stroking the baby's back. "She still feels so hot."

"The antibiotic will take a while to kick in. We can set the alarm and give her ibuprofen during the night. Go on," he urged. "You're weaving on your feet."

"Okay." Hattie took a quick shower and changed into a nightgown that was pretty but not overtly sexy. Now that they were home, her thoughts were in turmoil. She hated that she felt like an insecure teenager again, wondering if a boy liked her. Everything had seemed so simple, so natural out on the island.

But now…back on Luc's home turf, all her earlier reservations returned. Would Luc expect to share her room? Was she supposed to go to his?

The nursery was adjacent to Hattie's suite. Ana and Sherman had slept in a nearby guest room while Luc and Hattie were gone.

When Hattie returned to the baby's room, her steps faltered. She hung back in the hall, her heart wrenching painfully. In the room decorated with nursery rhyme murals, a night-light cast a soft, pink glow. Sitting in the maple rocker, his head leaned back, eyes half-closed, was Luc. And in his arms lay a sleeping baby.

Deedee was nestled against Luc's chest, one tiny hand clutching a fold of his shirt. The contrast between the big strong male and the tiny helpless baby twisted something deep in Hattie's chest. This was what Leo had feared. That Luc would fall in love with Deedee.

Luc himself had alluded to the fact that he understood the bond between parent and child. Clearly Hattie's niece had wormed her way into his heart. Seeing the two people Hattie loved most in the world…seeing them like this made her realize that she had backed herself into a difficult, if not impossible, corner.

Luc didn't believe in romantic love anymore. And Hattie alone was responsible for his cynicism. But if he loved Deedee, how could she take the baby away when the time came? How could she break Luc's heart a second time?

In the dimly lit room, Luc crooned a soft lullaby, his pleasing baritone singing of diamond rings and mockingbirds. The tender way he held the baby was poignant.

Hattie made herself step into the room. "I'll take her now so you can get cleaned up."

Luc's eyes, sleepy lidded, surveyed his wife. "Are you coming to my room to sleep?"

Wow. Trust Luc to cut straight to the chase. She steadied herself with a hand on the dresser. His meaning was crystal clear. But she had no clue how to respond. "Well, uh…"

His expression went blank, no trace of anything revealed on his classically sculpted features. "Don't sweat it, Hattie. We're both tired. But I'll be more than happy to help with the baby during the night if you need a hand."

Before Hattie could come up with words to explain the confusion in her heart, Luc gently placed Deedee in the crib, brushed by Hattie, and was gone.

Hattie rubbed her eyes with the heels of her hands, inhaling deeply. *Damn it.* Had she hurt his feelings? His male pride? She hadn't intended to say no to sleeping with him, but his artless question caught her off guard. This was uncharted territory.

They could no longer use a pretend honeymoon as an excuse to indulge in passionate sex. They were once again smack-dab in the throes of reality. Luc had married Hattie because she asked him to help protect an innocent baby. And perhaps because he could make Hattie dance to his tune and prove that she meant nothing to him. Did he also expect their physical intimacy to continue?

The baby was sleeping peacefully. Hattie made sure the volume on the monitor was adjusted and slipped out of the room, pulling the door shut as she left. Her big bed, which had seemed so luxurious and comfortable last week, was now a torture device. She tossed and turned, flipping the covers back in an effort to get cool.

She missed Luc, missed his big strong body snuggling with hers. What did he want from her? He'd seemed completely calm during their earlier conversation...not that it was much of a conversation. He'd taken her momentary confusion as a "no," and Hattie hadn't meant that at all, at least not completely.

Her befuddled brain had been scrambling to process all the pros and cons of maintaining a sexual relationship now that they were home. Ana and Sherman would know…and Leo, probably. Something like that was difficult to keep a secret.

So when the situation with Eddie was resolved and Hattie had to go, what then?

The next morning, Deedee was noticeably improved. Luc played with her for a half hour before announcing he was going to the office.

Hattie handed the baby off to Ana and frowned as she followed Luc down to the foyer. "You're still supposed to be on your honeymoon. They won't be expecting you…"

He shrugged into an immaculately tailored navy suit jacket, his expression impassive. "I'm back. Work will have piled up. I might as well get a jump start on things."

Hattie couldn't think of a thing to say to stop him from walking out the door.

As she stood at the window watching her husband's car move down the driveway, her cell phone rang. After ascertaining that it was an unknown number, she answered. "Hello."

"Mrs. Cavallo?"

"Yes."

"This is Harvey Sharpton. I work for your husband, and I have good news."

Hattie's chest tightened. "What is it? Tell me, please."

"Little Deedee's father has screwed up royally this time. Another DUI. A hit-and-run again, this time involving pedestrians. Fortunately, no one was fatally injured, but the judge threw the book at him. And when we came forward with the nurse's testimony, the one who heard Angela's request, the judge granted you sole custody."

Hattie could barely speak. "Thank you so much," she croaked.

"There are some papers you need to sign."

"I'll call you and make an appointment soon. I appreciate your calling me."

She sank down on the bottom step of the grand, sweeping staircase and put her face in her hands. The relief was overwhelming. She wanted to tell Luc immediately...needed to share her joy with the one person who would understand more than anyone else. But he was gone.

All day she rehearsed what she would say. Forty-eight hours ago, it would have been much easier. The Luc she had made love to on her honeymoon was far more approachable than the stern businessman he had reverted to upon their return.

When he didn't make it home in time for dinner, her stomach sank. Maybe she was foolishly naive.

Building castles in the air instead of planning for a future without Luc.

Finally, at eleven o'clock, she went to bed and fell into a fitful sleep. Something awoke her in the wee hours—a muffled thud, perhaps a door closing. She glanced at the clock on the bedside table. It was already time to give the baby a dose of medicine. Without bothering to put on a robe, she stole down the hall in her bare feet and opened the nursery door. For the second time, she found Luc with Deedee in his arms. He was standing beside the bed, the infant on his shoulder, patting her softly on the back.

Luc was wearing nothing but thin cotton boxers. Despite the hour and her fatigue, Hattie's body responded. It was conditioned now to expect searing pleasure, and Luc's scent, his masculine beauty, triggered all sorts of dancing hormones.

He turned to face her, speaking softly. "I've already given her the medicine. I thought you were asleep."

She shrugged. "I had a lot on my mind."

Ignoring Hattie's conversational gambit, Luc kissed Deedee's head before laying her back in the bed. He yawned and stretched, the corded muscles in his arms and chest flexing and rippling. "I checked her temp. It's almost normal. You don't need to worry."

Deedee wasn't Hattie's greatest concern at the moment. Instead, it was the way Luc was acting... aloof, unconcerned—about Hattie, that is. She took a step closer to him. "I never meant to imply that I wasn't going to sleep with you. You caught me by surprise, that's all. Do you want me to come with you now? I'm glad you're home."

He stilled, his dark eyes opaque, impossible to read. His shrug spoke volumes. "The baby needs you."

And I don't.

The unspoken words hovered between them. They might as well have been an aerial banner tugged through the sky by a plane.

Hattie didn't know what to say. It seemed as if he was trying purposefully to hurt her. And he was succeeding.

But she had learned a lot about him in the last week. Deep inside the coldly confident, unemotional man was a younger Luc. One who had been hurt repeatedly. One who had learned to shield his softer side. One who built walls. She took a courageous step in his direction. "The reason I wasn't able to sleep is because you weren't beside me."

Luc teetered on the edge of his own personal hell. Hattie was offering herself to him, coming to him of her own free will.

He was almost positive she was falling in love with him. Women couldn't hide things like that. Hattie didn't sleep around. And even though he was her husband, she wouldn't have shared his bed just for sex.

So why was he hesitating?

The dark knot of remembered pain inside him said, *Do it. Tell her to go to hell. Tell her you don't need a wife who's been bought and paid for. Tell her you don't want her.*

Would she see through the lie?

Could he instead reach for the rosy future that seemed almost within his grasp? A wife, a baby, a happily-ever-after?

People he loved left him. His parents. Hattie. If he brought her and the baby into his heart and home and then lost them, he wasn't sure he'd survive.

He clenched his fists, fighting the urge to grab her and pull her close. Instead, he shrugged. "We should probably reevaluate our relationship. See where things stand with the custody situation. I have a hell of a lot to catch up on at work…and you'll be spending time with the baby."

Hattie's face went white, her expression agonized. "So you were just using me in Key West because I was convenient?"

"Don't cast me as the villain in this drama," he said roughly. Sexual desire and searing regret choked him. "If anything, we used each other. You were wet and willing."

"You're a selfish ass," she said, tears choking her voice and welling in her beautiful eyes.

"I gave you what you wanted. You and the baby are safe. Don't ask for the moon, Hattie."

Chapter 18

Don't ask for the moon, Hattie. The careless words jangled in her head. She barely slept at all, and when dawn broke, she knew what she had to do. It would have to be a covert operation. Ana and Sherman couldn't be caught in the middle.

Breakfast was miserable. Despite Deedee's chortling happiness, Luc and Hattie barely spoke, concentrating on brief exchanges of information that left her grieving and heartsick.

By ten o'clock the house was empty. Ana and Sherman had gone to the market. Patti was back at school. Luc was at the office. As soon as Deedee went down for her morning nap, Hattie started packing. She walked the hallways back and forth, barely able to concentrate, her skin cold as ice. The pain was crushing. When the suitcases were in the car, she fled. Out the door, down the steps, the baby clasped to her chest.

Luc had sent Hattie's clunker car into the shop for an overhaul. The stylish new minivan that she was still learning to drive was backed into the garage. She snapped Deedee into the car seat, hands shaking, jumped into the driver's seat, put the car in gear and tore out of the driveway.

She drove on autopilot, her heart bleeding. Luc would never love her again. She had killed those feelings in him. He wanted her body, but with his iron control, he was clearly able to deny them even that.

If she stayed in his house an hour more, she might be reduced to begging. And Luc didn't deserve that. He had helped her when she needed it most, but that reason no longer existed. She and Deedee were on their own.

The miles flashed by as she cruised the interstate. Where would she go? What was the next step? She had credit cards galore, but what if Luc disabled them in order to force her home?

Hastily, she did a mental accounting of the cash in her purse…maybe four hundred dollars at the most. That wouldn't last long. But she had to go someplace where no one could find her. At least until she figured out what she was going to do.

Luc leaned back in his office chair and rubbed his neck. He had a killer headache. Thank God Leo was coming over for dinner tonight. His company would be a welcome diversion from the stilted, overly polite conversation to which he and Hattie had been reduced.

For the first time since the honeymoon, Luc arrived home at five-thirty. Leo was not far behind him.

Luc's brother wore a rumpled suit and offered a rueful apology. "Sorry for arriving unfashionably early. But I had a meeting in this part of town, and it didn't seem worth driving back to the office at rush hour."

Luc led him into the library and poured them each a finger of whiskey. "No worries. Deedee is starting to pull up on things, so Ana says she thinks Hattie and the baby went shoe shopping. They're not even back yet. We've got time to relax before dinner."

Leo settled his large frame into a spacious easy chair. After downing his drink in one gulp, he sighed, closed his eyes and spoke. "How are the two of you getting along?"

"No problems." Luc paced restlessly.

"Do you love her?"

"Who are you? Dr. Ruth? I'm not sure what love is."

"Then why did you marry her? Our lawyers have the ability to make mincemeat out of old Eddie. Tying the knot was totally unnecessary. So why did you do it?"

Luc had asked himself that same question a hundred times. The answer was clear, but it was too soon to tell his brother. Leo's propensity for mischief shouldn't be underestimated.

"It was the right thing to do. Protecting the baby."

"I'll give you that. You always did love playing the hero. But there's got to be more."

Sherman appeared in the door. "Excuse me, Mr. Luc. Ana found this note with your name on it. It was on the desk in the kitchen."

Luc ripped open the envelope and stared at the words without comprehension.

Leo came to stand beside him. "What is it? What's wrong?"

Luc had never been as scared as he was at this moment. "She's gone. She has custody, and she's gone."

His brother snatched the piece of paper and scanned it rapidly, cursing beneath his breath. "We'll find her. She can't have gone far."

* * *

But they didn't. One day passed. Then two. Then three. Hattie's cell phone was turned off, so the GPS locator was useless. None of her credit cards showed any sign of activity. It was as if she and Deedee had vanished off the face of the earth.

Luc was surviving on black coffee and three hours of sleep a night. His frustration with the police was enormous, but even he had to admit that there was no indication of foul play.

Hattie had left of her own free will. And she had taken his heart with her, dragging it in the wake of the speeding car, shredding it as the miles passed.

Leo was a rock. He moved in, and between the two of them, they hired the best detectives their considerable fortune could buy. But the P.I. reports were little comfort. When a person wanted to disappear, it could take weeks, months to track them down.

Luc lay in bed, night after night, dry-eyed, his body ice-cold. Pride. Injured pride had caused this debacle. All he'd had to do was tell Hattie he loved her more than life. Assure her that he had no plans to ever be parted from her or from Deedee.

If the lawyer had managed to give the news to Luc first instead of Hattie, Luc could have been prepared. But Luc had been too damn busy to listen to his voice mails.

On the fourth day, he caught a break. In her haste, Hattie had left behind the baby's antibiotic. Since Deedee had only been taking it a few days, there was a good chance the child's infection would return without the whole course of treatment.

Once Luc realized the omission, the detectives started monitoring the pediatrician's office with the cooperation of the doctor who was a friend of Luc's. At two-thirty in the afternoon of the fifth miserable day, a call came in requesting a replacement refill.

Luc practically grabbed the detective by the throat. "Tell me you got some information."

The grizzled sixtysomething veteran nodded, his gaze sympathetic. "The call originated from a Motel 6 in Marietta. Here's the address."

Hattie walked the floor, trying to soothe the cranky infant. Based on the last time she'd started the medicine, Deedee might not feel any better until at least forty-eight hours had passed.

Right after the honeymoon when the baby was ill, Hattie had been backed up with Luc's help and support. Now she was completely alone. The feelings of desolation and heartbreak were too much to bear. Her psyche adapted by shutting down all of Hattie's emotional pain sensors.

She was calm, too calm, but the unnatural state enabled her to function.

She had finally gotten Deedee to sleep late in the afternoon and had slumped onto the adjoining bed, craving a nap, when a loud knock hammered on the door of Room 106. Thankfully, the baby was dead asleep and didn't even stir.

Hattie peered through the peephole. *Dear God. Luc.* She wrung her hands, her brain paralyzed.

His distinctive voice sounded through the thin wood. "I see the car. I know you're in there. Open up, damn it."

Like a robot, she twisted the lock and turned the knob. As she stepped back into the room, Luc blew in with a barrage of rain and wind. A storm was brewing, the skies dark and boiling with clouds.

They faced off in the boxlike room.

He was haggard and pale, his shirt wrinkled, his hair a mess. Nothing about him suggested a successful entrepreneur.

Her heart iced over as the recollection of his deliberate cruelty flooded back.

"What do you want, Luc?" Fatigue enveloped her. She turned her back on him deliberately, sitting on the nearest bed and scooting back against the headboard. She pulled her knees to her chest, arms wrapped protectively around them.

His eyes were dark with misery. "I want *you*."

"Liar." She said it without inflection, but she saw him flinch as the insult found its mark.

He shrugged out of his jacket and swiped a hand through his wet hair. Thunder boomed, and the lights flickered. "I made a mistake. I was afraid to tell you how I felt. I never meant to drive you away."

Her fingernails dug into her legs. "I'm not stupid, Luc. I realized early on that one reason you agreed to help me was so that you could control things. You wanted the power this time. Lucky you. It worked."

He took a step toward the bed, but she stopped him with an outstretched arm.

Frustration carved grooves into his handsome face. "That idea lasted for about ten minutes. I told myself I wanted to hurt you…like you had hurt me. But I was kidding myself. I didn't want you to leave, Hattie."

"The lawyer called me. Eddie's not a threat anymore."

"I know. I read your note. It's wonderful news, but I'd rather have heard it from you face-to-face."

"You can give me part of that settlement now," she said calmly, her heart coming to life so that it could shatter into a million painful pieces. "We don't need your help anymore. We don't need you."

The look in his eyes made her ashamed. Spitefulness was not in her nature, but the need to lash out was inescapable.

He sat down at the foot of the bed, close enough

for her to smell his aftershave and his natural, masculine scent. His eyes were dark, but no darker than the shadows beneath them. And he hadn't shaved. The anomaly disturbed her.

He touched her knee. A brief flash of heat tried to warm her, but he took his hand away. "What if *I* need *you?*" he asked hoarsely.

Hope flared in her chest. She smashed it ruthlessly. "You can buy anything you need."

The tired, wry twist of his lips was painful to watch. "I'm pretty sure you believed that ten years ago. It wasn't true then, and it isn't true now. My money doesn't give me control over you, Hattie. You're the one with all the power in this relationship."

"I'm a single, homeless mom with no job."

Again he winced. "You have a home," he said quietly. "And a husband who loves you more than life."

A single tear found its way down her cheek. "You never told me. Not once. We had sex a dozen times, maybe more…but you treated it like recreation. Not at all like love. And I know that's my fault. I'm sorry, Luc. Sorry I treated your love so callously back then."

He bowed his head briefly. "I should have said the words you needed to hear. But I was scared," he said. "You had the power to destroy me, Hattie. You still do."

Her lips trembled. "You've played games with my feelings. You hate me for what I did to you."

"I *tried* to hate you," he said softly. "For years. But it didn't work. When you showed up in my office that day, it was as if life had given me another chance. For a very short while, I told myself it was revenge I wanted. But I lied even to myself, Hattie. I loved you. I love you. I don't think I ever really stopped loving you. You have to believe me."

"Or what?"

"Or I'm going to buy this motel and lock you in this room until you come to your senses and admit you love me, too."

Hattie was shaking so hard, she was afraid she might fly apart. She wanted so badly to be certain he was telling the truth. "I don't want a relationship where both of us are jockeying for control. I don't want to play mind games. I need to be in an equal partnership. If I decide to go back to my career when Deedee starts school, I don't want any flack about that just because you're too rich for your own good. I'll dress up for parties and I'll hostess for you, but I may still clip the occasional coupon…" She ran out of breath.

"Is that all?"

"Isn't that enough?"

"I'll let you make all the decisions from now on."

"Liar." This time she said it with rueful humor.

He leaned forward and found her mouth in a kiss so exquisitely tender it thawed the block of ice in her chest. Tears trickled down her cheeks, but he kissed them away. He took her face in his hands, his expression grave. "I love you, Hattie Parker."

Her lips trembled. Her arms went around his neck in a stranglehold. "I love you, Luc Cavallo. And remember…my name isn't Parker anymore. I belong to you."

She felt the mighty shudder that racked his body, struggled to breathe as his arms crushed her in an unbreakable grip.

"Have you forgiven me?" she asked quietly, still feeling the sting of regret. "I cost us so much time."

He pulled back to look her in the eyes, his own deadly serious. "Maybe we both needed to grow up. Maybe we needed to be the people we are now so we could love Deedee as our own."

She sniffled, having a hard time with the juxtaposition of soaring happiness and recent despair. "Take me home, Luc. Take *us* home."

He tucked her head beneath his chin, their heartbeats thudding in unison. "I thought you'd never ask."

Epilogue

Five months later, in a small villa in the south of France, Hattie caught her breath as her husband's rigid length entered her slowly. The sensation was exquisite.

His breathing was labored, his face flushed. He loved her gently, as he had in recent weeks.

She wrapped her legs around his waist and squeezed. "I won't break," she complained.

Late-afternoon shadows painted their nude bodies with warm light. In a nearby cheval mirror, she watched as he penetrated her with a lazy rhythm. The tantalizing pace sent her soaring. He waited until her peak receded slowly and then found his own release.

Afterward, Luc ran his hand over the small bump where her flat stomach used to be. They had made a baby that very first time in Key West. A fact that Luc continually referred to with pride.

He nuzzled her belly. "I think he's a boy." Their ultrasound was scheduled soon.

She sighed, feeling sated and content. "We're going to have our hands full with two little ones so close together."

"We have Ana and Sherman to help. We'll be fine."

She brushed a lock of dark hair from his forehead. "You're my knight in shining armor. You rescued Deedee and me. I'll never forget it."

Luc rolled to his back, taking her with him to sprawl on his chest. His eyes were alight with happiness. "You've got it all wrong, my love. The two of you rescued me."

* * * * *

KATHERINE GARBERA

USA TODAY bestselling author Katherine Garbera is a two-time Maggie Award winner who has written more than sixty books. A Florida native who grew up to travel the globe, Katherine now makes her home in the Midlands of the U.K. with her husband, two children and a very spoiled miniature dachshund. Visit her on the web at www.katherinegarbera.com, connect with her on Facebook and follow @katheringarbera on Twitter.

Look for more books from Katherine Garbera in Harlequin Desire—the ultimate destination for powerful, passionate romance! There are six new Harlequin Desire titles available every month. Check one out today!

BABY BUSINESS
Katherine Garbera

This book is dedicated to Courtney and Lucas
for always making me laugh.

Chapter 1

"You're a lifesaver," Cassidy Franzone said as she opened her front door.

At thirty-four weeks pregnant, she needed food when she wanted it. She was single and fine with that. She'd made the choice to have her baby on her own, but she hated going out in Charleston's August heat to pick up her favorite she-crab soup if she didn't have to.

Her father had put his employees at her disposal. If she needed anything, no matter what time of day it was, someone on the staff at Franzone Waste Management was available.

"Am I?"

The man standing in the doorway wasn't her father's employee. In fact, he was the father of her child.

Cassidy gaped at Donovan Tolley. He was still the most attractive man she'd ever seen. His thick hair—hair she'd loved to run her fingers through—lifted in the warm summer breeze. His designer clothes were tailored perfectly to his frame—not for vanity's sake, but because he liked quality.

"What are you doing here?" she asked. She hoped that she sounded nonchalant, as if the reason was not important, but she couldn't help but cover her stomach with one arm protectively. How had Donovan found out that she was pregnant? Or had he?

Maybe it was the fact that she was so hungry, or maybe it had just been so long—almost eight months, to be exact—since she'd seen him. But she felt a sting of tears in the back of her eyes as Donovan smiled at her.

"Can I come in? I don't want to talk to you in the doorway." He seemed a bit dazed. As he pushed his sunglasses up to the top of his head she saw in his eyes that he was busy processing her pregnancy.

"What do you want to talk about?" she asked. What if he didn't believe he was the father of her child? What exactly did he want? And why the hell was she still attracted to this man after he'd broken her heart and left her alone for almost eight months?

He eyed her belly and arched one eyebrow. "Your pregnancy, for starters."

She hadn't told Donovan that she was pregnant with his child, but then again he'd made his views on children quite clear when he'd made his rather businesslike marriage proposal to her. "I know everything I need to about how you feel about kids."

"I'm not so sure about that. Invite me in, Cassidy. I need to talk to you. And I'm not going away."

She hesitated. She would have shut the door on any other man, but then she wouldn't be pregnant with any other man's child. Donovan was the only man she'd ever loved. Still, she didn't need this kind of tension right now.

She was hungry, the baby was moving around and she wasn't exactly sure she wanted to send Donovan on his way. That wasn't like her. She'd always been very decisive, but lately she hadn't been herself.

She felt a bit faint, probably due to the heat. She made up her mind to send Donovan away. She'd deal with him after the baby was born, when she had her act together.

A late-model black-windowed Mercedes pulled into her driveway and Cassidy smiled. Finally her food was here.

"Got your soup, Ms. Cassidy."

"Thank you, Jimmy," she said as the young man handed her a brown bag. He nodded at her as she took the bag and then he left.

Donovan smiled. "Crab Shack?"

She nodded. She always tried not to focus on the fact that the soup she loved so much came from the place where she and Donovan had eaten at least once a week while they'd been together. The Crab Shack was a famous Charleston institution.

"I'll keep you company while you eat," he said.

"I don't think so. We can talk later this week. I'll call your assistant."

"I'm not leaving, Cassidy."

"Are you going to force your way into my house?" she asked.

"No," he said, bracing one arm on the door frame and leaning in over her. "You're going to invite me in."

His cologne was one-of-a-kind, made for him by an exclusive perfumery in France, and at this moment she really hated that company because Donovan smelled so good. The scent reminded her of the many times she'd lain cuddled close to his side with her head on his chest.

"Cassidy, baby, please let me in," he said, leaning closer so that his words were more of a whisper.

Everything feminine inside of her went nuts. Her breasts felt fuller and her nipples tightened against the fabric of her bra. Her skin felt more sensitive, her lips dry. She wet them with her tongue and saw his eyes narrow as he watched her.

"Is there anything I can do to convince you to go away?"

"No. I've missed you, Cassidy, and leaving is the last thing I want to do."

She hated the little thrill she got when he said he'd missed her. She tried to be nonchalant when she stepped back so that he could enter her house.

Donovan closed the front door behind them and she hesitated in the foyer of her own home. She should have never let him back into her house. She wasn't going to be able to keep any kind of distance between them. Face-to-face with Donovan again, all she could think about was sex. About being back in his arms one last time. Her hormones had been going crazy throughout her pregnancy, and once again they came rushing to the fore. She wanted this man. She hadn't even tried dating in the last eight months, though a few brave guys had asked her out. She didn't want anyone but Donovan.

She led the way to the first floor screened-in porch. It overlooked the wooded area behind her house, and with its tall ceilings and the shade provided by the nearby oak and magnolia trees, it was a cool refuge from the heat.

"Can I get you a beer or tea?" she asked.

"Beer would be great," he said.

She set her soup on the table and went to the wet bar to get Donovan's beer. He liked Heineken, same as she did. Though she hadn't had a beer since she'd gotten pregnant, she still kept her refrigerator stocked for when her brothers and friends visited.

She grabbed a bottle of Pellegrino for herself and came back to the table. Donovan stood up and held her chair for her. The gentlemanly courtesy was one he had always performed, and she appreciated it. That was one of the things that had always set Donovan apart from other men. She thanked him and sat down.

Food suddenly became unimportant as she realized the man she loved was sitting there next to her. She had to clasp her hands in her lap to keep from reaching out to touch him. To keep from leaning across the table and making sure he was really there.

"How are you, Cassidy?" he asked.

"Good. I haven't had any complications from the pregnancy." She was twenty-eight years old and in great shape thanks to a lifetime of exercise and eating right. The baby was healthy, something that she sometimes fancied was due to the fact that she and Donovan had been so much in love when he'd been conceived. But she knew that was her imagination running away with her.

"I'm glad."

"Are you?" she asked, trying for sarcasm but guessing she'd sounded a bit pleased that he was concerned about her health.

"Yes." He leaned back in his chair. "Why didn't you tell me about the baby? I'm assuming the baby is mine."

She suspected he knew she wasn't interested in any other man. She hadn't hidden her feelings for him when they were together.

"Yes, it is yours. I didn't tell you because it didn't seem like the type of information you'd be interested in."

"What do you mean by that?"

"Just that if something doesn't involve Tolley-Patterson Manufacturing or any of your other business interests, you usually don't pay much attention to it."

"I paid attention to you," he said.

"When there wasn't a crisis at one of your companies, sure, you did pay attention to me."

But she had always been aware that his position as executive vice president at Tolley-Patterson, the company his family owned, was the most important thing in Donovan's life. He was also consumed by his other business interests, and with increasing his holdings. He co-owned a sporting goods company with his former college roommate, and he had an interest in an island resort on Tobago with a friend from his boarding-school days. For a while his constant focus on business hadn't mattered. But during the last few months, while they'd been apart, she'd come to realize she had sold herself short in their relationship.

Donovan had always been obsessed with proving there was more to him than just his trust fund. And she wasn't interested in competing for his attention again. Getting over Donovan had been hard. The hardest thing she'd ever gone through. She'd thought she wasn't going to recover at first, and when she'd gotten confirmation that she was pregnant with his child, she'd made up her mind that the baby was the reason she'd been brought into Donovan's life. His child would be the one on whom she'd pour all the love that he'd never really wanted from her.

But now he was back, and she had this tingly excitement in the pit of her stomach that made her hope he might be back for good.

And that scared her more than facing the future alone.

* * *

"What does that comment mean? I never ignored you when we were together."

Donovan was still trying to process the fact that Cassidy was having his baby. He couldn't believe his good fortune in finding her pregnant. He'd come here today to ask her to marry him again, to convince her that he'd changed his mind about family. And he had to do it without revealing the circumstances that had brought him to her doorstep today.

Donovan had forgotten how truly beautiful Cassidy was. Her skin was like porcelain, fine and pale, and her hair was rich and thick. He knew from experience how soft it felt against his skin. Her lips were full, and though she didn't have lipstick on, they were a perfect deep pink color—the exact same shade as her nipples. God, he wanted to forget about talking and just draw her into his arms and kiss her. How he'd missed her mouth….

His body hardened and he adjusted his legs, trying to quell his erection. He'd never thought of pregnant women as sensual before, but there was something about seeing Cassidy's lush body filled out with his child.

"Only because I knew that you needed to be at work twelve hours a day and on weekends…I didn't make a lot of demands on your time," she said.

It took a moment for her words to register, because he'd been watching her mouth and wondering…if he leaned over and kissed her, would she kiss him back?

But then the words registered and he realized that she probably wasn't in the mood to be kissed. She was busy focusing on all the reasons they were no longer together. And he needed to get her thinking about why they should be again.

If there was one thing that Donovan was good at, it was winning—and winning Cassidy over was his first priority. He was competitive, and his drive for success went much deeper than wanting to make money. God knew, with his trust fund he never needed to work a day in his life. And the investments he'd made in the ventures with his friends had paid off handsomely. But he wanted more. He wanted his birthright—the CEO position at Tolley-Patterson.

Looking at Cassidy with her beautiful hair curling around her face made him realize that he'd missed her far more than he'd realized. He wouldn't have come back on his own, without the incentive of needing a wife and child, but being here now, he knew that coming back was exactly what he'd needed to do. Her pregnancy simply made his objective that much easier to attain.

"I'm sorry," he said. And part of him really meant the words. Another part—the man who was always looking for a way to turn every situation to his advantage—knew that being humble would help him win Cassidy back. Knew that even though he'd hurt her, there was a tentative hope in her eyes.

"For?"

"Making you feel like you weren't first in my life," he said.

She fiddled with her food bag and drew out a foam container of what he suspected was she-crab soup.

"Don't play games with me, Donovan."

"I'm not."

"Yes, you are. You're a master game player and everything you do is for a specific purpose."

She knew him well. In fact, that was one reason he'd let the distance grow between them when she'd walked out on him. She knew him better than he wanted anyone to know him. But she was the key to what he needed, and he wasn't going to let her walk away again. This time, he was better able to make room for Cassidy in his life.

"What? No snappy comeback?" she asked.

"Sarcasm doesn't suit you."

She shrugged. "I'm pregnant. Most of the time that means I get a pass on things like that."

"Does it?"

"Yes."

"From who?"

"Everyone." She gave him a grin that was pure Cassidy for sexiness. She had a way of accepting her feminine appeal and knew its effect on everyone she met.

"Is there a man in your life?" he asked, abruptly realizing that she might have met someone after they'd broken up. Oh, he knew the baby was his. Not just because she'd confirmed it, but because he knew Cassidy. She'd said she loved him, and he knew that, to her, that meant more than just words.

"My dad and brothers," she said, looking down at the table, the joy she'd exhibited a moment earlier totally extinguished.

"I meant a boyfriend," he said.

"Yeah, right. I'm pregnant out to here with your baby, why the heck would I be dating someone else?" she said, looking up at him with those clear brown eyes of hers.

"How long are we going to be dealing with the sarcasm? I didn't know you were pregnant," he said.

"I didn't think you'd care."

"Well, I do. So you're not dating?" he asked one more time. He couldn't help the rush of satisfaction that swamped him when he realized she'd been alone for the months they'd been apart.

"No. It didn't seem fair to get involved with another man right now. What about you, are you dating anyone?"

"Would I be here if I was?" he asked. The truth was he'd buried himself even more in work after they'd parted. That was one reason he'd had an edge over his cousin Sam, his competition for the CEO position. Sam had been married for more than ten years now and divided his time between the office and home. Then their grandfather's will had evened things up between them.

"Why are you here?" Cassidy asked.

He scratched the back of his neck. He knew what to say, but as he looked at her he began to calculate the consequences of what he was about to do. Lying to Cassidy wasn't something he did lightly. But if he told her the truth—that thanks to his grandfather's will, to take over as CEO of Tolley-Patterson, he needed to be married and have a child within a year as well as win the vote of the board—she'd tell him to hit the road.

"Donovan?"

"I missed you, Cassidy."

"I've been right here," she said.

"I wasn't sure you'd take me back."

"You want to date again?" she asked. "Once the baby is born that will be difficult."

"I don't want to date you, I want to marry you. The last eight months have made me realize how much I want you as my wife. I came here today prepared to tell you I've changed my mind about having a family."

He heard her breath catch in her throat and saw a sheen of tears in her eyes.

He pushed back from the table, standing up and walking over to her chair. He pulled it away from the table and turned her to face him. She looked up at him.

He leaned down so that their lips were almost touching. Framing her face with his hands, he suddenly knew that he really didn't want to screw this up. And not just because he wanted to beat Sam. He wanted to do this right because Cassidy was the key to a life that he'd never realized he might want until this moment.

"I want to marry you, Cassidy Franzone. I want to be a father to our child and have that family you dreamed we'd have together."

With Donovan so close to her, all Cassidy really wanted to do was kiss him and wrap her arms around him, feel his arms around her and maybe rest her head against his chest for a while. It was what she woke up in the middle of the night longing for, that touch of his.

But Donovan had been so adamant that he wasn't going to have a family, and this change, though eight months in the making, was drastic for him.

"Why? What made you change your mind?"

."I missed you," he said.

But he'd said that before. And missing her wasn't an explanation of why he'd changed his feelings about kids.

"That's not why you suddenly want a family." She was afraid to trust the sudden turnaround in his attitude.

He moved and dropped his hands from her face as he stood up. He grabbed his beer from the table and paced to the railing of the porch. Leaning one hip on the wooden railing, he tipped his head back and drained the bottle.

"What do you want me to say, Cassidy?"

She had no idea. Eight months ago when he'd proposed to her, she'd suspected she was pregnant—and she'd walked away when he'd made his opinion on kids and family clear. She'd walked away, because she knew that Donovan was the type of man who'd marry a woman he'd gotten pregnant—and that wasn't why she wanted to be married. She needed Donovan to marry her because he was in love with her. Because he couldn't live without her the way she couldn't live without him.

"I want to know why you changed your mind. You said kids were the major source of all arguments between married couples. You said that hav-

ing a child ruined many of the great relationships
you'd seen. You said—"

"Hell, I know what I said."

"And?"

"I've had a lot of time to think about you and me,
Cassidy. The way we were with each other, the way
we were both raised… I think we can have a family
and not lose the essence of who we are as a couple."

He was saying things that she wanted to believe,
things that she'd dreamed of him saying, and a part
of her wanted to just say yes. But being alone had
made her realize that being in love wasn't the be-
all and end-all of a relationship. And she couldn't
go through getting over him again.

"Are you proposing because you found out I'm
pregnant? I don't want you to marry me because
you feel obligated."

Donovan crossed the porch back to her. He set
his beer bottle on the table and drew her to her feet.
"Cassidy, I wouldn't insult either of us that way. I'm
here because I need you. I was coming to see you
today to beg you to take me back."

"Does it have anything to do with your grandfather's death?" she asked. "I was sorry to hear of
his passing." She'd sent flowers and felt awful for
not going to the service.

Donovan couldn't believe how close to the truth
she'd come with that one innocent comment. "Los-

ing Granddaddy did make me realize how quickly life can change, and I thought about how much he'd always wanted me to have children of my own while he could see them. I thought we had more time..."

Cassidy wrapped an arm around his shoulder and hugged him briefly then stepped back. "Did that make you realize there was more to life than work?"

Cassidy knew how hard it was for Donovan to talk about his emotions. But if she was going to take a chance on him again, on letting herself really love him and bring up a child with him, then she needed to know where he stood.

It wasn't just about her anymore. She rubbed a hand over her stomach, thinking of her baby—their baby. She wanted the best for this child, and that meant two loving parents.

"I guess it did. I don't want to talk too much about it. Granddaddy and I butted heads a lot, and his heart attack was so sudden...."

Donovan and Maxwell Patterson had had what could kindly be called an adversarial relationship. "Did you get a chance to make peace with him?"

"No, not really. Our last words were spoken in anger. I walked out on him."

"I'm sure he knew you loved him."

Donovan shrugged as though it wasn't important

but she knew that he'd always had a driving need to make his grandfather proud of him. To prove to the family that he was more than his sculptor father's son. To prove that he had the same blood in his veins as his grandfather did.

"That's why I need you. I need to have you by my side. You and our child. I don't want to get to the end of my days and find I have nothing but Tolley-Patterson to show for it. I want you to marry me, Cassidy."

Her heart melted. She still thought there had to be more to his change of heart, but she didn't care. He was offering her more than she'd ever expected him to. Donovan was the kind of man who honored his commitments. And with their baby on the way she knew that she could make their life everything she always dreamed it would be.

"Um…"

"What?"

"Getting married now, like this," she said, gesturing to her stomach, "isn't what I had in mind. I want to have a big wedding and all that."

"What are you saying?"

"Um…" What *was* she saying? She wanted their child to be born with Donovan's name. But a public wedding was out of the question until she delivered their child. "I think I'm saying let's get married in secret, with just our families present, and then after the baby is here we can have a big public commitment ceremony."

Donovan hadn't thought beyond getting Cassidy to agree to marry him. Married in secret didn't seem like a plan that would fulfill the conditions of his grandfather's will. His lawyer was working on finding a loophole, but Granddaddy had been a smart man—he'd made sure that his bizarre requirements for the next CEO of Tolley-Patterson were legally sound. It didn't matter that everyone who'd heard the will and read the new CEO description thought it was crazy. Legally Granddaddy had followed every rule.

"Why do you want to keep the marriage secret?"

Cassidy flushed and wrapped her arms around her stomach. One hand rubbed the top of her baby bump. "I just don't want the world to think that you're marrying me for the child."

"Cassidy, that's silly. Who cares what the world thinks?"

"I do," she said quietly.

"Then, okay, we'll do it your way."

"Really?"

"Yes."

"Thank you."

"You're welcome," he said, drawing her into his arms. The exhalation of her breath on a sigh brushed against his neck as she wrapped her arms around his waist and melted against him. Because of her belly, the embrace was different from all the ones they'd shared in the past, but Donovan felt a new sense of rightness to having her in his arms.

No matter why he was back here with her, this was where he was meant to be. She tipped her head back and he looked down into her brown eyes.

He cupped her face in his hands and lowered his mouth to hers. She rose on tiptoe to meet him. He brushed his lips over hers once, twice, and then he felt her lips part and her tongue touch his lower lip.

He'd never forgotten Cassidy's kisses. She was the only woman he'd ever found who fit him perfectly physically. There had never been any awkwardness to their sex life. She tasted wonderful to him, and as he slipped his tongue into her mouth he realized just how much he'd missed the taste of her.

She held on to him as she tilted her head to give him deeper access to her mouth. He tunneled his fingers into her hair, caressing the sides of her neck with his thumbs. She moaned deep in her throat, and the sound made him groan and slide one hand down to her hips to draw her closer to him.

She shifted against him, and then he felt a nudge against his stomach. It knocked him off track. He pulled back and looked down at her belly. A bump moved under her maternity top.

"Uh…"

She smiled. "He gets active in the afternoon."

"He?"

"Yes. We're having a son."

"A son," he said. Thinking about the baby as the means to an end was different than this. My God, he was going to have a son. That rocked him more than finding Cassidy pregnant. He sat down in the chair that Cassidy had vacated. She stood there watching him.

"Are you okay?"

"Yes. I just didn't think about the baby beyond you being pregnant. You know?"

She smiled at him. "Yes, I do. It's one thing to be pregnant but another to picture the baby in the future, isn't it?"

"Yes, it is. So I want to do this as soon as possible."

"Do this? You mean get married?" she asked.

"Yes. I'll take care of getting all the paperwork in order."

"Okay. I want to have our ceremony at my parents' house on the beach."

"That's fine. You can make the arrangements. When is the baby due?"

"In less than two weeks."

"Then I think we should get married over the weekend."

"So soon?"

"We don't have a lot of time if we're going to be married when our son is born."

"Does that matter to you?"

"Yes," he said, realizing that it did matter. He wanted to do everything by the book so that when the lawyers looked at his marriage to Cassidy and the birth of their son, they'd have no questions. And he needed to be married to her before she had his child. His primitive instincts demanded that she have his name.

"I'll give my mom a call and see if they can host the ceremony this weekend. Adam is in New York, so I'll have to see if he can make it back."

"Will both of your brothers be there?" he asked, guessing that the Franzone boys weren't too happy with him.

"I hope so. Don't worry, they understood about me having the baby on my own."

Somehow Donovan doubted that. Her two brothers were older and superprotective. He'd done his best to avoid them since he and Cassidy had broken up.

The late-afternoon sun spilled onto the porch, lighting the deep dark sheen of her hair and making him catch his breath. She was truly the most beautiful woman in the world. And he couldn't believe how easily this had all gone.

But then, this was Cassidy, and she'd always made his life brighter just by being near him. He would never admit it out loud, but maybe Granddaddy had done him a favor when he'd added that clause to the CEO requirements.

As he listened to her speaking with her mother, he realized that she was hopeful about their marriage. He made a vow at that moment to never let her find out why he'd come back. He'd do whatever it took to protect Cassidy from learning that he'd returned to her only to win the CEO position at Tolley-Patterson.

Chapter 2

Dwelling on details wasn't something that Cassidy was good at, and she knew it was one of the areas where Donovan and she weren't the same. He kept talking about all of the things that had to be done, but it was the first week in August and she was bigger than a beached whale—and about as comfortable as one, as well.

"Are you listening to me?" Donovan asked.

He'd coaxed her out of her house and to the country club where both of their families were members. They were sitting in a secluded alcove overlooking the ocean and she could feel the warm breeze stirring over the veranda.

"No."

"Cassidy, we don't have much time and I want everything taken care of before you go into labor."

"I don't understand what the rush is," she said, a part of her not believing that Donovan was back in her life. But here he was, and he was taking over the way he had before.

And she wasn't too sure she wanted to let him. The last time, she'd been more than happy for him to take the lead, but she was older and wiser—and crankier, she thought. She didn't want to talk about what kind of life insurance policy they should have for themselves to protect the baby if they died.

She didn't want to think about anything like that.

"We need to talk about guardians, as well. I think it would be best if the child went with my family."

"What do you mean, best? I've already asked Adam to be the guardian." Her oldest brother was very responsible and she knew that Adam would keep her child safe.

"You shouldn't have done that without consulting me first."

"Um…you weren't in my life, remember?"

"Again with the sarcasm."

"Yeah, I kind of like it."

"I don't."

"Then stop trying to run my life. I said I'd marry

you, but I'm not going to let you take complete control of everything."

"Cassidy…"

"Yes?"

"I'm not asking you to let me control your life."

"You're not?"

He leaned across the table. There was a glint in his eyes that was distinctly sexual and she had to fight not to smile. This was the Donovan she remembered, able to turn any situation into something fun and sexy.

"No, I'm not…I'm telling you."

She leaned closer to him. Her belly rested against the lip of the wooden surface. She reached out and traced his lower lip, and his mouth opened. She shifted farther in her chair and briefly pressed her lips to his. "You have to remember one thing, Donovan Tolley."

"And that is?" He brushed his mouth against hers. The soft kiss might have looked sweet and innocent, but a flood of hormones rushed through her body. Even though she was very pregnant, she really wanted this man.

"You aren't the boss outside of Tolley-Patterson."

He stroked a finger down the side of her neck, tracing the bead of sweat that had just taken the same path. "Once we're married I will be."

"How do you figure?" she asked, trying to ignore the way his finger felt as he stroked her skin just above the base of her neck. Her pulse was beating wildly. She had no idea where this conversation was going; she only knew that this was what she had missed. Having Donovan in her life meant she wasn't alone. And she could just be herself, no matter how crazy or silly she might seem to someone else.

"I'm going to insist that our vows have the word *obey* in them."

"I have no problem with that," she said. "I've always wanted you to obey me."

He threw his head back and laughed, drawing the attention of the other people on the veranda. Cassidy smiled at him and leaned back in her seat, taking a sip of the refreshingly cool lemonade she'd ordered.

Donovan's BlackBerry twittered and he pulled it from his pocket, glanced at the screen and then up at her. "I have to make a quick call. Will you be okay by yourself?"

She nodded. He got up and left the table, and she glanced around. Sitting alone at a table in a restaurant always made her feel exposed, something that she didn't like. She took a sip of her water.

"Cassidy?"

She turned to see her best friend, Emma Graham, and Emma's fiancé, Paul Preston. "Emma! How are you?"

"Good. Are you here alone?"

"No. I'm with Donovan."

Emma raised both eyebrows and told Paul she'd meet him at their table. Emma wasn't a subtle person, and Cassidy immediately knew her best friend was concerned.

"What's going on?" Emma asked, sitting down in Donovan's seat. "The man left you alone and pregnant. I can't believe he'd have the gall to come back to you now."

"You know he didn't know I was pregnant."

"Okay, I'll give him that. What does he want?"

"To marry me."

Emma's eyes widened. "Are you going to?" she asked.

For the first time, Cassidy felt a twinge about how easily she'd capitulated. But she couldn't have done anything else. Surely Emma understood— she was getting married as well. Cassidy wanted a partner—a husband—in her life. "Yes. I think so. I mean…"

"You still think you love him."

"Who's to say that I don't love him?"

Emma shrugged one delicate shoulder. "No one but you. Are we happy about this?"

Cassidy thought about it. "I don't know yet. I was going to call you in the morning."

"I've got an early flight to New York for a meeting. I can talk until eight tonight and then again after three tomorrow. I was going to stop by your place later today anyway."

They had grown up together and attended the same boarding school in Connecticut. Emma was like the sister Cassidy had never had and had always wanted. "Did you tell him about the baby, is that why he came back?"

"No. He just showed up."

"Why?"

"Um, he missed me," she said to her friend, feeling sheepish and suddenly wondering what Emma would say.

"And you believe that?" Emma asked.

"I—"

"Yes, Emma, she does believe me, because I told her that letting her walk out of my life was the biggest mistake I'd ever made."

"It's about time you realized it," Emma said. "Hurt her again and you'll deal with me."

Donovan nodded as Emma gave Cassidy a hug and then walked away. The threat should have seemed silly coming from the petite brunette, but

Donovan knew Emma Graham was more than capable of backing up her words.

"Sorry about that," Cassidy said as he sat back down.

"It's okay. She cares for you and wants the best for you."

"Yes, she does."

Cassidy took a sip of her lemonade and glanced toward the ocean. Donovan realized that getting her agreement to the marriage wasn't enough. He needed to...ah, hell, he needed to make some promises that would alleviate Cassidy's fears that he was going to hurt her again.

"I care, too," he said, realizing as the words left his mouth how lame they sounded. Lame-ass comments like that were exactly why he didn't talk about his emotions. He was much better keeping things light or talking about business.

"I'd suspected as much, since you asked me to marry you."

"See, you are a smart girl."

"Don't be condescending."

"I wasn't. You're one of the smartest women I know. It's what drew me to you the first time."

"Um...I thought that was my legs."

It had been everything about her. Her long legs in that impossibly short micromini she'd had on. Her long, dark curly hair hanging down her back in silky waves. But, to tell the truth, it had been her laughter that had first caught his attention. It was deep and uninhibited. He'd found himself distracted at the charity event. Instead of conducting business as he usually did at social functions, he'd followed her and joined her group just to hear that laugh again. And her intelligence was quickly evident as she debated and discussed myriad current events.

"Your legs were part of it," he said. He'd always been a leg man.

"I was drawn to your eyes."

"My eyes?" he asked, wondering what she saw in them.

"Every time you looked at me, there was this intensity that made me feel like I was the only person in the room that night."

"You were the only one I saw," he admitted.

"Yeah, until Sam entered and you remembered that he's your rival."

"That's not completely true." But it was partially true. He and Sam had always been in competition with each other. They'd been born a week apart and Donovan was the younger of the two of them. Every summer they'd been sent to live with their grandfather, and the old man had always challenged the both of them. Donovan had learned early on that the key to Granddaddy's praise was winning.

"Yes, it is. You even told me you'd do anything to beat him to the vice presidency, and you did it."

"That's right. You said you liked my ambition," he said.

"Did I?"

He nodded, wishing he knew what she was thinking at this moment. Because he had a feeling she was recalling the other things about him, the things she didn't like. Or had merely tolerated.

Part of the reason he'd let things lie between them was that she made him vulnerable, and only a man without any weaknesses could fully protect himself. Because then he had nothing for his enemies to attack.

He knew that sounded melodramatic considering he was an executive, but the modern-day business world was just as fierce as the ancient fiefdoms that had been defended by nobles and warriors. And Donovan had always known he was a warrior. The need to win was strongly bred into him.

"I like you when you're happy, and competing does that for you."

"You do that for me, too."

She tipped her head to the side. "Really?"

"Mmm, hmm. Want to get out of here and go for a walk on the beach?"

"No. Sorry, but my feet are swollen. I know that

sounds totally unromantic, but I'm not up to a long walk on the beach until it's cooler."

"How about going out on the yacht? You can sit on the deck and feel the ocean breeze in your hair."

She hesitated.

"What?"

"I can't believe that you're back in my life and going on about everything as if nothing has changed. As if the last eight months never happened…but they did, and I…I'm not sure if I can trust you the way I did before."

Donovan rubbed his neck and looked away. What could he say to her? He needed Cassidy and their child. And he needed them now. He didn't have time to seduce her or convince her that he was the man she wanted in her life.

He put his sunglasses on and stood up. "I can't just stand around and pretend we have all the time in the world to reconnect."

"Because of the baby?" she asked.

There was something in her tone and a kind of worry in her eyes that told him he had to say the right thing at this moment. Dammit, he sucked at saying the right thing.

"Not just because of the baby, Cassidy. Because you and I have lost eight months and we have only a short time to find *us* again before we are going to have our child."

Tears glimmered in her eyes and he shook his head. "You know I stink at saying the right thing."

She held his gaze. "Sometimes you say exactly the right thing."

"Don't bet on it happening too often."

She chuckled and gave him a weak grin. She looked tired and so achingly beautiful that he wanted to just pull her into his arms and hold her forever. Never mind the warning flashing at the back of his mind that he had a meeting with the board of directors to prepare for.

"Come out on the yacht, just for an hour," he said.

Cassidy loved being out on the ocean. The wind was cooler out here. Donovan had seated her on the padded bench and gone to make arrangements with the captain of the yacht. He hadn't come back since they'd left the dock.

She didn't mind, though; it gave her time to re-group. She put one hand low on her belly and felt the baby's foot resting against the outer wall of her stomach. She was overwhelmed by Donovan and everything that he was doing right now. A part of her knew that this was his way of ensuring she married him. That he would do whatever he had to in this week leading up to the wedding. That was the way he'd been when they'd first started dating. He was really good at making her feel like his top priority when he wanted to.

Had she trusted him too much?

Her cell phone rang and she glanced at the caller ID. Adam. She didn't answer it. She wasn't up to a lecture from her oldest brother at this moment, and that was exactly what she'd get from him. She guessed that their mother had put the word out to the family that she and Donovan were back together and getting married next weekend.

She had a feeling that her brothers weren't going to be very welcoming to Donovan.

Her phone beeped to let her know she had a voice mail. She would listen to it later.

"Who was that?"

"Adam."

"You didn't answer it?"

"I'm not really up to another demanding male telling me what he thinks is best for me."

"Demanding male? Is that how you see me?" Donovan asked.

"Yes. You've been bullying me all afternoon."

"It's because I do know best," he said, handing her a glass of sparkling water with a twist of lime.

She took a sip and watched him through narrowed eyes. She was glad that the sun was still drifting in the sky, because it gave her an excuse to keep her sunglasses on.

"You don't know me these days," she said. "How can you know what's best?"

"I do know you, Cassidy. I know that you are loving and caring. And that you've always wanted a family, and that despite having a career you love, work has never come first for you."

That was very true. Her job as curator at a small museum in Charleston was nice, but it wasn't anything that could compare with being a mom. She was going to stay on at her position in a part-time capacity once her son was born.

She had never tried to pretend that family and relationships weren't important to her. Her father and Adam were so consumed with their jobs that she'd been soured on that kind of career when she was a young girl. There had to be more to life than work, in her opinion.

"But you don't feel that way, do you? Or is that something else that's changed since we've been apart?"

"No. I haven't changed my focus. But I have broadened it to include more than just Tolley-Patterson."

"Like what? I know about your other business interests."

"Of course I still have those. I've also invested in Gil's team for the America's Cup. He has a new design that's going to revolutionize yacht racing."

"That's still an investment. How have you changed to put relationships and people first?"

"Gil is one of my oldest friends."

"I've never met him," she said. She had noticed that most of Donovan's friends didn't contact him unless they needed money. To be fair, he didn't exactly encourage anyone to stay close to him. He was a bit of a loner, despite his social connections and the parties he frequented. She'd realized early on that he was pretty much all about business.

"We'll invite him to our public wedding," he said.

"Fine, but you still haven't convinced me that you know what's best for *me*."

"I don't have to convince you with words," he said. "I'm going to show you with actions."

She raised her eyebrows. "How?"

He rubbed a hand through his hair. "You'll have to wait and see."

"I will?"

"Yes." He paused, and she braced herself, guessing she wouldn't like what was coming next. "I called my parents and they're both home this evening. When we get back to shore I think we should drop by and tell them about the wedding."

Cassidy tried to keep her face expressionless.

"It won't be bad."

"Your mom doesn't like me. She thinks my family are white trash."

"That's not true. She asked about you after we broke up."

"Really?"

"Yes. And we can't be married without my parents there. They would be disappointed."

Cassidy doubted that. But family was important and Donovan's parents would be her baby's grandparents. Maybe knowing that she was pregnant with Donovan's baby would make Donovan's mother like her better.

Not that being liked was *too* important to Cassidy, but she hated the fact that Donovan's family always acted so superior simply because they'd been in Charleston forever.

She gritted her teeth and mentally prepared herself to face Donovan's mother.

Chapter 3

Donovan's family had lived in the same house for more than six generations. The 1858 mansion was registered as a historical landmark. The first Tolley family had moved to Charleston just after the Civil War. They traced their fortune back to those days, as well.

His mother was a member of the Junior League and the Charleston Preservation Society, and she sat on the board for directors of Tolley-Patterson. She prided herself on the work she did with that group. She was the kind of woman who never had a hair out of place, and family image was very important to her.

"You're getting *married?*" she asked as she and Donovan sat in the parlor. She had a martini in one hand and looked every inch the genteel Southern lady that she was.

Cassidy was outside walking through the lamplit gardens with his father. His parents had both been shocked to see a pregnant Cassidy, and had covered their reaction only so-so. Donovan had been grateful when his usually withdrawn father had jumped up and asked to show his soon-to-be daughter-in-law his latest sculpture.

"Yes."

"I thought you broke up."

"We did, but now we're back together and getting married."

"Is this because of your grandfather's will? Even though she's pregnant, it might not be your child. Donovan, darling, there are a lot of women more suited to your social station that you could marry."

"Cassidy *is* suited to our station, Mother. And she's the one I chose."

"What about the baby?"

"Mother."

"Yes?"

"Stop it. I need you to just be happy for me and go along with this."

"I'll try, dear. It's just…I'm a little young to be a grandmother."

"And everyone will say that, you know that."

"Do you know if it's a boy or a girl?"

"A boy."

His mother took another sip of her martini. He couldn't read her thoughts. But she did smile for a second.

"Will her family be at the wedding? Surely you aren't going to have a big wedding with the pregnancy so far along."

"No, Mrs. Tolley, we aren't going to have a big wedding. Just an intimate ceremony at my parents' house. And we hope you'll both be there."

Donovan glanced at Cassidy to gauge her mood, but her face looked serene. She smiled politely at his mom. He had never thought before about the kind of attitude that Cassidy must have to endure from the oldest established families in Charleston. Her family, though wealthier than many, had accrued their fortune in the last twenty years and didn't have the kind of pedigree that the women in the Junior League approved of.

"I heard your parents were doing some remodeling," his mother said. "Would you consider having the ceremony here?"

Cassidy glanced at him and he shrugged. Everyone had heard about the bright pink stucco that had been used to repaint the Franzone mansion. Two weeks worth of editorials on the eyesore that their mansion had become had ensured that.

The Franzones were in the middle of a lengthy battle with their contractor to get him to repaint the house. The color was so bright and gaudy that the neighbors had complained to city hall in hopes of forcing the Franzones to do something immediately, instead of waiting for legal settlement.

"Thank you for that kind offer, but my mom has already started making arrangements."

"Very well. When is the ceremony going to be?"

Donovan knew from his mother's tone that she wasn't happy, but he didn't care. He needed Cassidy to be his wife. And his mother was never going to be happy to be related by marriage to the Franzones.

"This Saturday, Mother," Donovan said. He walked to Cassidy's side and wrapped his arm around her, pulling her close to him.

"Where is your father?"

"He went back to his studio," Cassidy answered. "He showed me the sculpture he's working on for the Myerson Museum."

"Did he?" Donovan and his father hardly had what anyone would call a close relationship, but he'd hoped that today, since he had come over to announce his engagement, his father would leave his studio for more than an hour and spend some time with him. But that wasn't the type of man his father was, and Donovan was old enough to accept that.

His parents had never had a close relationship. They'd married because his grandfather had wanted to merge Tolley Industries and Patterson Manufacturing. He'd always been aware that his parents didn't have a love match. His father's M.O. was to retreat to his studio whenever possible.

"Yes, he did. It's still rough, but you can see that it'll be breathtaking when it's done."

"I'm sure it will," Donovan said. "Mother, would you like to join us for dinner?"

"No, thank you, Donovan. I have a bridge game tonight."

"We will see you Saturday, then? At the Franzones'?" he asked.

"Of course. What time on Saturday?" she asked.

"Cassidy?"

She pulled her BlackBerry phone out and pressed a few buttons. "Six-thirty, Mrs. Tolley. There will be a dinner afterward."

"Do you need me to do anything to help?"

"No, thank you. We've got it all taken care of."

They said their goodbyes and were outside a few minutes later. Cassidy let out a breath.

"What?"

"Nothing."

"Cassidy, I know something's on your mind."

"Do I really need to tell you how snobby your mother is? She'll probably have a fit when she realizes that I've asked Emma to be one of the witnesses for the ceremony."

"Emma's not family."

"I don't have any sisters, and you know she's like one to me." She smiled shyly. "Do you want me to ask one of my brothers to be the best man?"

He stared at her. He hadn't thought about who should be his witness. "Which one?"

"Adam makes the most sense. You've met him."

He and Adam Franzone didn't get along. From the very beginning of his relationship with Cassidy, Adam had been telling him he wasn't good enough for her.

He didn't want her brother to stand up with him, but if it meant keeping Cassidy happy, he guessed he could do it. He shrugged. "Adam will do."

Donovan was silent as they drove away from his parents' house. Cassidy wondered if she was making the biggest mistake of her life. She'd been seeing Donovan as she wanted him to be. Seeing him with his mother, so arrogant and very much the wealthy son who'd always gotten his way...

"What are you thinking?" he asked.

"Nothing," she said. There were some doubts that she couldn't shake. She was waiting for the other shoe to drop, and that was exactly why she couldn't shake the panicked feeling deep inside of her.

"So it's something you don't want to share with me," he said, his voice a deep rumble in the cockpit of his sports car.

"How do you know I'm thinking anything at all?" Cassidy asked.

"Baby, you always have something going on in your head. Is it about work?"

"No. Lately I've been working with an artist, Sandra Paulo, who isn't coming in until a month after the baby is born. And she's been very cooperative. She shipped all of her paintings early so I'd be able to plan the display before I go out on maternity leave."

"Well if it's not the job, is it family?"

"Whose?"

"Mine or yours," he said.

"Not really. I mean, your mom *is* a bit of snob— that tone in her voice when she talked about the ceremony being held at my parents' place was a bit obvious."

"She's just used to things being a certain way."

"I imagine she is. You know your family is too caught up in pedigree."

Donovan shrugged. "So that's what you were

thinking about? I can't change my mother's attitude."

"I know, it's a part of who she is. It really doesn't bother me at all. I only mentioned it because you brought the subject up."

"I didn't bring it up. I asked what was on your mind, and you still haven't told me."

"That's because it's a nice day and I don't want to start an argument."

Donovan glanced over at her and arched one eyebrow at her. "I won't argue with you, Cassidy."

"I know that. You get quiet and clam up and act like nothing is wrong."

"I sound like a sulky two-year-old."

She forced herself not to smile. "Well…if the shoe fits."

He reached over and tickled her thigh, making her squirm in her seat. Laughing put too much pressure on her bladder.

"Stop, Donovan."

"Not until you take that back."

"Okay, I take it back," she said. He stopped tickling her, caressing the inside of her thigh before he removed his hand.

"You're so incredibly sexy," he said, his voice deepening with lust.

"I'm not sexy at all. I'm almost nine months pregnant. Big as a whale."

He pulled off the road under a streetlamp. "Cassidy, look at me."

She faced him. She'd never really had body issues, but the bigger her stomach had gotten and the skinnier her friends had stayed, the more conscious she'd become of her size. Being alone all these months hadn't helped, either.

He leaned over her and released her seat belt and then his own. He drew her into his arms and held her close.

"You are the only woman in the world who is always beautiful to me. First thing in the morning, after a workout, sunburned and swollen." He tipped her head back and leaned in to kiss her. "You've always been beautiful to me, but never more so than now. You are carrying my child."

He pulled back and put his hand on her belly. "I thought my life was meant to follow one path. Business has always been my focus. But when our baby kicked against me the other night…it was like an awakening for me."

"Awakening how?" she asked. This was what she wanted to understand. This was what she needed to know. Was Donovan really back because he'd had a change of heart and needed her the way she needed him? This moment could change everything. Put her doubts to rest for good.

"It made me realize that our futures—my future

and yours—were intertwined. And it made me see that I had a chance to leave behind a legacy outside of Tolley-Patterson."

Cassidy started to ask another question, but he stopped her with his mouth. The kiss was soft but not tentative. It felt like a promise to her. The promise of a life that they would build together with their child.

He sucked her bottom lip between his teeth and nibbled on her. She shifted in his arms, trying to get closer to him, but the close confines of the car made it impossible.

He groaned, his hands skimming up her belly to brush over her breasts. They were sensitive and his touch on them made her squirm as a pulse of desire speared through her body.

"Donovan," she said, holding tight to his shoulders when he would have pulled back.

"Baby," he said. "God, I want you."

"I want you, too," she said, thinking of all the vivid sexual dreams she'd had of him during her pregnancy.

He kissed her again and this time there was nothing soft or tentative about it. He was reclaiming her, and she knew that if they weren't in the front seat of his sports car this encounter wouldn't end until he was buried deep inside her body. But instead he gentled the embrace with some light kisses and eventually put her back in her seat, fastening her seat belt.

"Don't worry about us, Cassidy. We are solid this time. I'm not going to let you go."

As he pulled back out into traffic, she smiled, believing in Donovan and the future they'd have together.

Donovan dropped off Cassidy at her place and turned to leave. He had a meeting with his directors first thing in the morning and he still had a few hours preparation ahead. Something made him look back. Cassidy fingered her swollen lower lip as she stood in her doorway watching him. As their eyes met, he knew the promise he made to her in the car would be kept.

So that wasn't the reason for the churning in his gut. No, that was due to the fact that he knew the reason he'd made those promises wasn't because of his faith in their love but because he wouldn't be able to become CEO of Tolley-Patterson without Cassidy by his side.

He never lost focus, but right now he was torn. He wanted to stay with Cassidy even though he had reports to analyze.

He shook his head and got into the car. The job—his career at Tolley-Patterson—was the most important thing in his life. Winning the last challenge that Granddaddy had put before him and Sam was what he needed.

He glanced in the rearview mirror and saw Cassidy lean heavily against the doorjamb and knew he'd disappointed her.

Instead of going back, he hit the car phone button. "Call Marcus Ware."

"Calling Marcus," the car speaker responded.

Marcus answered on the third ring, exactly as Donovan expected of his right-hand man. Marcus had the same hungry ambition that Donovan did. The other man lived for Tolley-Patterson and the deals they both made.

"Catch me up on where we stand with the West Coast production problem," Donovan said without exchanging pleasantries.

"Not good. Someone needs to go out there and take care of the problem. Jose's been trying to negotiate with the workers, but he's made little headway."

The last thing he needed right now was a trip to the West Coast. It was Wednesday, and he and Cassidy were getting married on Saturday. "Marcus, I'm getting married this weekend."

"I know, sir."

He'd informed his second in command of the marriage to make sure that he covered all the bases for the terms of the will. He'd instructed Marcus not to mention it to anyone yet. "I need this problem fixed tomorrow."

"That's why I'm booked on the next flight to San Francisco. I'm not going to leave the table until we have this dispute resolved."

"Call me when it's taken care of."

"I will."

He disconnected the call. Donovan knew that Marcus was ambitious; in fact, the younger man reminded him a lot of himself, which was one reason he'd hired him. He had brought Marcus up the ranks with him each time he'd been promoted, and if Marcus got the West Coast operation back online tomorrow, Donovan intended to promote the man to his position when he became CEO.

And there was little doubt he'd be CEO with Cassidy already pregnant. Every detail was falling into place. So why then did he have this hollow feeling inside?

His cell phone rang and he glanced at the caller ID before answering it. "Hello, Sam. What's up?"

"My mother just called… So you're back with Cassidy Franzone." It was a statement, not a question.

"I am."

"You know that most of the board don't approve of her family."

"Granddaddy's will just said the CEO must be

married and have an heir. It said nothing about the type of family she had to come from."

There was silence on the line.

"But I think everyone assumes you'll marry someone from Old Charleston."

"Then they don't know me very well, do they?" He deliberately didn't tell Sam that the wedding was already planned. No need to tip off the competition.

"No, they don't. But I do," Sam said. "You sound confident."

"I'm the best man to take control of the company, and at the end of the day everyone is more interested in making money than social connections."

Sam cleared his throat. "You aren't the best man for the helm, Donovan."

"You think you are?"

"I know I am, because I know that to be successful in business you have to have a life outside of the office. You have to see the world in which we sell our products."

Donovan disagreed, but then Sam had lost his competitive edge four years ago when he'd married Marilyn. Since then Sam had become strictly a nine-to-five man, getting home to his wife every night. Donovan knew that a lot of people believed in balance, but he thought that theory was full of crap.

"Well, we'll see what the board decides in January when they meet."

"Yes, we will. Good luck," Sam said, hanging up.

Donovan continued driving, needing some time to figure out if there was value to anything Sam had said. He'd kept the news about Cassidy's pregnancy to himself and he wondered if his mother had, too. She probably hadn't said anything about it to her sister, Sam's mother, because his marrying his pregnant girlfriend wasn't exactly something she'd brag about.

For the first time in years, Donovan thought about his dreams and he realized that home and family had never been part of them. And with Granddaddy dead, he didn't know what he was searching for anymore. The old man's approval was always going to be just out of reach.

Chapter 4

"I don't like the way he's come back into your life," Adam said.

It was the same argument she'd heard many times since she'd called her brothers to tell them she and Donovan were getting married. At least her mother was thrilled for her. Her father had been out of town on business at the time and had sent her a text note to say that he hoped the house would be repainted by the wedding day. She tried to pretend it didn't matter that her father was more concerned about business than her, but deep inside it did.

"You promised you wouldn't start anything today."

"I'm not starting anything, Cassie," Adam said, sitting down next to her on the settee and putting his arm around her. "I just don't want to see you hurt again."

"I'm not going to be hurt again. Raising my baby with his father is what I've wanted since I found out I was pregnant."

"I don't understand why he left in the first place," her other brother, Lucas, said as he joined them. "And now he's back."

Eight months ago, she hadn't told her family that Donovan didn't want kids. She'd kept that to herself because it had been such a deep blow. Now she realized that they must have guessed anyway from the way the relationship had ended.

"It wasn't about the baby," she said.

"Of course not," Lucas said. "It was about him not being ready to be a father."

Lucas was married and had three sons. He had been a father since he was twenty-one and at thirty he felt that he was an expert on what men should do in family situations. Adam was three years older than Lucas and married to his job.

Her brothers had a lot in common with Donovan in that they seemed to exemplify the fact that men could be either family oriented or workaholics. Especially if their work involved a family business.

"Could be. Not every man is like you. Just because he needed time to consider everything doesn't mean anything."

"Having a wife and kids isn't an easy thing for some men," Adam said. "I couldn't do it. The job comes first for me the way it does with Dad."

Lucas nodded. Cassidy remembered every event their father had attended for them when they were growing up. Because there had only been two events—Adam's graduation from prep school and Lucas's college graduation. Their father had always put business first.

She put her head in her hands. The things that Donovan had said since coming back into her life made her believe that he was truly a changed man. That he was really going to be in her life and their child's.

Could she do what her own mother had? Could she watch her children's disappointed faces as their father once again missed out on an important school function?

"I need to talk to Donovan."

"Now? Why? Are you having second thoughts? We'll go and tell him the ceremony is off," Adam said, standing up and heading for the door.

"Adam, no. I just want to talk to him."

"Beth had the jitters on our wedding day," Lucas said. "Of course, our situation wasn't that different from yours."

Lucas's wife had been pregnant at their wedding—not as far along as Cassidy was, but pregnant all the same. "Are you happy, Lucas?"

"You know I am. But it was a struggle at first."

Lucas came over and hugged her close. "He wouldn't have asked you to marry him if he didn't want to make the relationship with you and your baby work."

She nodded. Lucas was always the sensible one. He'd made family his number-one priority, working a low-stress job so he could coach his kids' Little League team and be at every school event.

"Can you guys leave me alone for a few minutes?"

Lucas gave her another hug and then nodded. "Let's go."

Both her brothers left the room. Cassidy went to the French doors that led out to the garden, which had a beautiful white gazebo in the middle that overlooked the ocean. Chairs were set up for the few guests, and flowers decorated the white lattice around the sides of the gazebo.

The backyard looked fairy-tale perfect. Like something out of *Bride's* magazine—if you ignored the fact that the house in the background was bright pink. And Cassidy wanted to believe in the picture-perfect image. But she was a realist. Picture-perfect was just an image, not reality.

Not knowing exactly where Donovan was at this moment, she went to the house phone and dialed his cell number. While the phone rang, she tried to think of what she'd say, how she'd word her questions. The words eluded her.

"This is Donovan."

"Hey, it's me."

"Hello, baby. Is everything okay?"

There was caring and concern in his voice, bringing up her usual dichotomy of feelings toward Donovan. He was like this sometimes, and then she remembered the way he'd kissed her with all that passion and left her on her own doorstep.

Did he have a switch inside that he turned on and off when it came to her? How would having a father who did that affect their child?

"Cassidy?"

"I have to ask you something. I'm not even sure what I want you to say, but it's important, okay?"

"Sure. Go ahead."

"What kind of a father are you going to be? I mean, are you going to always be at work when our son has a school event, or will you take time off for him?"

"Just a second." She heard the scrape of a chair and then the ringing of his footsteps on a hardwood floor. He must be in her father's study. A second later she heard a door close, and then he said, "I don't know."

"Oh."

"Cassidy, less than a week ago I found out I was going to be a father. I came to your house that night planning to ask you to be my wife, but beyond that I haven't had time to think about our son."

"But just thinking about it now, what's your gut reaction?"

She heard him take a deep breath. "My gut is to tell you what I know you want to hear. But lying to you, Cassidy, isn't something I want to do. I have no idea what kind of father I'll be. I do know that I want to know our son and be a part of his life, but work has always been my focus... I can't promise to change that, but I can promise I will try."

She held the handset loosely and thought about what he'd said. "I'm not going to let you fail at this, Donovan. My dad...he wasn't there for us growing up. Now he's trying, but it feels like guilt. I'm going to insist you be a part of your son's life."

"Good," he said. "We'll make this life of ours work...together."

Donovan glanced over the small crowd of people gathered in back of the Franzones' gaudy pink mansion to celebrate his marriage to Cassidy. Tony Franzone was standing off to one side talking on his cell phone. The man was a better father than Cassidy realized—he'd come over to Donovan earlier and told him in no uncertain terms that if Donovan made his daughter cry again he'd put a hurt on him. The man had actually said that.

Donovan understood the sentiment that went behind it. He searched the crowd for his own parents and found them sitting alone, not talking to each other but each staring at the people around them. He saw his mother shudder when she took in the Franzone mansion.

His extended family had never been close-knit, and he didn't think they ever would be. He told himself it didn't matter that family had no place in his life and they'd never been particularly close, but a part of him was disappointed that more of his relatives weren't here.

Of course, he hadn't invited that many of them. He'd needed to keep the marriage quiet until he was ready to talk to the board.

Marcus had resolved the West Coast matter on Thursday and was back in the office Friday. Donovan had gotten a late-night call from his uncle Brandt congratulating him on taking care of the mess. Brandt had hinted that marriage was the only thing keeping Donovan from the CEO position. Donovan had almost told his uncle about the wedding, but had decided discretion was still wise at this point.

Donovan steeled himself as Adam Franzone approached.

"You sure about marrying my sister?" Adam asked as he came to stand in place next to Donovan at the stairs of the gazebo.

"As sure as any man can be," Donovan said.

"Hurt her again and I'll make sure you regret it for the rest of your life."

"I didn't hurt her on purpose eight months ago. I proposed to her, and she turned me down."

"She turned you down?" Adam asked.

"Yes, she did." He knew now that she had done it because of what he'd said about not wanting a family. From what Adam said, he must have hurt her. "I'll take care of Cassidy."

"Make sure you do."

"Are you threatening me?" He knew he'd do the same if he were Cassidy's brother and some other man had abandoned her. It was a sobering thought, and for the first time he was forced to look outside of himself.

"Yes," Adam said, totally unashamed of himself. "I should have done it the first time you dated her. I knew you were the kind of man who always put himself first."

"The same can be said of any successful businessman. And that's what women want, Adam. Success."

"They also want a guy to be able to balance that with family time."

"I don't see a ring on your finger. What makes you an expert?"

"The fact that I don't have a ring. I've spent my entire life avoiding the situation you're in because for me work always comes first."

Donovan knew it did for him, too. Always had. That was why he'd let Cassidy go. Because he'd known she could interfere with his success.

Donovan didn't want to have this discussion with Adam. The pressure he was under at work to make sure that every aspect of his division was running smoothly was tremendous.

"If it were any other woman, I'd walk away," Donovan said, realizing the words for the truth they were. It didn't matter that he'd had Granddaddy's will as an excuse to get back to her side. He'd wanted Cassidy for a long time. And now that he had her back where she belonged—in his life— he wasn't going to let her go.

The music started and Donovan saw Emma walking up the aisle. And then, Cassidy. She looked so lovely that for a second his breath caught in his throat. He was humbled by the fact that she was marrying him and having his baby.

Humbled by the fact that this woman was now going to be his. When she got to his side and he took her hand in his, he saw the joy on her face and knew he never wanted to disappoint her.

She could never know that he had come back into her life because of a will. That he was marrying her not only for herself but also because his job demanded it.

The lie of omission weighed on him. He would have to balance it with his actions. He was marrying her, and that was ultimately what she'd always wanted. And he would do his damnedest to be a good husband and father. But part of him—the man who was her lover—knew that Cassidy was never going to see a lie as balanced out by anything.

As he took her small hand in his and turned to face the pastor, he vowed to himself that he'd make their life together so fulfilling that, if she ever found out the real reason he'd come back to her, it wouldn't matter.

As the pastor led them through the ceremony, he felt the noose tighten. He heard words he'd heard a hundred times before in other ceremonies, but this time they sank in. This time they resonated throughout his body. His hand tightened in Cassidy's, and she looked up at him.

"You okay?" she mouthed.

He nodded. But was he? Marriage wasn't something to be entered into lightly. And this was the worst possible time for him to be having this thought, but maybe marrying Cassidy wasn't the only solution.

Then the pastor asked if he took Cassidy to be his, and the panic and the uncertainty left. Cassidy was already his, and this ceremony today would do nothing but affirm that to the world.

"I do," he said.

Cassidy smiled up at him, and that was it. That moment of panic retreated to a place where he would never have to think about it again. He wasn't a man who looked back and lamented the choices he'd made. He was a man who looked forward and shaped his own destiny, and this moment, with this woman, was where he was meant to be.

The rest of the ceremony passed in a blur and before he knew it, the pastor was telling him he could kiss his new wife.

He pulled Cassidy into his arms, felt the bump of her belly against his stomach. As he lowered his head to hers, she came up on her tiptoes, meeting his lips. He stroked her mouth with his tongue before pushing inside. She held on to his shoulders and he bent her back over his arm, kissing her and claiming her...Cassidy Franzone—no, Cassidy Tolley. His wife, his woman, the mother of his child.

* * *

"Cassidy, do you have a minute?"

"Sure, what's up?"

"I just heard something… I don't want to make waves on your wedding day, but—"

"Emma, just say it. Whatever it is."

"Um…there's something weird going on with Tolley-Patterson."

"Like what?"

"I don't have the details, but one of the attorneys at my father's firm, Jacob Eldred, handled Maxwell Patterson's will. I was talking with some of the firm's associates at a cocktail gathering the other night, and when I mentioned I was attending your wedding, they said something about Maxwell's will."

"His grandfather's will?"

"I couldn't ask more. I started to, and then they realized that they shouldn't be talking to me about the matter, so I asked my father, but you know how he is."

Cassidy sat down and Emma sat next to her, holding her hand. "I…I don't know what to think."

"I know, Cassidy. It may just be business, but I was thinking about how he came back to you out of the blue…."

"I don't think our marriage has anything to do

with his job. His grandfather liked the fact that Donovan was single."

"You're right. I just wanted to mention it."

"Mention what?" Donovan asked, coming up behind them.

"Nothing, Donovan. Just a comment I'd heard about you and your grandfather's will."

Cassidy wasn't sure, but it almost looked as if Donovan's face went white. "Like what?"

"Nothing specific, just that it was a bit strange."

"Well it's one of those old-time Southern wills. Nothing either of you has to worry about."

Emma and Donovan had never been great friends. She wished they'd find a way to get along, but it wasn't a main concern of hers. They didn't have to be best friends for her to continue her relationship with each of them.

"Of course it isn't. That's business and this is personal," she said to Donovan. Donovan reached for her hand and she gave it to him. He drew her to her feet. "Did you need me for something?"

"I wanted to dance with you," he said. "Will you excuse us, Emma?"

Her friend nodded, but Cassidy sensed that it wasn't over. There was more to what Emma had been saying, and she'd talk to Donovan about it later. Tonight, she wanted to enjoy their party. To hang on to the illusion that he was her Prince

Charming and she was embarking on happily-ever-after with him.

The band started to play "Do You Remember" by Jack Johnson, and Cassidy tipped her head back. "Did you request this?"

"I did. I couldn't think of a better song to be our first as husband and wife."

She'd always liked the song. It had a feeling of permanence to it. A feeling that the couple would be together forever. And she'd always wanted that for her and Donovan.

"I didn't think you'd remember I liked this song."

"I remember everything about you, Cassidy."

Sometimes, when he said things like that, she knew that her doubts about him were groundless. He drew her closer and sang along with the lead singer. His voice made her feel good deep inside.

She loved being in his arms. She'd missed that so much. She sighed and snuggled closer to him. His hands smoothed down her back and he shifted a bit to pull her even closer.

"Baby, you okay?"

"Yes. I've missed your arms around me."

"Me, too," he said. "We'll never sleep apart again."

She liked the sound of that. But she knew he traveled for business and doubted the words were the absolute truth.

She'd thought that getting married today would ease some of the doubts she'd been carrying inside, but instead she realized that more were being generated.

"Don't you want that?" he asked.

"Yes. I've missed sleeping next to you."

"I'm hearing some hesitation in your voice."

"There isn't any. I was just thinking how our lives sometimes don't follow the path we want for them."

"Even me?"

"Especially you."

"What can I do to alleviate those fears?"

She shrugged. "I don't know. I worry about a lot of things lately."

"What did Emma say to you?" he asked as the band switched gears to play an old Dean Martin song, "Return to Me." She suspected one of her brothers had requested it, since it was her parents' wedding song.

"Something about your grandfather's will."

"What about it?"

"Just that it was a bit strange," she said. "Don't my mom and dad look sweet?"

"Your mom does."

"Dad's not that bad. I'm just glad he was able to make it today. They were having some problems with the workers' union."

"Your dad's a tough guy, and he doesn't look sweet at all. I'm glad he made it today, as well."

"With Mom, he always seems different."

"He loves her," Donovan said. "That's why he's different."

"Yes, he does. Even when Dad disappointed us, he would never disappoint Mom."

"That's not a bad thing, Cassidy. He probably did what he could to be a good father to you."

"I know. I'm not complaining. It's just that if he'd been the way he is with Mom with me and the boys…"

She didn't know that it would have made a difference. But she thought about Adam and how he was sure he couldn't be a father and an executive, and then she thought about how Donovan was going to be both.

Donovan was a man who never let anyone get the better of him. Not her, not his cousin, not a business rival. What kind of father was he going to be? Someday, were they going to be dancing together at their child's wedding, or would they be divorced… two strangers standing across the dance floor, remembering this moment when they were young?

"Cassidy?"

"Hmm?"

"Don't worry about anything. We're together now, and that's all that matters."

   She wished she could believe him, but a part of her feared that just being together was never going to be enough for her.

Chapter 5

Cassidy had envisioned her wedding night many times when she'd been younger. Now, looking at herself in the mirror of the bathroom dressed in a maternity negligee, she felt...scared. She'd made love with Donovan many times, but he hadn't seen her body since she'd been pregnant.

And she wasn't even sure that she could make love to him now. Her stomach felt tight, and she couldn't stand still. Probably because of worry over what Emma had said to her. What did she really know about why Donovan had come back?

Only what he'd told her.

Did she trust him? Heck, she already knew that

she did trust him, now she just had to let go of the past and her fears and simply enjoy being with him.

He knocked on the door. "Are you almost done in there?"

"Yes. Just washing my face," she said, turning on the water to give her lie credence.

She heard the door open behind her and leaned down to cup her hands under the water, but then she froze. Donovan had removed his shirt and had on only his dress trousers. They hung low on his hips.

He looked incredibly sexy and she wanted nothing more than to get closer to him. To wrap her arms around his lean waist and rest her head against his chest and pretend that all the things she was worried about didn't exist.

"Why are you hiding out in here?"

"I'm not hiding. I just want… Okay, I am hiding. You haven't seen me all pregnant before. And this is our wedding night, which is supposed to be romantic, and I'm not sure I feel romantic at all."

"That's fine. Just come out and let me hold you," Donovan said.

He opened his arms and she stepped into them. The baby kicked as he drew her close, and Donovan's hand moved to her stomach, resting on the spot where the baby's foot had just been.

Donovan lifted her into his arms and carried her out of the bathroom and across the luxurious hotel suite to the king-size bed. He set her gently in the center of the bed.

He followed her down, lying next to her on his side. He propped his head up on his hand and stared down at her with a look of concentration.

"You seem very serious."

"I'm lying here with my wife…."

Her husband. She hadn't really let herself believe it, no matter how many plans they made, because a part of her hadn't been sure they'd get to the altar. Being married quietly with just family in attendance had sounded good when she'd insisted upon it, but now it made their relationship seem like a secret. That, and the fact that he hadn't wanted to put an announcement in the newspaper about the marriage.

"You're thinking way too much," he said, leaning down to trace her brow with one fingertip.

"Donovan—"

His mouth on her neck made her stop. She didn't want to have a heavy conversation tonight. She wanted just to lie in his arms.

She put her hands on the back of his head, felt the silky strands of his hair against her skin. His breath was warm against her, his mouth a hot brand as he kissed her neck.

She shifted onto her side and into his body. With

a hand on her hip he pulled her closer and raised the fabric of her nightgown up over her legs.

"Lift up."

She shifted her hips and he drew the nightgown over her head. And she was lying there completely bare except for her panties. He traced a path from her neck down over her breasts, which were bigger now than they had ever been before. Her nipple beaded as he drew his finger around the full globe of one breast.

He bent to capture the tip of her breast in his mouth. He sucked her in deep, his teeth lightly scraping against her sensitive flesh. His other hand played at her other breast, arousing her, making her arch against him in need.

He lifted his head. The tips of her breasts were damp from his mouth, and very tight. He brushed his chest over them.

"Is this okay?"

"Yes," she said, feeling cherished by the gentle way he was touching her.

"I want you, Cassidy."

She slid her hand down his body and wrapped her fingers around his erection. "I know."

"You are so damned sexy. I've been thinking of this moment all day."

"Have you?"

"Mmm, hmm," he said, his mouth on her

breast again. He kissed his way lower, following the mound of her stomach. He paused, whispering something soft that she couldn't hear.

He shifted on the bed, kneeling between her legs, and caressed her body from her neck, down her sternum to the very center of her.

"Do you want me?"

"Yes," she said, shifting her legs on the bed.

He drew her flesh into his mouth, sucking carefully on her. His hands held her thighs open, his fingers lightly caressing her legs as he pushed her legs farther apart until he could reach her dewy core. He pushed one finger into her body and drew out some of her moisture, then lifted his head and looked up her body.

She watched as he lifted his fingers to his mouth. "I've missed your taste."

Donovan had always been an earthy lover, and she hadn't realized how much she'd missed their lovemaking until this moment.

He lowered his head again, hungry for more of her. He feasted on her body, carefully tasting the flesh between her legs. He used his teeth, tongue and fingers to bring her to the brink of climax but held her there, wanting to draw out the moment of completion until she was begging him for it.

Her hands left her body, grasped his head as she

thrust her hips up toward his face. But he pulled back so that she didn't get the contact she craved.

"Donovan, please."

He scraped his teeth gently over her and she screamed as her orgasm rocked through her body. He kept his mouth on her until her body stopped shuddering and then slid up her.

He wrapped his body around hers. "That will have to do until after you have my baby. But you know that I've claimed you as my wife."

"Claimed me?"

"Yes. I don't want there to be any doubts. You are mine, Cassidy Tolley, and I don't give up anything that is mine."

Donovan woke aroused. He wanted to make love to Cass, and as she shifted against him he thought she was feeling the same way. He pulled her more fully against him and she turned her head into his shoulder, moaning softly.

He leaned down to find her lips. They parted under his and he kissed her. He knew he couldn't pull her under his body as he would have in the past. He skimmed his hands down her curves. Her hands tightened on his shoulders and her eyes opened.

"Hey, baby."

"Hey, you," she said, shifting in his arms and kissing him lightly.

He leaned in to kiss her again when she drew back. And groaned this time. "Donovan?"

"Yes."

"I think my water just broke."

"What the hell?!" He jumped out of bed, glancing around for his pants. He found them on the back of the chair. He wasn't completely unprepared for this. He'd had his assistant get him a couple of books on pregnancy, and he knew the layout of the hospital where Cassidy was expected to give birth…in two more weeks. He was even scheduled to attend his first childbirth class with Cassidy next week.

"Did it?"

She glanced down at the bed. "Um…yes."

He kept cool but inside he was panicking. What was he supposed to do with a pregnant woman? "Okay, let's get you dressed and we'll head out."

"Donovan?"

"Yes, baby?"

"I'm scared."

"Don't be. I'm here and I'll make sure everything goes exactly the way it's supposed to." He knew then that he couldn't give in to the uncertainty that swirled around him. He had to be the one to take control and present a calm front for her.

She smiled at him and he felt the burden he'd taken from her. He was scared, too, because he didn't want anything to go wrong. He needed Cassidy, and not just because he wanted to beat Sam in their quest for the CEO position.

He grabbed clean clothes for her from her overnight bag and called her doctor while she changed in the bathroom. He finished dressing and got his wallet. He also called the valet desk and had them bring his car around.

The door opened and Cassidy stepped out looking a bit dazed and scared. He didn't think of anything but Cassidy and the baby. Didn't think of anything but taking care of her.

This was a first for him, putting someone else completely before himself. He'd analyze that later. But for now, as they were riding in the elevator, he just wrapped his arm around her and held her close.

"I was so sure I could do this on my own," she said.

"You could have. Your mom would have been here with you, or Emma."

"That's true, but I was just thinking that having you here is exactly what I need. With you I can really relax and know that you'll take care of everything."

He really was a bastard for having walked out of her life the way he had and for only coming back for himself. There was so much he hadn't realized he was doing to her.

His car was waiting when they got downstairs and Cassidy started having some serious contractions while he drove them to the hospital. The decision to have their wedding night in Charleston instead of somewhere else outside the city had been a good one.

"Did you call my parents?"

"Not yet."

She pulled her phone from her pocket and dialed their number. He half listened to her conversation, thinking about the fact that this was his life now. This woman and the child about to be born.

He wasn't sure he was ready for his life to change this drastically.

He pulled into the parking lot at the hospital and got Cassidy out of the car and into the reception area. He pushed aside everything but Cassidy and the baby. He took control in the waiting area, got the nurses to see to Cassidy. He signed paperwork and talked to the doctor on call. Then there was nothing else to do.

He paced around the private room. It was nice enough, he supposed, with walls painted in neutral, soothing colors.

"Stop pacing," Cassidy said.

"Sorry. After all the stuff we had to do to get here, just standing around waiting for the monitor to do something…"

"Is making you crazy?"

"Pretty much. The next thing that should happen is your contractions getting more intensive. I'll help you manage them."

"You will? How?"

"By managing…distracting you," he said.

"I'm not exactly looking forward to this part," Cassidy said.

"What did you think when you found out you were pregnant?" he asked.

"Well, at first I was excited."

"When did you find out?" he asked. Everything had been going so fast since he'd walked back into her life that he hadn't had a chance to really talk to Cassidy about the baby. He'd been at the office as much as possible, shoring up his position with the board. Making sure that they knew he was the only man for the CEO position.

"The day you asked me to marry you," she said.

He crossed his arms over his chest. "Why did you turn me down? I mean, you knew about the baby, right?"

She closed her eyes for a second, and he checked the monitor and saw that she'd just had a contraction. "Sorry about missing that."

He went back to her side and took her hand in his. He kept one eye on the monitor. "Tell me why you didn't just marry me when I asked you to. Was it only because of what I said about children and family?"

"Yes. I didn't want you to feel trapped. I could have mentioned I was pregnant, and I know you, Donovan, you would have done the right thing."

He wasn't too sure about that. As much as he prided himself on being an upstanding man, a real gentleman when it came to women, he'd also seen what kids did to a man and his career. Relationships that had once been solid often folded under the pressures that a man inherited when he became a father.

"What's wrong about that?" he asked, truly not understanding what she was saying. He only knew that if she backed out of being married to him now, he didn't know what he'd do.

"I wanted you to marry me for me."

Cassidy didn't want to have a conversation about herself right now. The baby and marriage weren't exactly topics that she wanted to discuss during labor. She was interested in finding out what was going on with his cousin and Tolley-Patterson, but right now she didn't think she was up to an in-depth conversation.

Right now, she was figuring out that moderate pain wasn't as moderate as the books described—or maybe she was wimpier than the average woman.

Hell, she didn't care. The sensation in her abdomen was getting more intense and Donovan was standing over her, looking like a man who wanted to discuss the weight of the world.

"Baby," he said in a very low tone, and she felt a sting of tears in her eyes.

She turned away so he wouldn't see. He sounded as though he really cared. The man who could never and probably would never tell her how he felt had a voice that could melt her heart sometimes. She hated her weakness for tears. Especially now, when she was trying not to let him see how much pain she was in.

"I was speaking hypothetically. I was a man who arrogantly thought he knew what he felt about children."

"And you didn't?" she asked. Because Donovan was the kind of man who knew how he stood on every topic. She appreciated that he wanted to make her feel better and was trying to say something that would, but she saw through his words to the truth underneath.

And that truth was exactly what she'd feared. That Donovan would have married her and in fact probably *had* married her because she was pregnant with his child.

"Well, let's just say that I didn't anticipate anything to do with you and me and this child."

"What does that mean?" she asked, feeling her stomach start to tighten.

"You've got another contraction coming," he said, holding her hand solidly in his.

She gripped his hand.

"I just… Listen, Cassidy," he said once her pain subsided. He sank down on the bed next to her hip and took her hand in both of his. "My life was on a certain track, you know? Working my way to the top and proving to Granddaddy that I was his logical successor was always my focus."

He was trying to tell her something, but she had no idea what. There was too much going on inside her as her body prepared to give birth. She appreciated that Donovan was finally opening up to her but now was seriously not the time.

"I know. You've always been focused on your job," she said.

Her belly started to tighten again and she clamped down on his hand, her nails digging into his skin. "God this hurts."

Donovan held her hand through the long contraction and then stood up. "I'll take care of this."

She was amazed at how quickly he got the floor nurse into her room to take care of the pain. The technician who was supposed to be administering her epidural arrived and in a very short time she was resting comfortably. Donovan was commanding and in charge, making sure the hospital staff took care of her every need.

Her mother and Emma arrived. The women swarmed around the bed to ask if she was okay. Her father stood in the hallway, cell phone attached to his ear. She could hardly believe he'd come at this hour.

"I'll leave you alone with your girls for a little while. Have them call me on my cell if you need me." Donovan kissed her forehead.

She nodded, guessing he was uncomfortable and probably needed his space. But the last thing she wanted at this moment was for him to leave. She was scared that something would go wrong with the labor or that Donovan wouldn't get back in time to be by her side when she delivered.

"Where are you going?"

"Just down the hall. I want to call my parents," Donovan said.

"You'll be close by?" she asked.

"Yes," he assured her. Leaning down, he brushed the bangs off her forehead. "Emma?"

"Yes."

"You come and get me the moment anything changes in here. I want to be by her side."

Again she felt that melting deep inside. That certainty that Donovan had the same deep emotions for her as she did for him.

"If she wants you, I'll come and get you," Emma said.

Donovan kissed Cassidy again and left the room. Her mom and Emma both stood there for a second.

"Tonight?" Emma asked, a grin teasing her features. "On your wedding night you go into labor... that has to be the best wedding-night story ever."

"I don't know about best, but certainly the strangest."

"Oh, no, not the strangest," her mom said. "Cousin Dorothy's husband had an allergic reaction to the silk of her negligee and his entire body was covered in hives. He had to be rushed to the E.R."

Cassidy laughed at the story and once she started she found she couldn't stop. Soon her laughter changed to tears and she was crying.

Emma held her left hand and her mother leaned down to hug her from the right side. "Everything is going to be okay."

"Promise?"

"Yes. Childbirth is the greatest experience a woman can have."

"Greatest?"

"Cassidy, you are taking part in a miracle. You are going to be holding your son in a few hours and all of this will be forgotten."

Cassidy liked the sound of that. But then, her mother had always known how to say the right thing at the right time. She held tightly to Emma's hand and realized that as much as she appreciated her mother and her best friend being with her, she really needed Donovan.

She was afraid to ask Emma to go get him. Didn't want to seem too needy on this night, especially after she'd told him she hadn't wanted to be married for their child.

But when the door to her room opened a while later and Donovan poked his head in, she felt relieved. "Do you need anything?" he asked.

"You," she said.

Chapter 6

Cassidy woke from a sound sleep in a panic. Nearly three weeks had passed since she'd given birth and returned to her new home with Donovan and their baby boy. She glanced at the clock, and that only intensified her feelings. It was nearly 9:00 a.m. And Donovan Junior, or Van, as they'd decided to call him, hadn't woken her. She jumped out of bed and grabbed her robe on the way out the door.

She ran over the marble floor to the nursery door, which was closed. Who had closed the door? Her son wasn't even a month old, no way was she going to close the door to his room at night.

She pushed it open and stopped still in her

tracks. Van's crib was empty, and on the changing table were his pajamas. But no baby.

She walked back out to the hallway and made her way down the stairs. Hearing the sound of Donovan talking, she went to his home office and stood on the threshold, peering inside.

Van was in Donovan's arms, dressed in a pair of khaki pants and an oxford cloth shirt. He looked like a mini Donovan in his work-casual attire. Except that her son was drooling a bit as he slept.

The sight of the two of them, her two men together, made her heart stop. She just stared at them. And felt all the worries she'd had since her Donovan had come back into her life fade. Seeing him holding their son was all she'd ever wanted.

He looked perfectly at home with Van. Donovan had the baby cradled on his shoulder while he paced the room, talking to the speakerphone.

"Joseph has asked for a special board session to discuss Van."

"He can convene the board as often as he wants. Until the official board meeting, no changes can be made," Donovan said.

"He's positioning himself for the official meeting. There is only three months until the vote. And I have to tell you, what I'm hearing doesn't look good for you."

"Let me worry about my position, Sam. I've

heard the same things about you. Marcella isn't too happy with the way you've been handling the Canadian Group."

"You barely pulled the West Coast office through the latest mess."

"But I did. And that's what the board is looking for."

"You know, Granddaddy isn't here to set us against each other anymore."

"He left us one last challenge, Sam."

"And you think you won?"

"I know I did," Donovan said. Turning around, he paused as his eyes met Cassidy's.

She took another step into the room.

"I'll call you back, Sam."

He leaned down and hit a button on the phone.

"What was he talking about? Why does the board need to talk about Van?"

"It's nothing for you to worry about. Did you enjoy sleeping in this morning?"

"Yes," she said. "Though I did panic a bit when I woke up so late and couldn't find him."

"You have lunch today with Emma and Paul, so I figured the little man and I could spend all day together."

"That's very thoughtful," she said. She walked over to Donovan and kissed Van on his head. She hadn't known it was possible to love another being as much as she loved her son. Having him put everything in perspective. There was nothing in the world that was as important as taking care of him. She'd been disappointed when breastfeeding hadn't worked out for them, even though it gave Donovan more ways to help with his care.

"Are you sure you'll be okay with him?"

"Yes," he said. His cell phone rang and he glanced at the caller ID before turning back to her.

"Do you need to get that?"

He shook his head.

"Good. I've been wanting to talk to you about Sam and Tolley-Patterson… Emma heard some rumors about an odd stipulation in your grandfather's will."

"That's confidential information."

"She didn't know the details, just had heard a comment at a cocktail party her parents had." Cassidy had tried to bring up the will a few times, but she'd been tired from giving birth and taking care of her son. She hadn't really had time to investigate it further until now.

"From who?"

"Lawyers at her father's firm," Cassidy said. "Emma mentioned it because…"

"She was hoping to stir something up between the two of us," Donovan said.

"True, and I trust you, sweetheart. I'm just

worried Sam might be putting together something shady. And what I heard just now makes me even leerier of him."

Donovan hugged her to his side with his free arm. He kissed her. "Don't worry, baby. I've got everything I need right here."

"Really?" She was afraid to believe him when he said things like that. She knew that his life was business and everything else came second.

"Yes."

She tipped her head back and leaned up on her tiptoes to kiss him, but he dropped his arm and stepped away and she stood there awkwardly for a second. Donovan and she hadn't been out together since they were married, and he worked long hours. In fact, this moment was the most waking time she'd spent with her husband since they'd left the hospital.

She wasn't sure what was going on in his mind. Did he regret marrying her? They could have just as easily had Van and raised him without being married or even living together.

"What?"

"Nothing."

"Not nothing. You were staring at me like you wanted to say something."

She did, but how was she going to ask him if he no longer found her attractive since she'd given birth? How was she going to bring up the fact that she needed more one-on-one time with him?

"Just wanted to follow up on our plans for today. Are you sure that you can take Van this morning?"

"Yes, I can."

She stared at Donovan and realized that the love she'd always felt for him was getting stronger. She wanted him to be the husband she'd always fantasized about, and he was doing some things that made her believe he was that man. But then there were times like just now, when he'd pulled back from her, that let her know this wasn't a fantasy happy-ever-after marriage, but one based on necessity and reality.

Donovan wasn't the type of man who'd ever cared to be domestic, and carrying Van into the office didn't change his mind. The secretaries all cooed over the baby and the other men stood kind of awkwardly to one side while he set the baby in his car seat on the boardroom table.

"Never too early to start training the future generations," Marcus said as he entered the room.

Donovan laughed. "That was my granddaddy's creed. My earliest memories are of Sam and I playing on the floor of the executive offices."

"And now you're passing it on… I never saw you as the kind who'd bring a kid to work."

Donovan hadn't, either. He still wasn't one hundred percent certain of himself as a father or in the father role. But being in the office energized him, raised his confidence. Here he made no missteps. Here he knew exactly what he was supposed to do and how to do it.

As opposed to at home with Cassidy, where he was stymied by his own desire for her. It was all he could do not to make love to his wife. He knew she needed time for her body to recover from giving birth, but he was constantly aroused when he was around her.

This morning he'd woken up with a hard-on and had started to caress her when Van had cried out, stopping Donovan from making love to his wife.

"Let's get on with this meeting. I'm not sure how long Van's going to sleep."

"Don't you have a nanny or something?"

"Not yet. Cassidy is still interviewing them." Donovan didn't see how that was Marcus's business. He had the right to have his son with him in the office.

Marcus raised one eyebrow and shook his head. "This is why I always keep things casual."

"Why?"

"Look at you," he said, gesturing to Van's car seat, which Donovan had positioned directly next to him. "Your attention is divided now."

Donovan didn't like the way that sounded and glanced protectively at Van. Van was the future... his future. And he wanted his son to know from the start that he loved and cherished him. It was important to Donovan that Van feel comfortable in the offices of Tolley-Patterson and not as if he had to compete for the right to be there. "Have a seat, Marcus."

"Yes, sir." Marcus sat down as the rest of the staff started filing in.

Donovan moved Van's car seat to the credenza that sat against one wall, close enough so he could see his son but far enough away that the meeting wouldn't disturb the baby.

He brought the meeting to order, but his mind was only half on business. The other part was on Van. The baby had simply been a tool to beating Sam to the final prize his grandfather had dangled in front of both cousins. But now, as he watched his boy sleeping, he realized that the baby was so much more to him. Everything.

Marcus had been right on the money when he'd said that Donovan had changed. How had that happened? It seemed as if he'd become a different man. How could a few short weeks change a man's life?

"Donovan?"

"Yes?"

"We were discussing the budget for the next

quarter... Do you think we're going to need an increase in labor on the West Coast?"

Donovan pulled himself back into the meeting, pushing little Van to the side of his awareness, but it was hard. And as he tried to focus on the business at hand, he realized it wasn't just Van who was on his mind, but also Cassidy. He remembered her earlier kiss and how he'd gotten hard just from holding her. He could hardly think from wanting her.

He knew they still had a few more weeks before he could make proper love to her. And yet his body didn't seem to care. He wanted her. He needed to seal the bond of their new life together by thrusting into her sexy body and making them physically one.

He hardened thinking about the way her mouth had felt under his and her warm body had felt pressed against his side.

Was that why he was distracted? Because he hadn't been able to make love to his wife? He scrubbed a hand over the back of his neck, trying to release the tension he felt. But cold showers weren't working, and a quick massage wasn't getting the job done.

The only thing that would take care of his problems was Cassidy.

He suspected that this was what Marcus had been referring to. The need he felt to be with her every minute of the day. The way she was infiltrating this meeting without even being in the room with him.

The meeting adjourned thirty minutes later and Donovan picked up Van and went toward his office.

"Theo is waiting in your office," Karin said when he reached the outer office.

"Was he on my calendar for today?"

"No, but he wouldn't take no for an answer. He said it was highly urgent, regarding the upcoming board meeting."

"Okay. Anything else?"

"A few messages, I left them on your voice mail. And Sam wants five minutes of your time to discuss Canada."

"I talked to him at home this morning. When did he call?"

"Twenty minutes ago."

"Very well. When Theo leaves I'll call him."

"Do you want me to keep Van while you meet with Theo?"

Donovan set the baby seat on the edge of Karin's desk and set the diaper bag next to it. "Do you mind?"

"Not at all. My kiddos are all teens now, I miss little ones."

He left Van with Karin and entered his office. There was a sculpture in the corner that his father had made for him when he'd gotten the promotion to executive vice president. The desk that he used had been his great-grandfather's.

"Afternoon, Uncle Theo."

Theo was currently serving as interim CEO until the next board meeting when either Sam or he would take over that position. Theo was a bit of a cold fish and had at one time wanted to be appointed CEO, but he had given up that aspiration when Granddaddy had announced that either Donovan or Sam would be his successor.

"I'm not here for chitchat, Donovan."

"Why are you here?" he asked as he took a seat in the leather executive chair. He saw the picture of himself, Cassidy and Donovan that Emma had taken of the three of them in the hospital. Cassidy looked radiant as she looked down at their son and Donovan's stomach knotted thinking about how happy she looked.

In that picture they looked perfect, like a couple who'd finally made their lives complete by bringing a child into the world. Only Donovan knew the truth—that their life together was based on a lie.

"The board isn't pleased with your engagement to Cassidy."

"Engagement?" he asked. Surely his mother had told the other members of the board by now that he and Cassidy were married. She'd never kept anything from the board before. And even though he'd told her he wouldn't be announcing the marriage yet, he hadn't specifically asked her to keep it quiet.

"Yes. We understand that you want to marry her for Van's sake, but we strongly recommend you end all relations with Cassidy Franzone and find a proper woman to marry."

Cassidy enjoyed her lunch with Emma and Paul, but seeing them together underscored the distance between her and Donovan. She knew there was something missing from their relationship.

"So how's motherhood?" Emma asked when Paul went to get the car and they were both alone.

"Good. Tiring, but good."

"How's marriage?"

"Um…"

"Not good? What's up?"

"Nothing really. It's just that I don't see Donovan at all. And when he is home, I'm exhausted."

"That's to be expected, given how suddenly you two married. What about at night in bed?"

She looked at her friend. Only the fact that Emma was the sister of her heart allowed her to even think of sharing.

"I'm usually asleep by the time he comes in, and if I'm not he just rolls over on his side."

"He might be afraid to touch you since you had

Van. A lot of guys don't really know when it's okay to do that."

"This is Donovan we're talking about. He knows everything about...well, everything."

Emma pulled her compact and lipstick from her purse and touched up her lips. "I don't know what to say. Have you talked to him about it?"

"No." When she and Donovan had first started dating, he'd told her how much he loved her body, that her slim figure was one of the first things he'd noticed about her. Now she was afraid that her post-pregnancy belly was a huge turnoff for him. As soon as her doctor had OK'd it, she started doing sit-ups like a Marine going through boot camp, but her stomach had a little saggy bit that remained.

"That's what I'd do."

"Would you really, Emma? You wouldn't just let things ride to kind of keep the peace?" Cassidy asked her friend.

"Are you kidding me? There is never peace between Paul and I. We're always on about something."

Cassidy knew that. Emma's personality was a bit fierce and she didn't hesitate to speak her mind no matter what the circumstances. "What if you were afraid that you'd be bringing up something that would make Paul leave you?"

Emma nibbled on her lower lip. "Honestly, Cassidy?"

Cassidy nodded as she pulled her sunglasses from her Coach handbag. She hid her eyes behind the overlarge Gucci glasses.

"I'd do it. I'd probably be bitchy about it the whole time, though. I hate feeling unsure, you know?"

"Yes, I do. This entire relationship with Donovan has gone from nothing to everything in such a short span of time, I don't think I've had a chance to adjust." She hated how much she worried about everything with Donovan. Before, she'd known that she could make things right between them in bed, and now...that simply wasn't the case.

"He might be feeling the same way. I mean, he came back to you to try again, not expecting to have a baby and a wife so quickly. How is he adjusting to fatherhood?"

"I'm not sure. This morning he took care of Van so I could sleep in, and he does spend at least a half hour every morning with Van, talking to him and walking him around the house while I get ready."

"What does he say?"

Cassidy didn't know. She felt as if she was intruding and wanted to let Donovan have some alone time with their son. She knew the things she talked to Van about were personal. Things that were full of her love for her baby. And sometimes she talked to him about her dreams for him.

"Do you know?" Emma prodded her.

"Not really. But he does seem to be making time for Van. I mean, he's a busy executive and that's not going to change, but when I need him he's there."

Emma gave her a one-armed hug. "He's different than I thought he would be at this point. I don't know what happened when ya'll were apart, but he's not the same guy he was before."

That was what she kept telling herself. And a part of her was afraid to believe it. She wanted this new beginning to be what led them to happily-ever-after. But she knew she was steeling herself for the possibility that it might not work out. And that attitude was coloring everything, making it so much harder to just be happy in the moment.

Maybe because she was afraid to let herself believe in those dreams that she'd held for so long.

Paul pulled up but was on his cell phone so Emma gestured that she'd be another minute. "He talks so loudly when he's on that thing."

Cassidy laughed at that. Paul did talk loudly on his cell.

"Did you ask Donovan about Maxwell's will?" Emma asked.

"Yes. He said it wasn't a big deal. He's already

aware of whatever it was that Sam was talking about."

"That's all he said?"

"Yes. Why, did you hear anything else?"

"No. I asked my father about it, but he said it was none of my business."

"Well, he's right."

"He isn't. If it concerns Donovan then it concerns you and we're best friends."

"Uh-huh. Did that change your dad's opinion?"

"Absolutely not. But he can be a bit of a stickler when it comes to rules. Remember that time he went ballistic when we took his Mercedes for a test-drive?"

Cassidy did indeed remember the incident, which had happened when they'd both been thirteen. Emma's older brother, Eric, had been bragging about his abilities behind the wheel and Emma had had to prove she could drive as well as he did. To be fair, Emma was at least as good a driver as Eric. Unfortunately her father didn't care about that, he cared only that thirteen-year-olds weren't supposed to be behind the wheel.

They parted ways when Paul got off the phone. Cassidy left, wondering if she had let her reunion with Donovan change something essential inside of her. She'd never been a coward before this. From the moment she'd met Donovan she'd known she wanted to be his wife—why would she let anything intrude on her happiness now that she was?

She needed to take some action. No more waiting for Donovan to make the first move. Tonight, when he came home from work and Van was in bed, she was going to seduce her husband.

Chapter 7

Donovan drove home with Van buckled in the backseat of his Porsche Cayenne. He'd bought the SUV the day after they'd brought Van home from the hospital. The Cayenne had the engine power he was used to in his Porsche 911, but the safety and room needed for an infant.

He hadn't met with Sam or anyone else after Theo had left. His family made the Machiavellis look like inhabitants of *Mr. Rogers' Neighborhood*. He was angry and frustrated and ready to take on the entire board. This mess was getting out of hand. Granddaddy had started this fiasco with his ridiculous will and the way he'd always pitted his sons and grandsons against each other.

He dialed his parents' number and got their housekeeper, Maria, who informed him that his mother was out for the evening with her bridge club and that his father was in his studio.

Without thinking twice Donovan drove to his parents' house. He needed to talk to his father. He took Van out of the car seat when they got there and found that the baby needed his diaper changed. Donovan took care of it and then carried the baby around the back of the mansion he'd grown up in to his father's studio.

He knocked on the door but then opened it and entered, knowing his father never answered the door. His dad held up one hand in a gesture that Donovan knew meant he'd be a minute.

So he took Van on a walk around his father's studio, showing his son the pictures that had been taken of his father at different exhibits.

"What can I do for you?" his dad asked.

"I'm not sure. Uncle Theo visited me today and warned me against marrying Cassidy…. Dad, what's up? I thought for sure Mom would have mentioned the wedding to more of the family."

His dad wiped his hands on the front of his shirt and then walked over to where Donovan stood.

"I have no idea. Your mother votes my shares

and has the active seat on the board. I haven't said anything to anyone because I've been in the studio. I have a show in three months and really don't have time for any of the Tolley-Patterson business."

It was a familiar scenario. Donovan had never really had any of his father's attention or his father's time. Sculpting came first for his father, and then family.

He looked down at little Van sleeping so quietly in his arms.

"I remember when you were that size," his dad said, gesturing to Van. "I used to keep you in here with me during the day."

He didn't remember that. "Really?"

"Well, your mother was still an active executive at the company so it made sense for me to keep you. I had a playpen for you over in that corner."

His father turned to look in the direction he'd indicated and Donovan stood there awkwardly, realizing that he and his father had never been close so he'd never considered that he might have had dreams for him to be an artist. He thought of it now only because he knew he wanted Van to follow in *his* footsteps and one day take over running the family company.

"I need to talk to Mom about this. Will you ask her to call me when she gets home?"

"Yes. What did Theo say?"

"That I needed to marry a proper girl. One from the right sort of family."

His dad chuffed. "Sometimes I think the Tolleys forget that they were carpetbaggers."

"Dad, watch out, that kind of talk will get you disinherited."

"Wouldn't be the first time that I was threatened with that. That might not be a bad thing. Always remember that you aren't a clone of your grand-father."

"I know that."

"Do you? I think you've always wanted to be better than he was, but you know he took the company from a nearly bankrupt run-down business to where it is today. He carved his own path, Dono-van, and I think a part of you has always hungered to do the same."

"Did he want you to do that, too?"

"We had a big argument about it when I decided to go to the Art Institute of Chicago instead of Har-vard. He said that I was letting him down by not following in his footsteps...called me weak."

"That sounds like Granddaddy. He never could understand anything that happened outside the walls of Tolley-Patterson."

"I told him I wasn't his clone and I couldn't fol-low his path. I needed to follow my own."

Donovan's family didn't just live in Charleston,

they were steeped in the history of this town. He'd grown up surrounded by his past the same way his dad had. But instead of shunning what was all around him, Donovan had embraced it.

Today, though, he'd seen another side of being a Tolley, and he acknowledged that Uncle Theo and the board might never come around to accepting Cassidy.

He left his father's studio with nothing resolved and more questions in his own mind. Had he been just as guilty as Uncle Theo and the board of discriminating against Cassidy and her family and friends? He had kept their marriage quiet so that he could use her and Van to the best advantage when it came to beating Sam.

He sat in the front seat of the Cayenne and glanced over his shoulder into the backseat. Van was awake and waving his fist in front of his face.

"What do you think, buddy?" he asked the baby. "Should I tell the board to go to hell?"

The baby cooed and looked up at him with eyes that were shaped like Cassidy's. He knew he had his answer. The thing was, he didn't know if he could let go of the goals that had been a driving force in his life for so long. Could he give up beating Sam and taking over as CEO for Cassidy?

Not that she would ask him to. But if his family wouldn't accept her, he couldn't allow anyone to treat her with disdain. All she'd ever done was love him and give him a son.

He leaned over to brush the drool off Van's lower lip with his thumb and realized that his life had already changed, whether he wanted to admit it or not.

Cassidy was ready for Donovan that night. She'd gone to the salon to get her legs waxed. She'd taken a long bath and taken time with her appearance. She'd gone shopping after she'd left Emma and purchased a new wardrobe that fit her postpregnancy body.

She'd even cut her hair and had it highlighted. She looked more like her old self than she had in a long time. She *felt* more like her old self. She glanced in the mirror and saw the flirty woman she used to be.

Cassidy gave the housekeeper the night off and was prepared to fix a simple supper of grilled salmon and watercress salad whenever Donovan got home. She even had a shaker and ingredients ready to make martinis as soon as he walked in the door.

She heard his car in the back driveway and realized she was standing around, staring at the back door as if she were waiting for him. Which she was, but he didn't need to know that.

But she had no idea where she should go. She

didn't watch TV and the study was on the other side of the house. Dammit. Why hadn't she planned this part better?

She went into the living room to the wet bar and started mixing the drinks.

"Cassidy, we're home. Where's Mrs. Winters?"

She went over to Donovan and gave him a kiss on the cheek before taking Van from him. "I gave her the night off. I thought it would be nice to have a family night."

"Sounds good. We need to talk anyway."

"About what?"

"My family… What were you making here?"

"Gin martinis."

"I'll do that. Are we doing dinner?"

"Yes. Salmon steaks on the grill and salad."

He grinned at her and she felt the groove she'd been searching for between them. "I'm going to go change Van out of his work clothes."

"I'll come with you. I need a change, too. Is the baby too small for the pool?"

"To be honest I have no idea. I think he'll be fine as long as we hold him."

They walked up the curving staircase in the front of the house. Donovan touched her shoulder and then caught a strand of her hair. She turned and looked at him eye to eye since she was a step higher than he was.

"I like your hair."

"Thank you," she said, her voice sounding a little hoarse to her own ears.

"God, Cassidy, you are so gorgeous." His mouth found hers and he kissed her the way she'd been longing for him to. His lips moved over hers with surety, his tongue teasing first her lips and then brushing over the seam of her mouth and thrusting inside. He tasted faintly of mint and something that she associated only with Donovan.

She leaned toward him, wanting to feel his chest pressing against her breasts, but instead felt Van's little hand on the bottom of her neck. She pulled back and stared at her husband for a long moment, remembering the orgasm she'd had on their wedding night. Man, that felt like a lifetime ago.

Donovan kissed the baby's hand and then walked around her on the stairs and continued up toward the master suite. "He was good for me today. Slept through two meetings and flirted with all the secretaries."

"Then he's a lot like his father."

"Funny. You don't get to the executive office by sleeping through meetings."

"But flirting helps?" she asked, teasing him, trying to find some kind of lightness to take her mind off of the physical ache she felt. Oh, how she wanted him.

"It doesn't hurt."

They entered the master suite and Donovan went into his closet, to change, she supposed. She laid Van on the center of their king-size bed. She took off his khaki pants and button-down shirt and then checked his diaper, which was dry.

The baby lay on his back cooing and chewing on his fingers until she handed him a little plastic pretzel chew toy. She wanted to go change but didn't feel safe turning her back for even a second while the baby was up on the high bed.

She took the bolster pillow from the head of the bed and put that on one side of Van and then used the other pillows to create a barricade around the baby. He wasn't crawling yet so he should be fine, she thought.

Her bathing suit was in the dresser in this room. She grabbed it quickly and then went back to the side of the bed. Van had fallen asleep in the midst of the pillows, the toy on his chest. She watched him as she got changed next to the bed.

Instead of the daring bikini she used to wear, she donned a new tankini, and when she caught a glimpse of herself in the mirror she thought she looked pretty good.

She turned back to Van, leaning over him to adjust one of the pillows. She felt Donovan's breath on the back of her neck a second before she felt his lips on her skin.

He nibbled down the length of her neck. She shivered under his touch as his hands found her waist and he drew her back against his body. His chest was bare and felt wonderful as he wrapped his arms around her and pulled her fully against his body.

"Can we make love?" he asked. "Because I'm aching to be inside you."

"I can't take you," she said. "Not yet. But in a few more weeks I can."

"Then we'll have to do something else, because I can't keep my hands off you for another day."

Cassidy turned in his arms. "I want you, too."

"I know."

She arched one eyebrow at him. "How?"

"Your pheromones have been making me crazy since I walked in the door."

She started to respond but he kissed her mouth, cutting off her words and making it impossible to do anything but kiss him back.

Donovan couldn't keep his eyes or his hands off Cassidy as they prepared and ate dinner. Van was sleeping happily in his portable crib and for a moment Donovan felt that everything in his life was perfect. There was none of the intense competitive need to be better than anyone. To keep reaching for that elusive whatever that was always missing in his life.

Instead, as he looked across the table at Cassidy sipping her pinot grigio and wearing that bathing suit, he felt something close to contentment. And that scared him as nothing else could. Content men weren't hungry or successful. Content men sat on the sidelines while others made things happen, and Donovan knew he could never be the kind of guy who did that.

He wanted Cassidy, wanted this peace she brought to him and his life, and yet he knew that this was false. That there was no way they were going to have this moment for too much longer. His job was going to come between them.

She had her iPod plugged in to the Bose speaker system that surrounded the pool and the songs that were playing were romantic. After holding her and kissing her earlier, he wanted nothing more than to make love to her.

But he needed to talk to Cassidy. Needed to tell her that most of his family didn't know they were married. He needed to come clean about what had been going on.

Part of him didn't want to. That was work re-lated and shouldn't be something for her to worry about. This marriage was what she'd wanted. And he was going to make everything at Tolley-Patterson work out.

"You're staring at me."

"Am I?" he asked.

She nodded. "Why?"

"Because I want to."

She arched her eyebrows at him. "Why do you want to?"

One thing that had always drawn him to her was the way that her eyes sparkled when she laughed or teased. It wasn't even just when she teased him. He found her joy of life attractive no matter whom she was teasing.

"I'm surprised someone with your upbringing would do something as rude as staring."

"Well, I'm a rebel."

"I've always liked that about you."

"What else do you like about me?"

"Your butt."

That surprised him and he leaned back in his chair. "I like yours, too."

"I know," she said, mimicking him from earlier.

The music changed and "Brown-Eyed Girl" by Van Morrison came on. Donovan was pushing back his chair as Cassidy got to her feet. "This is my song."

He knew that. It was always Cassidy's song. With her vibrant brown eyes and her shorter hair dancing around her shoulders, she started to move to the song. And he knew that, no matter what he'd been telling himself, this brown-eyed girl was important to him. At least as important as Tolley-Patterson.

He took her hand in his and drew her into his arms. She sang a bit off-key as they danced around the pool. Her limbs were silky and cool against his as he held her.

She tipped her head back. "I've been afraid of being myself with you."

"How do you mean?"

"Our marriage felt like it was so rushed, and I'm still not entirely sure why you came back when you did…." She pulled out of his arms. "I guess that part of me didn't want to rock the boat."

"I can understand that. I've been doing the same thing. Just working and keeping to my old routines."

"That's it exactly, but because I'm not working I've been sitting at home stewing and going a bit crazy because I couldn't figure out what was going on with you."

"And now you have me figured out?" he asked, sliding his hands up and down her back. It never ceased to amaze him how small she was or how right she felt in his arms.

"Not you. I figured *me* out. I was lost for so

long, not sure what I was going to do, just waiting for Van to be born so I could figure out my next move. But now he's here and you're here, and I had to get here, too."

Listening to her talk made him feel like a bastard. He was here not because of any great philosophical development but because he needed her. "I didn't journey to you like that."

"It doesn't matter. This isn't about you really."

"Should I be offended?"

She shrugged. "If you want to be."

"Nah. Tell me more about being afraid to be you," he said. The music changed to Jamiroquai's "Virtual Insanity." And as Cassidy danced around him, he realized that she was a bit buzzed. She smiled at him each time she turned to face him.

"I think I didn't know if you could still want me, because I'd changed so much as a woman."

"In what way? By being a mother?"

"No. I mean my body. I've put on some weight and I'm never going to have that flat stomach I used to have."

He pulled her to a stop. "I love your body, Cassidy. Flat stomachs don't attract me—you do."

She tilted her head to the side and eyed him with that level stare of hers. The one that he was sure could see straight into his soul. "Really? The first thing you complimented me on was my slim figure."

"That's only because I thought I'd sound ridiculous if I told you that I loved your laugh and the way you smile when you're teasing."

She quieted and got really serious. "Do you mean that?"

"I don't say things I don't mean."

She wrapped her arms around him and squeezed him so tightly that he felt it all the way to his soul. "Being married to you has made me so incredibly happy."

She rested her head on his shoulder and he held her loosely because he desperately wanted to clutch her to him. And men who were afraid to lose what they held were a liability. They stopped looking to the future and only looked to the present, his Granddaddy used to say. Those kind of men were the kind that life left behind.

Chapter 8

Cassidy was seated at her vanity table when he came into their bedroom from putting Van down in his crib. He set the baby monitor on his nightstand and tried to calm his raging libido. Traditional sex was out of the question; she'd said she couldn't for a few more weeks. But he wanted to make love to her tonight. To seduce her with his lips and hands and give her the concrete reassurances that he still found her attractive.

"Thanks for tucking Van in."

"You're welcome," he said, watching her in the mirror. He walked over to her and put his hands on her shoulders. Her skin was smooth to the touch—

he never got over how soft she was. She smelled sweetly of flowers.

He leaned in low to brush his lips over her shoulder. Her nightgown had spaghetti straps and he kissed his way toward her neck, moving that thin strip of fabric out of his way so that he dropped kisses on every inch of her flesh.

"Donovan," she said his name on a sigh.

"Yes, baby?" he asked.

She turned on the stool and twined her arms around his shoulders, drawing his mouth to hers. Take it slow, he told himself. But slow wasn't in his programming with this woman. She was pure feminine temptation. He lifted her from the padded bench she sat on and set her down on the vanity counter. He slid his hands down her back, finding the hem of her nightgown and pulling it up until he caressed between her legs. She was creamy with desire, and hot.

She moaned deep in her throat and he hardened painfully. He thrust against her, rubbing their groins together until he thought he was going to explode.

He slid the straps of her nightgown down her arms until he could see the tops of her breasts and the barest hint of the rosy flesh of her nipples. He lowered his head, using his teeth to pull the loosened fabric away from her skin.

Her nipples stood out against the cool air in the room. He ran the tip of one fingertip around her aroused flesh. She trembled in his arms.

Lowering his head he took one of her nipples in his mouth and suckled her. She held him to her with a strength that surprised him. But shouldn't have.

Her fingers drifted down his back and then slid under the T-shirt he'd put on to sleep in. She tangled her fingers in the hair on his chest and tugged, spreading her fingers out to dig her nails lightly into his pecs.

He liked the light teasing of her fingernails. She shifted back away from him, and he kept his hands on her breasts. His fingers worked over her nipples as she pushed the shirt up to his armpits. He let go of her for a minute to rip the shirt off and toss it across the room. He growled deep in his throat when she leaned forward to brush kisses against his chest.

She bit and nibbled and made him feel like her plaything. He wanted to sit back and let her have her way with him. But there was no room here. No time for seduction or extended lovemaking.

He pulled her to him and lifted her slightly so that her nipples brushed his chest. Holding her carefully he rubbed against her. Blood roared in his ears. He was so hard, so full right now that he needed to be inside of her body. But tonight he'd have to focus on other things.

Impatient with the fabric of her nightgown, he shoved it up and out of his way. He caressed her creamy thighs. She was so soft. She moaned as he neared her center and then sighed when he brushed his fingertips across the humid opening of her body.

She was warm and wet. He slipped one finger into her body, felt the walls tighten around him and hesitated for a second, looking down into her heavy-lidded eyes. She bit down on her lower lip and he felt the minute movements of her hips as she tried to move his touch where she needed it.

He was beyond teasing her or prolonging anything. He plunged two fingers into her humid body. She squirmed against him.

He needed to taste her *now*.

He dropped to his knees in front of her, kicking the vanity chair out of his way.

"What are you doing?" she asked, looking down at him.

"Taking care of you," he said.

She murmured something he didn't catch as he lowered his head and touched his tongue to her center. Her thighs flexed around his head and he thrust his fingers in and out of her warm body. Her hands tangled in his hair as he caught her sweet flesh lightly between his teeth and nibbled on her.

He guided her hands to the cool surface at the rounded edge of the table. "Hold on."

"Yessss..." she said. And then he heard those little sounds she made right before she came. He felt her body tighten around his fingers and was careful to keep the pressure on until he felt her shake and tremble around him.

He stood up and braced his hands on the vanity, trying to catch his breath.

She reached for him and he pulled away.

"Donovan?"

"Don't touch me, baby. I want you too badly right now."

She reached between their bodies and took him in her hand. "Let me—"

"Not tonight," he said. "This night is for you. I wanted you to sleep in my arms knowing how much I want you and how attractive you are to me."

"Thank you," she said.

"You're welcome, baby."

Cassidy never felt as wanted as she did that night in Donovan's arms. He brought her to orgasm after orgasm, and only took pleasure for himself when Cassidy finally insisted that she needed to enjoy the sensuality of his body as well. She fell into an exhausted sleep wrapped in his arms. Cuddled up against his side with his body pressed to hers she found a strength and peace that came from him.

But that peace faded at breakfast when she read an article in the business pages about her son's birth in which she was named as Donovan's former girlfriend. She read the article twice and learned a little more about the situation that Donovan was facing at work. The reporter speculated that either Sam Patterson or Donovan Tolley would be appointed CEO of Tolley-Patterson at the next board meeting in January.

Cassidy finished her juice while she waited for him to come down from getting ready for work.

She heard the phone ring and a moment later Mrs. Winters came in with the cordless phone. "It's your mother."

"Thank you," Cassidy said, waiting until Mrs. Winters left the room before she lifted the phone. "Hi, Mom."

"Did you see this morning's paper?" her mother asked. It was noisy at her parents' house. Loud music and the sound of her mother's treadmill vied for dominance.

"Just now."

"What's going on? Why does this article make it sound as if you and Donovan aren't married?"

"I don't know, Mom. Donovan's still upstairs getting ready."

"Your father is outraged…. I think Adam is going to call the editor of the paper."

"Don't let him do that, Mom."

"Why not?"

"Because I wanted to keep the marriage quiet."

"Cassidy…"

"I needed time to adjust to everything and I didn't want there to be any speculation that Donovan married me because I was pregnant."

"Who cares what anyone has to say?" her mother said.

"Donovan's family."

"They're too full of themselves. It shouldn't matter to you what they think."

"I know, Mom."

Her phone beeped, letting her know there was another call waiting. She promised to call her mother back as she switched over to the other call.

"Hey, girl, brace yourself before you open up the paper this morning," Emma said.

"I've already seen it." She really should have thought through the consequences of keeping her marriage to Donovan secret. She'd just wanted a quiet ceremony and time for them all to adjust to being a family. How weird was it going to be for Donovan when he realized that his uncle had lied to protect their secret? She knew that honesty was one of the cornerstones of Tolley-Patterson. They had a public mission statement that reiterated that value.

"Okay. So what's up?"

"Um… Remember how I wasn't sure if Donovan was being real with me when he came back and proposed?"

"Yes."

"Well, I asked him to keep quiet about us. I just didn't want Charleston society to see our wedding as him marrying me for the baby."

"Why not?"

Cassidy wrapped one arm around her waist. "In case he changed his mind."

"Oh, Cassidy."

"I know. This is a mess."

"What's a mess?" Donovan asked. "Van?"

He entered the breakfast room and kissed her on the head. "You okay?"

"Emma, I'll call you back."

She hung up the phone as Donovan poured himself a cup of coffee. How was he going to react to the article? From their time dating, she knew he hated for any personal information to make its way into articles about him.

"There's an article about you and Van in today's paper."

"Just me and Van?" he asked, reaching for the newspaper. She handed him the Business section.

"Yes. It mentions me as your former girlfriend."

"Who mentioned you that way?" he asked, flipping to the article.

"Theo Tolley," Cassidy said. She'd only met Donovan's uncle once, and from the article she'd learned that he was the interim CEO until the next board meeting.

"Dammit. It's not the way it might seem to you."

"What's not? Your parents were at the wedding, right? I mean, I know I wanted to keep it quiet, but I didn't mean that you had to pretend that we weren't even together."

Donovan skimmed the article and then turned away.

"I'm not pretending we aren't together," he said.

"It's okay," she said. "I suggested we keep things quiet. I just had no idea how it would feel to read something like this. It makes me feel like I'm not even a part of our son's life."

"There's a news van in front of the house," Mrs. Winters said, entering the kitchen.

Cassidy didn't like the sound of that. "Where?"

"At the edge of the property."

Cassidy had a feeling that more than the business journalists were interested in their story. For a society as staid and steeped in tradition and history as Charleston's was, this was a scandal. Especially since Donovan's family and hers were like oil and water.

"This is crazy." The last thing she wanted was to have to deal with the media today. Last night had felt like a real beginning in her relationship with Donovan.

"I agree," Donovan said. "This is a huge mess."

"Yes, it is. This goes way beyond an article in the business pages. If anyone does a records search, they're going to know that we *are* married, and then your uncle is going to look foolish. I'm not sure what to do. I should call my father and tell him what's going on."

"Cassidy..."

"I'm sure you'll have a plan for this. But talking to the reporters is something my father is used to doing. He can help."

"Your father can't comment on this. You aren't to say anything to the media. In fact, no one in your family is."

"You're kidding, right?"

"No, I'm not. Call your folks right now, tell them to say nothing."

"Donovan."

"What?" he asked, impatiently. She knew he'd probably already moved on to the next order of business in his head, but no way was she going to call her parents and tell them what to do.

"We have a problem. I don't take orders, and neither does my family."

"Until we have this sorted out, you both do," he said, walking away.

Donovan's first call was to an old college roommate, Jamie, who worked for the local NBC affiliate in Charleston.

"You are one hot story right now," Jamie said. "The stipulations of your grandfather's will were just leaked."

Donovan stilled. "By who?" he asked, his legendary cold, calm reaction coming to the fore. He automatically prioritized the situation and knew getting the media off his back was number one. Talking to Cassidy…oh, man, that was going to take more time.

"I don't know. I just wanted to give you the heads-up."

"Thanks, Jamie."

"You're welcome. I don't suppose you have a comment…"

"Not right now."

He hung up and called his uncle. Theo was on voice mail, and who could blame the man. His grandfather's will wasn't the first to have the kind of stipulation it did, but no one on the board wanted the media or the world to know about it.

"What is going on?" Cassidy said as she entered his study.

She held Van in her arms, and she looked upset.

Cassidy took a deep breath and released it slowly. Donovan watched her and realized for the first time that his priorities were wrong. He didn't care what the board did or what the media knew. He needed to make this right for Cassidy.

"I think it'd be better for me to handle this," she said. "I can say that I wasn't ready to talk to the press since I just gave birth and that your family, out of concern for me, kept quiet." She gazed at him. "What do you think?"

He was speechless. That Cassidy would take the blame for something that wasn't even her fault was beyond his comprehension. He had to act. He hadn't anticipated Theo going after Cassidy in such a public way. Donovan was going to have to go in front of the entire board to get to the bottom of this.

Judging by his mention of Cassidy in the paper, Theo was up to something, and the power play wasn't one that Donovan was going to respond to.

"I think that you're extremely generous, but you should let me take care of this," he said.

"Well, I think we should handle it together. I'm going to issue a statement so that it doesn't seem as if I'm ignoring the media."

Donovan didn't want the story to go any further

than it already had. He needed to get Marcus on the phone and have his team meet him at the office. It didn't matter that it was a Saturday.

"No. You will not do anything of the kind," he said. He pulled his cell phone from his pocket and sent a text message to his staff. He looked back up to see Cassidy glaring at him.

"What?" he asked, distracted.

"Did you just tell me what to do? *Again?*"

"Yes, I did. And I'm going to continue doing it."

"Excuse me?" Cassidy asked.

"You heard me."

"You are acting like a…"

"Jerk? I know. But you aren't prepared to deal with reporters shouting questions at you. And you're too old to have your father do it. I'll take care of it for us. This mess—"

"Mess? Do you mean our marriage and our son?"

Cassidy was on the verge of breaking down. He saw it in her eyes and in the almost desperate way she was holding their son close to her.

"No, of course not. You and Van are the best things to ever happen to me."

The words were meant to bring her solace, but they resonated with him, as well. He did need Cassidy and his son.

The doorbell rang but Donovan ignored it. "I

think it would be best if you and Van kept a low profile until I talk to my people. Please."

"Fine," Cassidy said shortly.

Mrs. Winters knocked on the study door. "Sam Patterson is here."

The last thing he wanted was to have Sam here, but in light of the will being made public, the two of them would have to address the stipulation together.

"I'll be with him in a minute. Ask him to wait in the conservatory."

"No," Cassidy said. "Show him in here. I'll go upstairs and leave you both to it."

There was too much left unresolved between the two of them. He hadn't come close to explaining anything to her, and it was only a matter of time until she found out the entire truth.

"Cassidy?"

"Yes?"

"There's something I have to tell you—"

Sam entered the room without knocking. He gave Cassidy a vague smile and turned to Donovan. "We need to talk."

"Not now," Donovan said.

"Yes, now. You and Cassidy can finish your conversation later. Tolley-Patterson comes first."

"Not today."

"Really? Well then, our conversation will be

short," Sam said. "I guess this means I'll be the new CEO."

"No, it doesn't," Cassidy said. She turned to Donovan. "Talk to your cousin. We can finish our discussion later."

Cassidy walked away, and as he watched her go, he began to understand just how much he loved her.

Loved her.

Chapter 9

"Oh my God. You aren't going to believe it, but Donovan needed you and your baby." Emma burst into the sunroom.

"What are you talking about?"

"That's the weird will thing. The thing I told you I heard at the cocktail party? Maxwell's will said that either Sam or Donovan would be his successor and left them both some very challenging business objectives to accomplish."

"Of course he did. That was what he always did with those two," Cassidy said. "And it makes sense that either Sam or Donovan take over. They're both young and have the drive and experience to take the company to the next level."

"I'm not arguing that. But there was one more thing in the will...the reason why there are news vans outside your door."

Cassidy waited. She felt a trickle of apprehension, because there *was* something that Donovan hadn't told her. Some secret he'd been keeping.

"They each have to be married and produce an heir before they can be appointed CEO!"

Cassidy was glad she was sitting down. She felt faint and her stomach knotted. She thought about the new bonds she and Donovan had forged last night, and she realized that he had just been playing his part. Doing what he thought he needed to do to keep her happy.

She had feared being married for her child, but had believed that he'd only do that out of a sense of responsibility. She'd had no idea that he'd stoop this low. She knew that his company meant everything to him, but he should never have married her without revealing this.

"Cassidy? Are you okay?"

"Yes, I'm fine," she said, but she knew that wasn't true. And yet it was. Because she'd loved Donovan Tolley from the moment she'd met him and he'd smiled at her. She'd loved him even though he always put his job and career in front of her.

She'd loved him even though he'd left her alone all those months.

And finally, she thought, she didn't love him anymore.

Well, that wasn't true. She still loved him, but she finally had the proof she needed that *he* didn't love *her.* That he wasn't ever going to love her the way she wanted him to.

"I'm sorry," Emma said.

"What for?"

"Being the one to tell you. But I couldn't let you find out from some nosy reporter."

"Thanks, Emma. I did need to know this. What am I going to do?"

"Take Van and leave. Let Donovan know that he doesn't have a wife or heir as far as you're concerned. Get him back for what he's done to you."

"Emma...I can't do that."

"Why not? He obviously didn't care about hurting you."

Was that true? She didn't know, and right now she really couldn't figure it out. She only knew that she hurt so much she couldn't think of what to do next. She needed some space.

Her cell phone rang and she glanced at the caller ID. It was her mom.

"Are you going to answer that?"

"Not now," Cassidy said, hitting the ignore button on the phone. She put it on the table and then reached for Van, pulling him into her arms. She tucked him to her and let the love she felt for him soothe her. But it didn't, completely. When she looked into his eyes, she was struck by how much he was a part of both Donovan and her.

That he was a part of the lies that she'd been telling herself for so long.

Emma was staring at her, and Cassidy knew she needed to do something. "Thanks for telling me everything. I'm going to…"

Do what? She wanted in that instant to make Donovan feel the same kind of pain she was experiencing. Because the more she thought about that article she'd read, the more she began to suspect that he'd deliberately kept quiet about their marriage, possibly to use it to his advantage when the time came.

"I'm not leaving you. We'll fix this. I think the first thing to do is—"

"Nothing," Cassidy said. "I want to see what Donovan's going to do next. I mean, he's had a plan all along and I want to wait until he gets to his final move."

"And then tell him it's all over?"

Cassidy thought about that. Essentially, they *were* all over. This was the kind of blow to a relationship that she couldn't fix. The only thing that would fix it would be for Donovan to love her more than he did his job. More than he did the one thing he'd always turned to and found solace in.

Her anger mellowed as she realized they were both trapped in this thing together, because Donovan couldn't change the man he was. And she didn't want to stop loving him. The only way they'd both be happy was if that happened.

Because Donovan was never going to love her, and she wasn't going to be able to endure the humiliation of knowing that he'd come back into her life and married her simply to beat his cousin to the finish line.

Emma watched her and Cassidy realized she had to start detaching herself from her emotions. It was time for her to seriously move on. Or at least create the illusion that she had.

Deep inside, where she kept those dreams of happily-ever-after alive, she wept, but on the outside she simply smiled and stood up with her son in her arms.

"Let's go out," she said to Emma. She wasn't about to hide.

Sam paced around Donovan's office. He'd always seen his cousin as an adversary, and nothing in either of their lives had ever really changed that. The few times they had worked together, they'd both done so in their own way and with their own agenda.

This situation was no different. They were never going to be friends. But when it came to Tolley-Patterson, he knew that they both would do anything to make sure the company prospered and its profits continued to grow.

"We need to find the leak. This kind of press leaves us vulnerable and the investors aren't going to be too happy with the fact that a wife and child are the main requirements for their new CEO."

"Indeed," Sam said. "I've got Kyle from my team using his contacts to try to locate the source of the leak."

Donovan nodded. He was going to check with Jamie later to see if he'd found out anything more on the media side.

"I'm going to ask Theo and the rest of the board to address this. I already sent a message to Franklin in PR. I had asked him to draft a press release in case this situation arose," Donovan said.

"Why did you do that?"

"Granddaddy's will was too sensational for someone not to talk about it. Cassidy's friend Emma already had heard some rumblings, so it was only a matter of time."

"You should have kept me in the loop on this."

Donovan shrugged. He probably should have,

but the will had been one of the things that he and Sam had never seen eye to eye on. If they'd both protested it, they could have gone to the board and had it thrown out. But Sam had steadfastly refused to do that.

"It's too late now. Franklin will issue an official statement from the company, and I think you and I should say 'no comment.'"

"I've asked the board to schedule an emergency meeting for tomorrow afternoon to give everyone time to get into town. I think we should both be prepared to make an argument for a new CEO appointment. Theo isn't equipped to deal with this, and I think our investors are going to need some reassurance," Sam said.

"I agree. I've got two of my guys monitoring our competition to ensure we know what they're doing."

Sam cocked an eyebrow at Donovan. "I guess we're working together on this."

"Seems like it."

"Did you ever wonder why Granddad always set us against each other?" Sam asked.

"Not really. I imagine you and I were always competing. I can't remember a time when we weren't."

In college, he'd gone to Harvard and Sam to Yale. They'd both interned at Fortune 500 companies, Sam at a company owned by one of Maxwell's cronies, Donovan at another one. For every major moment in his life, Donovan realized he'd basically been alone.

He was simply better by himself than working with others. And that was part of what made him leery of this current situation with Sam and the company.

"I don't know if I can work with you on this," Sam said. "My instinct is to go to the media and do my own thing."

"But that wouldn't be best for Tolley-Patterson," Donovan said.

"No, it wouldn't," Sam said a bit ruefully. "Do you ever wish we were just two normal guys?"

"Hell, no."

Sam laughed. "I wonder if Granddaddy had any idea that our path to the chairmanship would go this way."

"Who knows? The old man was good at thinking through every variable. But I don't think he could have predicted what happened with Cassidy and me."

Sam leaned back in his chair. "I'm not so sure about that."

"What do you mean?"

"Just one look at Cassidy and everyone could tell she loved you. And I think Granddaddy always wanted that for you."

Donovan wasn't sure what Sam was getting at, but he didn't want to discuss Cassidy or how she felt about him with his cousin.

Donovan took control of the discussion and soon had the feeling that even Sam knew he was the right choice to lead the company. They spent the rest of the day in his home office on the phone with the board and different investors, working together to assuage them.

"Thanks for all your hard work today, Sam," Donovan said as his cousin prepared to go.

"You don't have to thank me. It's my company, too."

"True, but after today I think we both know that I'll be taking the helm."

"How do you figure?"

"You heard Theo say that they refused to waive the stipulations from the will. And with the board all meeting tomorrow, I'm going to push for a vote for the new chairman. Clearly I'm the best candidate."

Sam got to his feet. "Keep telling yourself that. If I ask the board to postpone the vote or to consider the fact that my wife may now be pregnant…"

"Whatever you do, I think we both know that waiting isn't the best course of action. We need to take the stand as a company that we have a bigger story than Granddaddy's will, and the only thing bigger than that is a new CEO. And I'm the most logical choice," Donovan said. He opened the door to his office to show Sam out.

"Don't bother," Sam said. "I know the way."

Cassidy collided with Sam on his way out the door. She had Van strapped to her chest in a baby carrier and her arms were laden with packages from her and Emma's shopping trip.

He steadied them both and glared at Van. "I hope you know what you've gotten yourself into."

"What do you mean?"

"By having a child with a man who lives only for the company."

Cassidy wasn't sure what had happened, but she'd never seen Sam so hot under the collar before. Though she wasn't happy with Donovan right now, she wasn't going to talk trash about him with his rival.

"Donovan always does what he thinks is best for Tolley-Patterson because he wants what's best for his family."

Sam's eyes narrowed. "I can't believe you're defending him. You know he used you."

"How do you figure?"

"He came back to you to beat me. How does that make you feel? You're nothing more than a broodmare to an egomaniac."

He wasn't telling Cassidy anything she hadn't already figured out for herself. And though she was angry with Donovan for his actions, she wasn't about to condemn him.

"You're nothing but a bitter man who's afraid to admit that he isn't as good as the competition," Cassidy said, desperately trying to hold on to her composure. Sam had just vocalized everything that she'd been thinking for a long time.

She believed, just as Sam did, that Donovan had been using her. Probably from the very beginning when they'd dated over a year ago. Long before Van had been conceived and his grandfather's will had demanded an heir.

Even her realization that Donovan probably couldn't help being the way he was didn't change the fact that he'd lied to her. That he'd made her believe that he'd come back to her because of a change of heart. But she'd begun to comprehend that maybe she hadn't really loved him as well as she thought if she hadn't understood that his love and focus was always going to be on work. She *knew* that. She had known that forever.

"I feel sorry for you," Cassidy said at last, running her hands over the back of her sweet, sleeping baby. No matter why she and Donovan had come together, she had Van, and that counted for a lot in her book.

"Why?"

"Because you're so busy looking at Donovan and blaming him for your failures that you haven't looked at yourself. You're the only one who can control your actions."

"I could say the same of you."

"How so?" she asked, setting down her packages so she could remove Van from the carrier.

"You see him as you want him to be and not as he really is," Sam said. "Turn around and I'll unhook the carrier for you."

Sam's entire demeanor changed and suddenly he was the rather mild-mannered man she'd met a few times before. It was odd to think that he was the competition for Donovan, because personalitywise the two men were polar opposites. Sam was more easygoing and inclusive…more of a team player than Donovan would ever be.

Donovan was a loner. And that was something she should have realized a long time ago.

"I don't know if I trust you with my back turned."

"Look," Sam said. "I'm sorry I attacked you like I did. Seeing your son…he reminded me of a conversation I had with Granddaddy last Christmas."

"What did he say?"

Sam shook his head. "That we had to remember Tolley-Patterson was looking to the future. That we weren't going to be the last generation to run our family's company."

"Maybe that's why he was so determined that his next CEO produce an heir," Cassidy said. It seemed to her that Maxwell Patterson had wanted to control his grandsons for as long as he could.

"Perhaps. I *am* sorry for what I said. It seems as if you do know what you're getting into with Donovan."

She smiled and tried to appear confident. But she wasn't sure she'd pulled it off. Because to be honest, she had no idea what to expect from Donovan. "I guess."

"The rest of the family isn't going to accept your marriage, Cassidy."

"Why not?"

"Uncle Theo's quote in the business section... Did you see that?"

"Yes, I did."

"Well, he knows you and Donovan are back together. He's trying to push the two of you apart."

"Why?"

Sam shook his head. "I can honestly say that it has nothing to do with you."

"Who does it have to do with? Van? I'm not going to let your uncle or Tolley-Patterson be the focus of his life. I don't want him to grow up like that."

Sam smiled at her. "I can see that Donovan chose the right woman to be the mother of his children."

It was such a change from where Sam had been before that she almost didn't trust him. "Thanks, I think."

"Do you need a hand with your bags?" he asked.

"No, thanks."

"Good night then," Sam said, and he walked down to his Mercedes and drove away.

Cassidy watched him go, wondering desperately what she was going to do about both the mess that was her marriage and her son's future.

Chapter 10

Donovan didn't leave his office until well after midnight. Even though he hadn't spoken to Cassidy, he knew she was aware that he'd married her to fulfill the requirements of his grandfather's will. Her lack of contact spoke volumes. He rubbed a hand over his eyes. They felt gritty and his back ached from sitting in one position for too long.

The house was quiet and air-conditioned cold as he walked up the grand staircase to the second-floor landing. One of his father's sculptures was displayed there. This one was of him, from when he'd been in his first year of college. The cold marble seemed startlingly like him. The eyes were vacuous, though, something he'd never noticed in his own.

Seeing himself in stone like this always made him strive harder. Work harder. His grandfather used to say that the boy in that sculpture had so much potential and fire to change the world. And Donovan was reminded of those words each time he walked past it.

But he was fifteen years older and he'd changed. He'd had to change. Hadn't he?

He entered the master suite and found it empty and quiet. He stood in the doorway feeling the hollowness of his victory. His long hours in the office this last week had assured that victory. Tomorrow there would be a public announcement officially declaring him the new CEO of Tolley-Patterson.

And he was all alone.

He strode to his nightstand and reached for the fine quality embossed note card that had Cassidy's monogram on the front. Not the one from when she'd been a Franzone, but the new one that reflected her married name.

He opened the card and traced his finger over her signature. It was flowery and pretty, very feminine and reflective of the woman she was.

Donovan,
I hated to leave without saying anything but

I couldn't wait around for you. I need to get away so I can think about everything that's happened. I think I made a mistake in marrying you so quickly, without understanding exactly what your needs were.

Van and I are moving back into my house so I can have space to figure this out. I know you'll be busy with the company and your new role. Somehow, without even asking, I know you will be the new CEO.

I pray it's everything you hoped it would be.

Love, Cassidy

He tossed the note on the bed and left the bedroom. The house was a monument to his success. He had every "thing" anyone could possibly want. And for what?

He shook it off. Cassidy was just a woman. He'd lived just fine without her for the eight months they were apart. He went downstairs to the wet bar and poured himself a stiff drink.

He heard a sound behind him on the marble floor and turned to see a shadow in the doorway.

"Cassidy?"

She stepped into the room.

"I thought you'd gone."

"I did."

She wore a pair of faded jeans and a scoop-neck, sleeveless top. She looked tired. Her eyes were red, and he suspected that she had been crying. *He had made her cry.* He tried to think how he could make it better for her. She'd come back, so that had to mean that she didn't really want to be apart from him.

"Where's Van?"

"With my parents. I needed to talk to you. I want to make sure you understand why I left."

"I run a multimillion-dollar company. I think I can figure it out," he said, not really up to discussing all the things that were wrong with him when it came to relationships.

"You can be a real bastard."

"I know," he said, rubbing the back of his neck. "Listen, I didn't mean it that way. You know how I am. I'm not the kind of guy who talks about his emotions…."

He trailed off, hoping that she'd rescue him. That she'd give him a pass the way she had so often before. But she didn't.

"I do know how you are."

"Then why are you surprised?"

"Because…listen, I can't explain it any better than to just say I love you. And I think in loving you I made you into the hero I needed you to be.

I have always been drawn to men who are driven, and you are that in spades."

"So what's the problem?"

"I thought you were different from my dad. That you had all of his strengths and none of his weaknesses."

"I've never talked on the phone all through a dinner with you."

"Donovan...do you care about this relationship, or do you want me to just walk out the door?"

It would be so much easier to have a clean break with Cassidy. She complicated things, complicated his life endlessly because she made him want to be that white knight she thought he was.

But he wasn't naive and never had been. He couldn't be the man she wanted him to be. His life was this empty house. His life was Tolley-Patterson.

"Donovan?"

"Yes?"

"What are you thinking?"

"About letting you go," he said honestly.

"That's funny," Cassidy said, feeling calm for once. No tears burned in her eyes. She felt nothing but a sense of unreality. "I think you probably already let me go...almost a year ago."

He shook his head and walked to her. He looked so tired and drained, and she wanted nothing more than to open her arms and offer him the comfort of a hug. But this was the man who kept breaking her heart, and solace wasn't something she should even be thinking of giving him anymore.

Yet to quit loving him was hard. She couldn't just fall out of love with him in less than one week. She couldn't stop the emotions that had been there from the moment their hands had touched. But she was determined to let him go. Determined to make a new start for herself. One where Donovan was nothing more than her baby's father.

"Baby, I have been holding on to you in ways you can't even imagine," he said.

The words sounded true, but she had learned during their brief marriage that Donovan wasn't above manipulating the truth.

"It feels to me more like you're pushing me away. You lied to me, Donovan. Flat-out lied when I asked you why you came back."

She'd come back for closure. Writing a note to him and leaving the way she had had left her feeling as if…oh, God, as if maybe there was still a chance for the two of them. The only way she was going to be able to move on was through some sort of final conflict.

"What did you want me to say, Cassidy? That I needed a wife and a baby for the company?" he asked, sarcasm dripping from every word.

"Well it would have been the truth." She wasn't about to take the blame for this. He had lied to her, and he had planned to keep on lying to her.

"You were happy to believe I was back for you."

"I was happy to believe that, because I wanted it so much. But I think maybe I was lying to myself. Listen, I just came back tonight because I didn't want things to end the way they did last time." She thought about telling him about her other stop that day—at his parents' house—and decided against it.

"I'm not sure what you mean," he said. "There isn't any reason for our marriage to be over…but that's what your note meant, right?"

"Yes. Our marriage *is* over." It was mainly pride talking, but she didn't care. She was tired of loving Donovan too much and him caring for her too little. She was never going to be able to compete with Tolley-Patterson. She was never going to be able to challenge him and fill his life the way that company did. She was never going to be anything more to him than the mother of his son.

"Why?" he asked.

He seemed perplexed, and frankly she didn't understand it. He had to see that she was more than a cog in the wheel of his plans for the future.

"What do you mean, why? Honestly, I think you can see why we can't stay married."

She wanted to say because he'd hurt her when

he'd lied to her, but it was more than that. Tonight, as she'd tucked Van into his crib at her parents' house and seen the picture her parents had placed over his crib of her and Donovan holding the baby in the hospital—she'd wanted desperately for the emotions she felt to be real on both sides.

"No, I can't, Cassidy. Nothing's changed."

"Everything's changed."

He came over to her and took her hand in his, lacing his fingers with hers. She noticed the way their wedding rings nestled together.

"I married you, and we had Van together. My grandfather's will was in place before he was born."

"I didn't know that that was why you married me."

"Haven't you been happy?" he asked.

She *had* been happy. Had been finding her way in this new role. She still had to go back to her job, and they'd never made a public announcement of their marriage, but she'd been happy with Donovan.

"Well, yes, but…" How to explain? "I kept hoping you'd come back, and then you did. I set myself up for it."

"Set yourself up for what?"

She swallowed hard, hating to admit once again that she'd wanted to be wanted, to feel special, for herself. To be the one thing that he hadn't been able to live without.

"For you. I set myself up to be totally vulnerable to you. And that's what makes me mad. I made everything so easy for you."

Donovan cursed and dropped her hand, pacing away from her. She watched his back, watched him walk away, though he didn't go too far. She made herself watch that view and remember it. He had walked away from her, and from her love.

"Nothing about this has been easy, Cassidy. Lying to you didn't sit right with me, but as long as you seemed happy I told myself that the ends justified the means."

"Of course you would say that. You've never needed me the way I need you."

Silence built between them, and she realized how much she'd hoped he would argue with her about this. Hoped that he'd suddenly confess to loving her and needing her. And the last of her dreams around Donovan Tolley died.

She pivoted on her heel and walked toward the door.

"Cassidy, wait," he said.

She stopped where she was but didn't turn around. The numbness she'd wrapped herself in when she'd come back to this house was fading, leaving behind the kind of aching pain that she'd experienced only one other time…when he'd let her down before.

"How can I fix this?" he asked.

That he'd asked made her feel marginally better. That he couldn't figure out what she needed from him negated those good feelings. No one wanted to have to tell someone that they needed to be loved. That they needed to be first in their life.

"I don't think you can."

There were a few moments in a person's life that defined him, and Donovan knew this moment with Cassidy was one. This would determine for the rest of his life what the balance of their relationship would be. And he had only to think about that feeling he'd had when he'd walked into the empty master suite to know that losing her now wasn't an option.

"*Can't* isn't in my vocabulary," he said.

She glanced back at him, that long curly hair of hers swinging around her shoulders. "What are you trying to say?"

He didn't blame her. He'd used evasion and half-truth for so long. They'd become his standard way of communicating with everyone. It was simply easier to play his cards close to his chest. He could protect himself and use the knowledge he collected to his advantage.

And the knowledge he'd collected about Cassidy was simple and straightforward. She needed some kind of emotional reciprocity. And it was about time that he delivered it.

But laying bare his soul…

"That we aren't done talking yet. Don't walk away while there are still things to be said." No response. "Please."

She turned to face him, arms crossed. "I'm listening."

"Let's go outside. I'm tired of being in the house."

She nodded and followed him out onto the patio. The soothing sound of the waterfall in the pool area eased the tension that was riding him.

He didn't lose. He wasn't going to lose Cassidy. He just had to do the right thing. He'd always been able to fix things that way.

This was no different. He was going to win Cassidy back. He'd come back from worse situations. It wouldn't be the first time that he'd been down like this. She wouldn't have come back tonight if she hadn't wanted to.

"I know that I haven't exactly been your knight in shining armor, but I can change that. This stuff with Granddaddy's will was making me a bit crazy, and I had to focus on that and outplaying Sam. But that's behind me now, and I want to make you and Van the focus of my life."

Cassidy watched him and he didn't even kid

himself that he had any idea what she was thinking. But he did know that she was no longer walking away. It eased the ache that he'd felt when he'd stared at her back.

"You're talking about starting over?"

"If that's what you want. I'd prefer to start from here," he said, meaning it. "We've had some good times, haven't we?"

"Yes, we have. But I can't—"

"What?"

"Listen, I want this to work. I mean, I love you, Donovan, but you have been a jerk about certain things in our relationship, and I'm not about to put up with it anymore."

"Fair enough. You tell me what you want me to change and I'll change it."

"It's not that easy."

"Why not? That's what makes the most successful relationships work."

"What relationships?"

"Business partnerships, mergers."

He felt her go quiet. She stopped leaning toward him and even though she didn't turn away he felt exactly as he had earlier when she'd walked away.

"Mergers? Was this a hostile takeover, or a friendly acquisition?"

"A friendly merger," he said, drawing her into his arms.

She held herself stiff and he realized that the situation was slipping away from him again. Was it time to pull back and regroup? Hell, he'd never done that and wasn't about to now.

He leaned down to kiss her but she put her arm between them. "This will change nothing. Physical compatibility isn't the issue between us."

"Prove it."

"*Prove* it? You're supposed to be the one giving ground and wooing me back."

"Am I?"

"Yes," she said. "And frankly, I'm not that impressed right now."

He pulled her back into his arms and didn't hesitate to take her mouth. He kissed her slowly and deeply, reminding her with passion of the bond they shared. Reminding her that it was deeper and stronger than anything she'd experienced before. Than anything *he'd* experienced before.

He wasn't going to accept defeat. He swept his hands down her back to the curve of her hips, holding her tightly to him. Dominating her with the passion that had always been so much a part of their relationship.

She moaned, a sweet sound that he swallowed. She tipped her head to the side, allowing him access to her mouth. She held his shoulders, undulating against him. He wanted more of her and hardened in a rush. Making love to Cassidy was an addiction.

He brought his hand between them, cupping the full globe of one breast. She shivered in his arms as he brushed his thumb over her nipple.

He lifted his head so that their eyes met. Slowly he raised the hand between them and unbuttoned her blouse. She arched her shoulders and let him push the blouse off. She reached for the front clasp of her bra, opening it and baring herself to him.

He pushed back a little to see her. Her breasts were bare, nipples distended and begging for his mouth. He lowered his head and suckled.

He held her with a hand on the small of her back and buried the other in her hair. She arched over his arm, and her breasts thrust up at him. Nothing compared to the way she made him feel.

Her eyes were closed, her hips moving subtly against him, and when he blew on her nipples, gooseflesh spread down her body.

He loved the way she reacted to him. Her nipples were so sensitive he was pretty sure he could bring her to orgasm just by touching her there. He kept kissing and caressing, gently pinching her nipples until her hands clenched in his hair and she rocked her hips harder against his length. He thrust against her and bit down carefully on one tender, aroused nipple. She cried his name, and he hurriedly covered her mouth with his, wanting to feel every bit of her passion, rocking her until she quieted in his arms.

He held her close. Her bare breasts brushed his chest. He was so hard he thought he'd die if he didn't get inside her. Yet this was the perfect moment. Because he knew that he'd turned a corner, and that Cassidy was the one negotiation that he couldn't bear to lose.

Oh, hell, he loved her.

Chapter 11

Cassidy got out of bed late in the morning. The room was empty and it was clear that Donovan was gone. She dressed in last night's clothing, since she'd packed all of her other clothes the day before. She heard Mrs. Winters in the kitchen and smelled the enticing aroma of coffee wafting through the house.

She felt small and alone, ashamed that she'd let herself fall once again for Donovan's silver-tongued charm.

She was in the foyer when Mrs. Winters came out of the study. "Good morning, Mrs. Tolley."

"Morning."

"Mr. Tolley left this for you."

"Thank you." She took the small, oblong-shaped box and put it in her purse. She'd received enough jewelry in her life to recognize the box for what it was. And it felt like a bribe. She needed to get out of this house and back to her own.

She walked out of the house. There was a News 4 Van parked at the end of the circular driveway. As she approached her car, a reporter and camera-man scrambled toward her. She hated this part of being an heiress and a magnet for news.

Deciding she wasn't going to talk to anyone, she got into her car and put on her dark glasses. They ran toward her, but she waved them off and drove away.

But she had no idea where to go. Her parents' house, she imagined, was the best place. She called her mom to let her know she'd be there soon to pick up Van. She could collect her son and then plan a trip out of town for a few months. Until the local media had something better to report on than her and her Donovan.

When she pulled into her parents' house, her older brother, Adam, was standing in the portico.

"What are you doing here?"

"Waiting for you."

She stared at him, nonplussed. "How'd you know I'd be here?"

"I was with Mom when you called. I thought we should talk," he said, taking her arm and leading her to the back gardens.

"About?"

"Tolley-Patterson. It seems that the stipulation of marriage wasn't the only thing in that will of Maxwell Patterson's. He also left it up to the board of directors to approve Donovan's choice of wife."

"That's ridiculous."

"Exactly. I don't know what's going on today, but according to what I've been able to piece together, Donovan called for an emergency meeting to force the board to make a decision on the CEO."

"Why are you telling me this?"

"Because I have a man on the inside—"

"You sound like a secret agent, Adam. What does that mean?"

"A guy who works for Tolley-Patterson is keeping me abreast of what's happening in the meeting."

"Why would he do that?"

"I asked him to."

"Oh." No further explanation seemed to be forthcoming. "What did he say?"

"That the board will only accept Donovan as CEO if he doesn't marry you."

She heard the words as if from a distance and realized what they meant. Donovan had to choose between her and that position he'd always craved.

Her and the last chance he had to prove himself to his grandfather over Sam.

"Thanks for letting me know."

"Cassidy?"

"Yes?"

"Mom and Dad have suggested having your marriage annulled quietly so that you don't have to go through the humiliation of a divorce."

She nodded. "Are they waiting for me?"

"Yes."

"I'm not going to let them take over. I need to do things in my own time."

"What will you do?"

"Talk to Donovan. Who's your source?"

Adam turned away from her. "I don't think I should say."

"I think you better. Is he reliable?"

Adam faced her again, taking off his sunglasses. There was a seriousness in her brother's eyes that she was used to seeing, but she also noticed that he seemed angry. She knew it was on her behalf, and she realized how deeply she was loved by her family.

"Very reliable."

"Who?"

"Sam Patterson."

"*Sam?* He hates Donovan! Adam, I wouldn't

trust anything that he said. He's always working an angle."

"Hell, I know that. That's why I contacted him. I wanted to know more about what was going on."

"Why would he talk to you?"

"I have no idea."

"Liar."

"Liar?"

"Yes. You wouldn't make a deal with a man you didn't trust and there has to be more to this than Sam keeping you in the loop out of the goodness of his heart."

Adam looked uncomfortable for a moment before he put his sunglasses back on. "You're right. There is. I'm helping Sam with a contract he's working on in Canada using some of our contacts."

He didn't elaborate, which just made her mad. She was sick of the men in her life. Just plain sick of them and the way that everything in their worlds revolved around business.

"Did he say when we'd know what the board decides?"

"We should know soon. They're due for a lunch break in a few minutes."

Theo's power play was going to net Donovan the results he wanted. Donovan had no doubt about that. The board of directors had been unmoved by Theo's presentation, he suspected.

"What are you going to do?" Sam asked him as they both stood outside the boardroom. They'd been asked to leave while the board had a final vote.

"About what?"

"If they insist that you not marry Cassidy."

"Sam, I'm already married to her, so there's little the board can do. Even they can't insist I get a divorce."

"You're *married?* I thought she was just living with you."

"Do you honestly think I wouldn't marry her?"

"Well...yes. We all believed—"

"All? Who else? Theo? Have you been in league with him?"

"No. Theo has his own issues because Grand-daddy left him out of the running for successor."

Donovan agreed. Maxwell Patterson had left them all with a heck of a mess. The company wasn't in the best financial shape, but with him and Sam working as they had for the last few months, Tolley-Patterson was finally on the right track.

"If not Theo, then who?"

"Um...Adam Franzone."

"Then you must have known I was married to Cassidy," Donovan said.

"No, I didn't. Adam and I have a very limited

agreement—I'm keeping him informed about what's going on in the board meeting today, and he's using his contacts to get us the land we need in Canada for our new facility."

Donovan was surprised that Sam had thought to use Adam for help in the land acquisition, which had been progressing very slowly. "Did you go to him?"

"No. Adam came to me."

Donovan realized that after all the years he'd spent competing with his cousin, he really didn't know the man. He had always just looked at Sam's weaknesses and tried to exploit them. But now he saw a glimpse of a future.

"I'm not going to leave Cassidy. I've just figured out how to get her back into my life. The board is going to have to accept some kind of compromise. I suggest you and I go in there united."

"What do you have in mind?" Sam asked.

"A joint venture. Granddaddy knew you and I were the future, and I'm not sure that he didn't mean for us to somehow work out an agreement."

Sam laughed. "He didn't. He set us against each other because we both respond to a challenge."

"True. So can you do it?"

"If you can convince the board? Then, yes, I'll go for it."

"If the board doesn't meet my terms, I'm walking. I've given this company everything, and to have them tell me who I can marry is going too far."

Donovan had thought about it good and hard before he'd come to the office today. Leaving Cassidy behind in bed had been difficult. He'd wanted to be there when she woke so he could make sure she understood that he wasn't letting her walk out of his life.

"They won't respond to a threat," Sam said.

"They will respond to the bottom line. You and I have already impacted revenues in ways that Theo never could and won't be able to. He's too stuck in the old way of doing business."

"Right. Do you have documentation to back up the figures?"

"I do," Donovan said. He took out his Black-Berry and sent a quick text to Marcus. Then he sent another note to Cassidy. Just a quick one to tell her that he needed to see her as soon as he was done with this meeting.

Because if this morning had done one thing, it had reinforced to him how much he loved her—and he needed to tell her that.

"We're ready for you both now," Theo said from the doorway.

"I need a word with Donovan." His mother stood behind his uncle.

"Fine. We can wait five minutes," Theo said.

His mother began walking down the hall toward his office. "Mom?"

She turned. "We can't talk in the hallway."

He nodded and followed her past Karin, his assistant, who glanced up, arching her eyebrows at him. He signaled her to hold his calls.

His mother walked over to the window overlooking downtown Charleston and crossed her arms.

"What is it?" he asked.

"I owe you and Cassidy an apology."

Okay. *That* he hadn't expected. "Why?"

"For hiding your marriage from the board and Sam. I know that you meant to hide it from the public just temporarily until Van was born, but I kept hoping that the marriage would fall apart."

"It isn't going to," Donovan said. "Her family isn't as bad as you make them out to be."

"I know. That's why I'm apologizing. I told the board that you two are married and that the marriage is a solid match."

"Did that sway them?" he asked, aware that his mother had in her own way gone to bat for him. And he appreciated it more than he'd thought he would.

She shrugged. "It was a written vote, not vocal, so I have no idea of the outcome."

"Thanks, Mom. What changed your mind about Cassidy and the Franzones?"

"Cassidy did. She brought Van by to visit us yesterday. She was very frank with your father and I about the lies you'd told her and how that made her feel. She said she had no idea how much longer your marriage would last, but she wanted Van to know his grandparents."

Donovan wasn't surprised. Cassidy was kinder than he deserved. And if she had any idea of the things his mother had done, apparently that hadn't stopped Cassidy from doing the right thing.

"That girl is a keeper, Donovan," his mother said.

He agreed with his mother, which didn't happen that often.

As his mother left and he prepared to go to the boardroom, his BlackBerry vibrated. He glanced at the screen to see a message from Cassidy, informing him that she was aware that he had to divorce her to become CEO. He stared at the words, wondering how she knew what had happened in the boardroom.

He dialed her number and got her voice mail. He left a message, but had the feeling that Cassidy wasn't interested in listening to anything he had to say.

Cassidy and Van were having a quiet evening at home. Well, at her home. She hadn't been able to go back to the mansion she shared with Donovan. She also wanted to be away from her family, as they were acting as though they had a right to make decisions in her life. She'd set them straight and told Adam to mind his own business.

The doorbell rang just before seven and she opened the door to find Jimmy standing there.

"What are you doing here?"

"Delivery again."

"I don't need any soup."

"It's not soup."

He handed her a padded envelope and gave her a smile before he walked back to his car. She closed the door and stared bemusedly at the envelope in her hand. It had her name written on it in very distinctive handwriting—Donovan's.

She wasn't ready to deal with anything else from him right now. The jewelry box sat on the table in the foyer, still unopened. She tossed the envelope next to it and walked back to the family room, where Van was sleeping in his playpen.

Ten minutes later her cell phone rang and she checked the caller ID before answering it. "Hey, Emma."

"Hey, girl. Did you open the envelope?"

"Which one?"

"The one Jimmy delivered."

"No, and how do you know about it?"

"Because I'm coming over to babysit."

"I don't want to talk to Donovan."

"Trust me, on this you're going to want to at least give him a chance to explain."

"I've already given him three chances with my heart, and each time he's let me down."

"I know. If you didn't love him then I'd say to ignore him, but you do, so give him a chance to explain and make things up to you."

"What does he have planned?"

"I don't know. Open the envelope. I'm going to be there in fifteen minutes."

Cassidy hung up and went back to the foyer. She brought the envelope and jewelry box into the living room and sat down where she could see Van.

She opened the envelope first and inside found an invitation requesting her presence at the yacht club tonight at nine.

She shook her head. Romance and romantic gestures weren't going to win her over. But a part of her…okay, all of her, wanted her relationship with Donovan to work. As hurt as she was by his actions, she still hadn't had time to fall out of love with him. She didn't know if she'd ever be able to.

She opened the jewelry box and found inside a platinum charm bracelet. There was only one charm on it. A photo of her, Van and Donovan, a small version of the photo that hung by Van's crib at her parents' house. On the back of the charm was a small engraving that read, This is my world.

She felt a sting of tears as she read it. She wasn't sure what Donovan had in mind for later this evening, but she knew now she was going to go and hear him out. She owed it to the both of them to give their relationship one last chance.

She took the baby monitor down the hall to her bedroom and got changed out of her jeans and shirt into a cocktail-length sundress. She put her makeup on with a steady hand and touched up her curls.

When Emma arrived a few minutes later, she was almost ready to go. She put on her wedding rings and her charm bracelet.

"I'm going to take Van to my place for the night," Emma said.

"Emma…"

"If you need to come and get him before morning, don't worry. But I have the feeling you're going to be otherwise occupied."

She bit her lower lip. She needed more than another sexy night in Donovan's arms. But she had no idea if he could give her anything more. Romance was fine, but she needed his heart. She really needed him to be the man she'd always believed him to be.

A limo arrived just after Emma, and she hugged

her friend and dropped a kiss on Van's head as she left.

In the backseat of the limo she found another envelope. She opened it, and a piece of vellum paper dropped out. On the paper was a poem written by Christopher Brennan called "Because She Would Ask Me Why I Loved Her."

The poem was beautiful and sweet, and the scrawled *I love you* at the bottom made her heart beat a little faster. She wanted to believe that Donovan was making this gesture because he loved her, but a part of her—the part jaded by his betrayals—feared he was going to ask her to remain his secret wife.

Chapter 12

Donovan was waiting on the dock when the limo pulled up. He had spent the evening making sure every detail was in place. For once, he was nervous, but not because he was afraid of the outcome. He'd always been a winner, and there was no way he'd settle for anything less than complete victory with Cassidy tonight.

"Good evening, Cassidy," he said as he took her hand and helped her out of the back of the car.

"Donovan."

The night sky was filled with stars and a warm tropical breeze stirred off the water. "Thank you for joining me."

"You're welcome. I'll admit I came only because I want to hear what you have to say."

"Did you read my notes?"

"I did."

"And?"

She hesitated.

"I love you, Cassidy."

"Did you lose your job today?" she asked.

Not exactly the response he'd been looking for.

"What does that have to do with anything?"

"Adam said—"

"Adam doesn't know everything."

"No, but I thought Sam did."

Donovan shook his head. "Let's go onto my yacht. I'll tell you all about the day if you want."

She followed him onto the yacht. His chef had prepared some hors d'oeuvres and they were set out near the stern.

"My uncle and the board gave me an ultimatum, which you obviously heard about—leave you, or forfeit the chairmanship. I declined their offer and countered with a joint chairmanship.

"Sam and I have really made a difference in the company bottom line, and we decided we both should be at the helm."

"And they didn't go for it," she said.

"Why are you so sure that they said no?"

"Why else would you be trying so hard to hold

on to me unless you lost the company? That was your number one priority."

He shook his head, regretting the fact that he'd let her down and made her feel as if she didn't mean as much to him as his job did. He'd wanted his grandfather's respect, had craved a chance to make his mark in the world, but over the short course of his marriage, he had realized that being a husband and father was the one thing that mattered most.

"They took our offer. Sam and I are co-CEOs. I'm telling you how I feel about you because, when I thought I was going to lose everything, I didn't feel devastated."

"You didn't?" she asked.

He shook his head and drew her into his arms. "Instead, I thought about you and Van and the family we were starting, and I looked at my relatives who sit on the board. Even though they also represent the investors in the company, I knew that family was the most important thing.

"That *you* were the most important thing in my life," he said, leaning down to kiss her. "You and Van.

"I love you, Cassidy Franzone Tolley. And I want to marry you again in front of the world so that everyone knows you are mine."

Cassidy was crying, but she was also smiling—

the brightest smile he'd ever seen. "I love you, too, Donovan."

"Will you marry me again?"

"No," she said, and his heart nearly stopped. "I don't need a ceremony in front of the world."

He let out a breath, overwhelmed by his love for this woman. "What do you need?"

"You," she said.

* * * * *

We hope you enjoyed reading

THE BILLIONAIRE'S BORROWED BABY

by *USA TODAY* bestselling author

JANICE MAYNARD

and

BABY BUSINESS

by *USA TODAY* bestselling author

KATHERINE GARBERA.

SPECIAL EXCERPT FROM

HARLEQUIN

Desire

*Read on for a sneak preview
of* USA TODAY *bestselling author*
Janice Maynard's
STRANDED WITH THE RANCHER,
the debut novel in
**TEXAS CATTLEMAN'S CLUB:
AFTER THE STORM.**
*Trapped in a storm cellar after the worst tornado to hit
Royal, Texas, in decades, two longtime enemies need
each other to survive...*

Beth stood and went to the ladder, peering up at their
prison door. "I don't hear anything at all," she said.
"What if we have to spend the night here? I don't want
to sleep on the concrete floor. And I'm hungry, dammit."

Drew heard the moment she cracked. Jumping to his
feet, he took her in his arms and shushed her. He let her
cry it out, surmising that the tears were healthy. This
afternoon had been scary as hell, and to make things
worse, they had no clue if help was on the way and no
means of communication.

Beth felt good in his arms. Though he usually had the
urge to argue with her, this was better. Her hair was silky,
the natural curls alive and bouncing with vitality. Though
he had felt the pull of sexual attraction between them
before, he had never acted on it. Now, trapped in the dark
with nothing to do, he wondered what would happen if
he kissed her.

Wondering led to fantasizing, which led to action.

HDEXP0914

Tangling his fingers in the hair at her nape, he tugged back her head and looked at her, wishing he could see her expression. "Better now?" The crying was over except for the occasional hitching breath.

"Yes." He felt her nod.

"I want to kiss you, Beth. But you can say no."

She lifted her shoulders and let them fall. "You saved my life. I suppose a kiss is in order."

He frowned. "We saved *each other's* lives," he said firmly. "I'm not interested in kisses as legal tender."

"Oh, just do it," she said, the words sharp instead of romantic. "We've both thought about this over the last two years. Don't deny it."

He brushed the pad of his thumb over her lower lip. "I wasn't planning to."

When their lips touched, something spectacular happened. Time stood still. Not as it had in the frantic fury of the storm, but with a hushed anticipation.

Don't miss the first installment of the

**TEXAS CATTLEMAN'S CLUB:
AFTER THE STORM** *miniseries,*

STRANDED WITH THE RANCHER

by USA TODAY *bestselling author*

Janice Maynard.

Available October 2014 wherever Harlequin® Desire books and ebooks are sold.

HDEXP0914

HARLEQUIN®

Desire

POWERFUL HEROES... SCANDALOUS SECRETS... BURNING DESIRES!

THE CHILD THEY DIDN'T EXPECT

by *USA TODAY* bestselling author

Yvonne Lindsay

Available October 2014

Surprise—it's a baby!

After their steamy vacation fling, Alison Carter knows
Ronin Marshall is a skilled lover and a billionaire businessman.
But a *father*...who hires her New Zealand baby-planning service?
This divorcée has already been deceived once;
Ronin's now the last man she wants to see.

But he must have Ali. Only she can rescue Ronin from the upheaval
of caring for his orphaned nephew...and give Ronin more of what
he shared with her during the best night of his life. But something is
holding her back. And Ronin will stop at nothing to find out what
secrets she's keeping!

This exciting new story is part of the Harlequin® Desire's
popular *Billionaires & Babies* collection featuring
powerful men...wrapped around their babies' little fingers!

Available wherever books and ebooks are sold.

Talk to us online!
www.Facebook.com/HarlequinBooks
www.Pinterest.com/HarlequinBooks
www.Twitter.com/HarlequinBooks

HARLEQUIN®

Desire

POWERFUL HEROES... SCANDALOUS SECRETS... BURNING DESIRES!

TEMPTED BY A COWBOY
by Sarah M. Anderson

Available October 2014

**The 2nd novel of the *Beaumont Heirs* featuring
one Colorado family with limitless scandal!**

*How can she resist the cowboy's smile when it
promises so much pleasure?*

Phillip Beaumont likes his drinks strong and his women easy.
So why is he flirting with his new horse trainer, Jo Spears,
who challenges him at every turn? Phillip wants nothing but
the chase...until the look in Jo's haunted green eyes makes him
yearn for more....

Sure, Jo's boss is as jaded and stubborn as Sun, the
multimillion-dollar stallion she was hired to train. But it isn't
long before she starts spending days *and* nights with the sexy
cowboy. Maybe Sun isn't the only male on the Beaumont
ranch worth saving!

Be sure to read the 1st novel of the *Beaumont Heirs*
by Sarah M. Anderson
NOT THE BOSS'S BABY

Available wherever books and ebooks are sold.

HD73346